ZERO HOUR

ZERO HOUR

JORDAN CASTILLO PRICE

jcpbooks.com

Second print edition published in the United States in 2018 by JCP Books.

WWW.JCPBOOKS.COM

ISBN 978-1-944779-02-3

We know what we are, but know not what we may be.

-William Shakespeare

⌐⌐⌐CHAPTER ONE⌐⌐⌐

THE HATCH CLICKED OPEN. Ernest stepped outside his POD and took a long, deep breath. The fresh air was bracing. (That's what they said in old-time data feeds, wasn't it? That the air was bracing? He was fairly sure, though there was nobody nearby who could verify his impression that the air was, indeed, bracing.) "Louise," he said. "Is the air bracing?"

"Now, I wouldn't know about that, Ernest."

That's what L0U15E said every time he asked a question outside her parameters. She used to actually say, "That question is not within my parameters." But Ernest had saved up his discretional income for nearly three months to pay for a personalized re-program of her reply.

Three months of his life was a large tradeoff for one simple sentence. But every time he heard it, he smiled. Even now. Since he enjoyed rhetorical questions, he got his money's worth.

The historic district was fascinating. Ernest looked up one side of the street, turned, then looked down the other. The buildings were old and full of character, crafted from wood and stone and brick. They cracked here and bulged there, and some even had ivy growing up the side. Spectacular.

He gazed at a rustic crack that zig-zagged up between the bricks of a building's foundation, and then turned toward the street. L0U15E was staring at him...he could tell. "Aren't you going to go dock?" he asked.

"All the way over there?" An arrow appeared on the front viscreen of Ernest's POD. "Public parking is way down at the other end of the block. Can't we go someplace with its own POD docks?"

The "soft argue," as it was called, was another add-on he had purchased. POD-minds were artificial intelligences with a single purpose: to run a personal overland device, and most people's POD-minds didn't talk back. They did what their operators told them to do unless the actions reached a certain threshold of potential harm for the owners, or for others. When L0U15E did the "soft argue," it meant that Ernest's action—in this case, entering a crumbling old building where she wasn't docked into the computer system to keep track of him—had scored as moderately risky. The risk was probably mitigated by the fact that this was a public building, heavily monitored.

"Don't worry," he reassured her. He knew that AIs didn't have emotions, but wasn't assessing risk and broadcasting a warning as close to actual *worry* as a computer could get? "I'll be careful."

He could have *commanded* L0U15E to stop second-guessing him and go dock, but he let her sit there, parked right in the middle of the magnetic strip, and watch him go inside his very first coffee shop. If L0U15E had possessed actual emotions, maybe she'd feel proud of him for finally striking out on his own.

The front door opened for Ernest, and the smell hit him. It was strange and divine, rich and somewhat burnt. The interior was full of right angles and furniture, with philodendrons spilling from every surface. He waited for the shop's AI to tell him what to do, figuring it was on a time-delay to give him a chance to soak up the ambiance.

The main room held five round tables with two chairs apiece. Mundane tables with no interface. Interesting. Someone could sit at one of those tables and do anything that came to his mind—anything at all.

A tiny thrill fluttered in his belly.

A few customers were packed into the right-angled corners or against the far wall, each in his or her own world. Three were hooked into portable VR units that obscured their eyes and most of their faces. Their arms and legs twitched and waved, but gave no indication as to what they were experiencing.

Another man had a hanging bag tubed into his arm-shunt. He bent over an object that it took Ernest a moment to recognize. Ernest blinked. A book! That man was reading a portable monitor shaped like a book while he had his coffee!

Ernest smiled wistfully. Coffee and a book. All that was missing was a cigarette. They'd been illegal ever since 2323, but undoubtedly someone, somewhere, could produce one—for a price.

The reading man probably had only a few more days left, judging by his parchment skin, the wispy gray of his hair and the way his head nodded along as he read.

Maybe they had cigarettes here. Or maybe a martini. Shaken, not stirred. Ernest hugged himself with glee. The coffee shop was everything he'd hoped it would be, and more. Maybe it would be worth draining the rest of his savings to see what a cigarette was all about. Or a martini. Or—

"Can I help you?"

Ernest whirled around and looked at the counter. He'd expected an AI to guide him, give him a list of choices and prices, and possibly a recommendation based on a quick scan of his public domain personality profile, but instead he found...a man.

Staring at him.

How uncomfortable.

But wasn't that the way of things in old-time data streams? "Here's looking at you, kid," from a time when people did, in fact, look. At each other, no less.

"Hello?" said Ernest.

The man rolled his eyes. "Yes, I'm real. No, I'm not a holo. Yes, this is an actual coffee shop and not a historical re-creation. And no, I can't be bothered to parse the tedious characters of your public profile to determine what it is that you want. You're going to have to tell me."

Ernest looked back. He figured he might as well, since he was being scrutinized himself. The man behind the counter had to be third decade if he was in a job so public, probably closer to twenty-nine than nineteen. He was tall, blond and lanky, with sinews that showed in his jaw, neck and forearms. He looked as if his feed program needed some tweaking.

"I thought you just asked if you could help me," Ernest said.

"Figure of speech. Sort of like, 'How are you?' or 'I could eat a horse.' And no, we don't serve horses here."

Ernest's head spun. He wondered if he was giddy from the bracing air he'd just inhaled. It had probably been full of all kinds of unidentified compounds.

The clerk raised an eyebrow. "First time at a shop, huh?"

Ernest nodded. "Never got out of my POD much."

"Name's Will." The clerk held out his hand. His pale eyebrows tilted up as if he expected something.

Ernest stared, puzzled, until he matched the gesture with one he'd seen on an old-time feed, and then he grasped Will's hand and pumped his arm up and down precisely three times. "I'm Ernest. Pleased to meet you."

"First handshake?"

Ernest felt his face grow warm. "Was it that obvious?"

Will shrugged. "No, I guess not. Most virgins just stand there with their mouths hanging open and stare at my hand. At least you knew what to do. Helpful hint: don't squeeze so tight." He pointed at a series of screens behind the counter with lists of tiny characters and glyphs, prices beside them. "There's the menu. I'm guessing that's new to you, too?"

Ernest nodded.

"Take your time. I'll clarify whatever you don't get."

"Could we...could we try that handshake one more time? It's just that...you really seem to know what you're doing."

Will shrugged. "Whatever trips your switch."

Ernest led this time, presenting his hand boldly.

"Other hand."

Ernest felt his cheeks heat up again. He ignored the sensation and concentrated on learning the handshake.

Will slid his hand into Ernest's. He moved more deliberately than Ernest had, and Ernest felt the pads of Will's fingertips glide along his palm. A thrill raced down his spine and the tiny hairs on the back of his neck stood on end.

"Harder than that," Will said. "Otherwise you'll come off as a wuss."

Ernest deduced that being a "wuss" wasn't good. Yet another bit of data to research later. He applied more pressure to Will's hand. "Nice," Will purred. "Now shake it like you're not counting. And vary the height a little."

Ernest did his best to be random. It was easier than he would have thought. He was so focused on the feel of Will's hand inside his that he'd forgotten how to count as high as three.

"And there you go," Will said. He let go of Ernest's hand, which now felt completely foreign. "Just like something out of a paperback novel."

"A what?"

"Never mind. C754s are supposed to be smart. I thought you'd parse the reference."

"A novel? As in a book? On paper? Paper-back. Paperback. Yes. What's the rest of it made from?"

Will leaned over the counter on both hands as if he was about to divulge a great secret. Ernest leaned forward and met him halfway. Will pressed his mouth to Ernest's hair just beside his ear and whispered.

"Paper."

Ernest straightened back up, disgusted. He hadn't come to the coffee shop to be mocked. He'd come for coffee. "Very funny."

"You don't believe me? But it's true. All the books upstairs are made from paper...and maybe a little glue and ink."

Books. Actual books. Upstairs. Ernest had scanned feeds about bibliophiles cracking open the spine of a freshly bound book—which sounded incredibly violent, yet somehow satisfying—and breathing deep of the "new book smell."

He supposed that Will's books wouldn't smell like that anymore, not after centuries of...what did books do? They moldered. Not after centuries of moldering.

Unless they'd been sealed, preserved somehow.

"What do they smell like?"

Will's eyebrows twisted up and he...what was that called? Smiled? Grinned? Smirked? "Not like anything your POD can synth up, that's for sure."

Ernest would need to access the feeds on facial expressions if he wanted to get through the next twenty-nine days with any comprehension whatsoever of what was going on around him. He felt a pang. It made no sense. It was several hours until his next meal was scheduled. So why the...longing?

"Same for the coffee," said Will. That was probably a smirk, Ernest decided. "Some things just can't be replicated by nanos. So, what'll it be?"

"Can I see the books?"

Will's eyebrows plunged low, forming a straight line over the top edge of his eyelids, with a vertical crease dead center. "Top floor's for customers only. You understand. Gotta make a living."

"Oh. Yes. Of course." He'd need to order. That was what he'd come for anyway, wasn't it? The coffee: mythic elixir, beverage of commoners and kings. He tore his gaze away from Will's eyebrows and looked back at the LCD board, with its singles and doubles, mochas and lattes. Someone might as well have handed him a schematic and told him to build his own POD. "Um...Will...Not that I expect you to analyze my public profile, but based on your own experience, what would you recommend?"

"That depends on how much you wanna spend. We got hypos. We got IVs. Of course, if you're really flush, I can set you up a brew."

Ernest's attention snapped back to Will. "Brew? You mean, to drink?"

Will waggled his eyebrows.

Ernest guessed that was a *yes*.

ııı CHAPTER TWO ııı

"Is it true that once you drink, you can never use your shunt again?" Ernest asked.

Will made a flicking motion with his hand. He'd draped himself over his side of the coffee bar with a bend to his spine that made it look as if his POD's posture-correcting function had been disabled long ago. "Nah. That's just Deaconist propaganda they circulate to stop you from putting stuff in your mouth. Besides, what've you got to lose by trying? You've only got, what, how many days left?"

"Thirty. I mean...twenty-nine. I guess. I mean...it's my first day."

"And you chose my humble little shop for your inaugural outing? I'm flattered."

Ernest looked up at the LCD, tucked his hair behind his ear and tried to read the price list, but found he was too flustered to make anything of it. He stared, and he read, and he stared some more. Will went about wiping down a perfectly clean section of the corner with a spotless cloth.

"You can tell?" Ernest blurted out.

Will looked up at Ernest. His eyebrows shot up quizzically.

"I mean, well...I didn't think I'd look *retired* quite so soon." Ernest glanced over at the white-haired retiree in the seating area, the man with the book and the IV, wondering if maybe he'd stopped breathing during their conversation.

Will stared at the old retiree for a moment, then re-focused his attention on Ernest. "No, of course not. I figured you were probably somewhere in the first week."

Ernest could see the gleam of the old man's scalp through his hair. How long had he been retired? Twenty-five days? Twenty? Ten?

"But you could definitely tell just by looking at me," Ernest said. "That I'm retired, I mean."

"Look. I read body language. That's what I do. This is a customer service job, and I interact with people all day long. You've got the air of someone fresh out of his POD. That's all. Don't go reading something into it that I didn't say."

Ernest focused on the sign behind Will's head. Its lettering looked like meaningless squiggles and marks. As he did his best to parse it, Will strode out from behind the counter and rounded the room. He gave everyone's hanging drip bag a couple of squeezes, then leaned over the shoulder of the retiree with the book-shaped monitor and said something soft in his ear. The old man smiled to himself. Will gave his bony shoulder an absent, trailing touch and returned to his post at the counter.

He certainly was tactile.

"Really." Will picked up the conversation right where he'd left off. "You look great. The long hair's spiffy on you. No grays yet. I would've taken you for a PODless worker...a mechanic or a Deacon or something...if you hadn't been so excited about the coffee and the books."

Ernest felt his adrenaline level ebb. He let his shoulders relax. "Really?"

"Sure. You don't look a day over twenty-five. I swear on my Deacon's electromagnetic field. So what'll it be? I can unseal a pack of pure ground arabica for you for just eighteen credits."

Ernest's adrenaline surged again. He'd be out of money in less than a week if he dropped eighteen credits on a unit of coffee, genuine or not. "Let's, ah, let's save that for one of my milestones. Tenth day of retirement, maybe twentieth."

Will shrugged. "Whatever you say. I hear the taste buds die off pretty quickly. Shame to let yours go to waste without even beta-testing them."

"I'll think about it. Maybe tomorrow. For today, I think I'll try...." Ernest looked up at the menu and selected the second-cheapest item. He didn't want to seem too obvious. "A decaf half-syringe."

Will stared.

Ernest forced himself to meet Will's eyes. "What?"

"Do you even know what 'decaf' means?"

"It's...ah...something about ten. Ten flavors?"

"No. The root word's not *deca-*. It's *de-*, as in 'no.' No caffeine. Here you are, retired after thirty years' faithful service, and you're gonna waste your time on a decaffeinated syringe?"

Ernest blinked. "No?"

"No. Of course not. What you want is a nice shot of espresso, black. I'll throw in some sugar, too, so you get a really good kick."

Ernest checked the menu. The espresso syringe cost three and a half credits, double what he'd meant to spend. But Will was already at the cool-storage, rifling through the color-coded packets. Ernest could hardly change his mind now.

"Swipe your chip there," Will said, and Ernest inserted his thumb into the slot. His balance flashed as the cost of the syringe was deducted, and he withdrew his thumb, now warm at the nail bed from the laser scan.

Will peeled the wrapper from the syringe, staring hard into Ernest's eyes and smiling. Probably smiling.

"Maybe you should sit down."

Ernest thought it would be a good idea to take Will's advice, even though his choice of coffee had cost an extra 1.75 credits.

Ernest turned toward the seating area. One of the people in the VR masks had collapsed over a table, limp, an arm dangling over the side. Another VR viewer, this one female, still twitched. The man with the wispy gray hair was now watching Ernest, though his expression was difficult to read with all the sags and wrinkles around his features. When he saw Ernest had noticed him, he looked back down at his book-shaped monitor as if it contained all the secrets of the universe.

"Hey."

Even though he saw Will coming, Ernest still jumped when

Will's hand came down on his shoulder. He did his best not to flinch; people slapped and clapped each other all the time on old-time feeds. He didn't want Will to know that no one ever touched him but his health monitor.

Will shoved at his shoulder until Ernest turned to face him. Will leaned in close. He smelled exotic, earthy and burnt, like the shop, only headier. "I said the upstairs was for customers only. Now you're a customer. Come on."

Will paused at the shop's front door. He wriggled his fingers beneath the door's keyscan and the lock clicked shut. "Just in case a caffeine junkie on the street gets any funny ideas," Will said.

Ernest had absolutely no idea what that meant, but it sounded terribly thrilling.

Will turned to the old man and said, "Come grab me if anyone wants out...you can do that much, can't you?"

The man gave a grunt that seemed annoyed. Or maybe phlegmy. Ernest supposed his joints felt none too good when he attempted to walk. Without waiting for any more of an answer, Will turned and marched down a dark, narrow hallway, all angles and planes, and gestured distractedly for Ernest to follow. He pulled out a key, an actual metal key, and unlocked an ill-fitting wooden door set in the hallway's perpendicular terminus.

Ernest's heart pounded in his throat. All these exotic things— the key, the door, the coffee—they were straight out of old-time data feeds. Will handled them all as if they were the actual facets of his life, not artifacts or curiosities.

The door opened onto a tiny hall with a back door on the far wall, a closet to the right and a stairwell to the left. Will went left and took a couple of steps up, and then turned and looked down on Ernest. A tiny window at the top of the stairs backlit him, and he looked like a Grand Deacon about to deliver a sermon on obligation and duty.

"You do know how to use the stairs, don't you?"

Ernest's cheeks went hot. "Yes. Of course."

"Okay, just checking."

Will turned back and bounded up the stairs two at a time.

Ernest watched him pass the small window with the light streaming through it, round the corner of a landing and disappear.

Ernest had thought he was supposed to step on each riser. He felt terribly ignorant, relieved that Will wasn't there to see him use the stairway. Staircase. Stairs. He followed, placing his feet exactly in Will's footsteps.

A narrow, angular hallway at the top of the stairs stretched deep into the upper floor of the old building, and along that hallway, one door was open. An arc of yellow light spilled out over the worn floorboards. Ernest wove toward the light unsteadily. He felt as if he'd gone to sleep and woken up in an old-time feed. His heart hammered against his ribcage. His hands shook. He wiped the perspiration from them and stuffed them in his pockets.

Once he reached the doorway, he stood inside it and simply looked. There was so much to take in. Furniture made of fabric and wood, and maybe even leather (which was actually just a synonym for processed animal hides). And stacked everywhere, on shelves, on tables, on the windowsill and even the floor...were books. Hundreds? Ernest scanned. No, thousands.

He took a deep breath, and sputtered.

"Yeah, sorry," Will said. "It gets a little dusty up here from all the cellulose fibers."

Ernest flinched. He'd been so distracted by the stacks and stacks of precious antique books, he'd forgotten about Will.

"Have a seat." Will took Ernest by the elbow and guided him to a sofa. There was a wad of fabric at one end, a cushion on the other.

"Do you...sleep here?" said Ernest.

"No, no. Of course not. I sleep in my POD. That's just there for historical reference. Sharp eye you got there. Can't put anything past a C754."

Ernest felt his cheeks grow warm again. There must have been something wrong with the temperature monitor in the shop. "I watch a lot of feeds."

"Sit, enjoy the brocade. That's velvet, circa 1932."

Ernest sat. He touched the arm of the sofa.

"Well, roll up your sleeve and I'll inject you. Though it really is a shame you didn't go for the drinkable coffee. The syringe isn't historically accurate."

Ernest stared at the room in a daze. If he'd known he could have his coffee like this—on a sofa, surrounded by actual books—well, maybe he would have gone ahead and purchased it, madly expensive or not.

"Do you think I could hold a book while you do it?"

"Sure, why not?" Will took the top book from a pile and placed it in Ernest's hands. Ernest read the title. *Zen and the Art of Motorcycle Maintenance.* He didn't parse either 'Zen' or 'Motorcycle,' but it fascinated him nonetheless.

"I can give you a cup to hold, if you're really after the most authentic experience you can have. With a syringe, anyway."

"Yes, please."

Will pulled a cup off one of the crowded shelves and set it on top of the book that Ernest was holding with both hands. "You put your fingers through the handle and steady it with your thumb."

"I know. I've told you: I watch lots of feeds." Ernest curled his fingers through the ceramic loop. The cup felt heavy and strange. He couldn't imagine the concentration it would take to keep from spilling if it were full of hot liquid. Old-time *homo sapiens* must have been more dexterous than he'd always thought. That notion bordered on heresy, though. Ernest quickly searched for something else to focus on.

Will obliged him by sitting so close to him on the sofa that their thighs touched. And not just a passing brush, either. Will's thigh pressed into Ernest's so firmly that Ernest actually needed to move over. Even that didn't seem to help. Will just pressed himself closer.

"You might want to hold on to something," Will said. "It can be pretty intense."

Ernest squeezed the cup more tightly. "I'm ready."

Will put the syringe's protective cap between his teeth and yanked. Ernest stared. He'd never seen a *homo consummatus* put something in his mouth. Before he could ask about it, Will spit the cap onto the floor. "Brace yourself."

Ernest grit his teeth.

There were no nerve endings in an arm shunt, of course, but he swore he could feel the needle anyway as the tip of the syringe pierced the self-healing membrane. Will looked at him, smiled, and pressed the plunger.

Probably smiled.

Ernest almost reminded himself to look up the feed on facial expressions. But not quite. Because the caffeine hit his system, and he forgot everything. Where he was. Who he was.

He pitched forward, face between his knees. The room spun, and spun, and spun. All he could do was breathe. Or at least try to.

He didn't know how long he'd been out. He came to stretched out on the sofa, the cushion under his head, and the length of fabric covering his body.

"Oh, are you with us again?"

Will.

"What did you do to me?" Ernest tried to sit up. The room spun some more. He pressed his hand into the sofa and forced himself upright. He shivered. There was definitely something wrong with the temperature-control.

"I told you to brace yourself."

"That wasn't coffee. It was something else—a drug."

"What do you think caffeine is? A food group?"

"I think I need to see my health monitor."

Will grabbed him by the chin and made sure Ernest was focused entirely on him. "Sure, I can load you into your POD, send you rocketing off toward your health monitor. No problem. But, see, then you can't come back here."

"No, no, it's not like that. I'm not trying to get you in trouble. I think I'm really sick. Maybe there was something wrong with the coffee. Maybe it was tainted. Maybe it was old."

Will took him by the shoulder, both shoulders, and leaned over him so they were face to face. He had the most fascinating hazel eyes.

"It's not up to me. If coffee doesn't agree with you, they're not gonna let you keep sampling it, retirement or not. Listen, pal. That's what it's like the first time. It's called a rush. It's an acquired taste."

"But I didn't taste anything," Ernest said in a quiet voice.

"Yeah, well, you would have, if you'd just taken it by mouth." Will peeled a small foil square off the syringe's wrapper. "Here, give me your chip."

Ernest held up his trembling hand.

Will pressed the square onto Ernest's thumbnail. A taste exploded in his senses that was a lot like the smell that had first hit him as he opened the shop door. It was similar to that of the shop, but not quite the same. Sweet. Burnt. Earthy. Terribly bitter. But something was definitely missing. It was nowhere near as complex as the scent of the store, or even the smell of Will himself.

"Sorry," Will said. "I forgot. I don't get into the shots, myself. I guess the synth-taste makes it go down easier."

"Is that really what coffee tastes like?"

Will shrugged. "Kinda sorta. You know how it is with synths."

Ernest assumed he knew how it was. Everything he'd ever tasted had been synthetic, a surge of carefully programmed nanos that tickled the taste center of his brain and then died, coursing through his bloodstream to his lungs, where he'd exhale their spent carcasses within the next three breaths.

That's how it was with synths?

Ernest had no idea how it was *without* them.

ıııCHAPTER THREEııı

"I'D BETTER GO DOWNSTAIRS," Will said. "It's not a good idea to leave the shop unattended."

Even as Ernest's head spun, he had to agree that the old man had seemed more likely to watch his book than mind the store. He listened as Will's footsteps thudded down the stairs, and then cautiously sat up and looked around the room. It felt huge. Terrifying. All of the books, the stacks and stacks of them, were suddenly intimidating, as if they might cascade from their teetering piles and bury him—without any AI to observe, or call for help.

Down in the shop, the notion of being unplugged from the grid had felt thrilling, in an illicit sort of way. But here, without anyone around, anyone at all? It was creepy. If the books did indeed take a topple, he'd be at Will's mercy...and who was to say when Will would come back upstairs again? Hours later? Days? Ernest only had twenty-nine days left. He couldn't afford to spend them trapped in a room—even an antique room full of precious artifacts. He pushed the fabric that covered him to the end of the sofa, swung his legs over the side, and crept to the door, down the stairs, and along the downstairs hall.

He paused in the doorway and scanned the room. The old man was gone. Will stood behind his counter, "chatting" with a new customer, a woman. "Oh, just ignore him," she was saying, "he's probably getting into the cranky phase." Her hair was black, threaded through with a few glittery strands of iron gray at the temples. The skin at the corner of her eyes crinkled subtly. How old was she? Thirty and five? Thirty and ten?

She turned to look at Ernest. "Oh, a C754—with long hair, how cute. That's my favorite—"

Ernest was so overwhelmed, he couldn't bear to hear another word. He not only walked past her without acknowledging she was speaking to him—he broke into a run.

He burst through the front door and onto the sidewalk. "Louise!"

Down the block, his POD snapped out of its dock, propelled itself to the magnetic strip that ran down the center of the street, and glided toward his location. He scurried along to meet it, casting furtive glances back over his shoulder.

"Hello, Ernest. How was your—?"

"Let me in," he snapped.

A series of lights flashed on the POD's front viscreen. "Ernest? You don't look well." There was a small click, and the POD's hatch swung open. Ernest climbed in and LOU15E shut the hatch.

"Take me out of this neighborhood. Somewhere far away that won't use up too many credits."

"Far away? How far?"

"I don't know. Fifth Street."

What would LOU15E have done if he'd requested to go to Casablanca? Ernest wasn't sure.

He felt some clicks as Louise relayed a destination to the track, and the gentle hum of the POD as it began to pick up speed. "Your cheeks are flushed," she said. "We should do some bloodwork."

"No. Not now."

"Are you sure? I could take you to your health monitor."

His heart was pounding, whether from the running or the caffeine, he didn't know. "It's fine." He forced himself to smile. It wasn't fine, but he didn't want his health monitor to start restricting his activities. "It's...great, in fact. I'd like to access all the free feeds you can get me on caffeine. And facial expressions, smiles in particular, if there's a subfeed."

LOU15E's interior viscreen rippled with data that assembled itself into neat columns. Ernest hoped he could lose himself in his research enough to bring his heart rate back down—or at least occupy LOU15E until it did so on its own. "Let's see," he said. "Add 'psychology' to the smile feed. And 'smirk,' too. And I'd like something with pictures. Diagrams, if you can find them."

Ernest settled into the POD and pretended his heart wasn't trying to hammer through his ribcage. LOU15E could read his body temperature, analyze his facial expression, but she couldn't do any bloodwork until he shunted in. "Ah, here it is." He pointed to the screen. "Caffeine raises the heart rate. That's all it was, Louise. A physiological reaction."

"I don't think it's safe to experiment with something like that."

"What can it hurt? I've only got another twenty-nine days. Any sort of addiction I might form would be short-lived."

"That's morbid. Don't say things like that."

Ernest studied a diagram on facial expressions that had been developed for the treatment of autistic individuals. "Free feed on *autistic*," he said, unfamiliar with the term. The diagram was good. Ernest could see the subtle nuances of each expression in the tilt of the eyebrows, the shape of the lower eyelid. "Do you think I'm autistic?" he asked LOU15E.

"Autism was bred out of *homo sapiens* in 2098. It's never existed in *homo consummatus.*"

"Oh. Well, I like the diagram anyway. Tile and commit to background."

The POD's interior lit up with dozens upon dozens of small, almost-smiling faces. *Amusement*, read one with lazy-looking eyelids. *Delight*, read another, lips parted, eyes wide. *Sardonic*, read the face with quirked eyebrows and only one corner of the mouth turned up.

"Louise?"

"Yes, Ernest?"

"Can you put blond hair on that one? And make the cheek-bones higher?"

One face out of every hundred sprouted a yellow-blond crew cut. "A little longer?" The hair grew. "There. That's good."

Ernest pondered "sardonic." Now that it had spiked blond hair, it looked an awful lot like Will.

o ◎ o

"Look what the cat dragged in."

If Will was trying to confuse Ernest with idiom, it wasn't going to work. Ernest had given himself a "crash course" on expressions (both verbal and facial), caffeine, handshakes, and the alimentary canal. He wasn't normally able to pack in so much study, but after the shot of "espresso" he hadn't slept for two days.

He looked up at the menu and told himself that it was acceptable to splurge three or four credits, since he'd stayed in the POD for three days straight without spending anything except his most basic maintenance costs.

"Today," Ernest said, "I'd like an IV."

An expression fleeted across Will's face, too subtle to match with one of the many diagrams Ernest had committed to memory. "It's a piss-poor substitute for the real drink," he said nonchalantly.

"What about the book-shaped monitor?" Ernest asked. "What does that cost? That customer the other day, he was reading a book while he had his coffee. I want to do that."

Will stared. He was thinking—Ernest could tell as much because his eyes flicked side to side as he did so, and one of the psychology feeds Ernest had recently read said that people did that when they were accessing their temporal lobe—and then he shrugged. "It's a good approximation of authenticity."

Ernest waited for Will to tell him it wasn't anything like drinking with your mouth. And it wasn't exactly like a book made from paper and glue. And it would be nothing at all like going upstairs and sitting on that dusty couch that felt somehow shameful in a way Ernest didn't quite parse.

Will didn't argue, though. Not a word.

He turned and glanced up at the LCD menu. "What about French Roast? That'll give you a long, slow buzz you can sit with for hours."

Ernest felt his face settle into grim lines. He tried to match it to something he'd seen on his viscreen. Disgusted? Depressed? It seemed to have less to do with sorrow and more to do with... he didn't know.

"How about Colombian?" Will said. "A little sour, to my taste, but then again you won't really be drinking it. You'll just have the nanos tickling your brain."

Disappointed. There it was. He'd wanted Will to lure him up to that mysterious room again. He should have stayed when he'd had the chance. Now? Now he was just another customer. Ernest found the cheapest drip, and then the second-cheapest. "How's the house blend?"

Will shrugged. "Bland."

"I think...I think I'll try that. I started a little too strong last time."

"Suit yourself." Will opened a cabinet and selected a hanging drip. Ernest scanned his chip. His remaining credits flashed on the screen. He could make them last for twenty-five more days if he was very careful about where he went, what he bought. From now on, he'd only order free feeds. He'd visit the coffee shop no more than every other day. And maybe, if he was very careful, on day twenty-nine he could try drinking some actual brewed coffee.

"Go ahead," Will said, "pick a seat. I'll bring the bag out to you."

"Don't forget the book. The book-shaped monitor, I mean." Ernest turned and looked at the tables. Only two were occupied today, both of them with VR-helmeted customers. He didn't think either of them were the people he'd seen speaking with Will, though possibly one customer had been there last time, judging by the outfit, body type and position. The other wore the uniform of a second-decade tech—someone on a vaca-day.

The tech snickered at something in his VR. It wasn't merely a laugh. Ernest had recently played and analyzed enough laugh files to know; there was something condescending about the way it sounded. Ernest took an instant dislike to him, and chose a seat as far away as possible.

Will came around the counter. His pants hung low on his hips. He was definitely too thin. Didn't his POD-mind care? Not that AIs could actually care, but it was certainly against their programs to let their charges waste away. Maybe Will's job was just too physical, and his interface needed to be tweaked.

Will cleared his throat. Ernest blinked and looked up from Will's hips.

"Here." Will dropped the monitor on the table. It clattered. He snapped the hanging drip onto an overhead hook and unkinked the tubing. "Shunt."

"Wait...uh...." Ernest searched for something to say. Wasn't Will supposed to *chat* with him? He was a customer. He'd just paid. There was a fine line between Will's eyebrows. Ernest couldn't match it with an emotion; it wasn't enough of a clue to go on. "How do I hook into a feed on the book?"

"You don't. This is a freestanding monitor. It's not on the W3."

"Wow. I mean, I've never...."

"I'll load some feeds for you," he said, while gazing out the window at the street where PODs did their stop-and-start creep down the magnetic strip. "I've got all kinds of wild stuff. What're you in the mood for?"

Ernest had no idea. Psychology, perhaps? It had seemed like interesting enough company when he'd been unable to sleep.

"How about porn?" Will suggested. "The W3 was practically made of porn before the big Purge."

"Sure. That sounds fine." If Ernest couldn't parse what the feed was supposed to be about, he'd just have L0U15E help him look it up later. The exact feeds wouldn't be available to him, of course, if they'd been Purged. But he could at least gain some historical context.

Will put his hand in his pocket and pulled out a thin case. "Your first time off the grid?"

"Well...I suppose."

Will raised an eyebrow. "If you had your own port-a-player, I could copy you some feeds that'd really curl your toes. And not just porn. Politics. Religion. History. You'd be surprised at all the things that're nothing like you've been told." He snapped a datachip into the book-shaped monitor. "Here ya go. Hetero pairs, homo pairs, group and solo. It's all in the menu."

Ernest nodded, scrambling to parse. He'd understood the

word "menu." That would need to be enough.

Will rolled up Ernest's sleeve, bit the tip off the hanging drip's tubing needle, spat the tip on the floor and shunted in. "I'll set it for a slow feed. You won't get a nice rush like last time, but you'll last longer."

Ernest watched the clear fluid drip into the tube. Shunting had always been routine for him, but the workings were hidden inside his POD. He felt his pulse begin to race after the first dozen drips. The room seemed brighter. He felt...good. Invincible. "Yes," he whispered.

Will looked at him for a moment, squinted, and made a smallish smile that didn't match any of the ones Ernest had studied. "Okay, then. If you need anything, just yell. That's a figure of speech. A wave'll do."

Will checked the hanging drips on the VR customers, glanced out the window again, then went back behind the counter and began fingering sequences into the scanner. He kept his eyes on the door as he worked.

The less objectionable VR customer murmured something softly and curled onto his side in the chair. The tech tapped his foot. Ernest looked down at his book-shaped monitor. There was the menu. He figured he should just start at the beginning. "Hetero Pairs," he told it. It did nothing. He repeated himself. "Hetero pairs."

"It's a touchscreen," Will called from behind the counter. "Old-time, I know, but think about the privacy factor."

Ernest had never considered it. He'd never watched a feed outside his POD before.

He touched the menu item and a submenu fanned out. Missionary. Oral. Anal. Kink.

Missionary was first on the list, but it seemed too religious to mark the occasion of Ernest's first successful coffee-and-book excursion. Oral. That seemed appropriate, given that old-time coffee was taken by mouth.

Ernest was first struck by the fact that the people in the feed had no clothing on. And then, by the bizarre, distended penis of the man. It was huge, and stiff. There was a woman with him, in a plain room, crouched on a bed. The angle of the feed changed without Ernest's input, zooming tight on the woman's face. "Zoom out," he said, but the feed stayed trained on her mouth.

Maybe the feed couldn't zoom. It must have been ancient. The man and woman must have been *homo sapiens*, though none of the *sapiens* in Ernest's studies had ever looked quite like them. Especially that penis. Ernest wondered how the man could even walk.

The woman ran her tongue down the man's stomach, and Ernest blushed. Tongues are for talking, as his Deacon always said. Was there even a word for what she was doing? There must have been, once.

The man seemed to enjoy it. He sank his fingers into her hair and pulled her closer, prodding her face with his gigantic, stiff penis.

The feed zoomed out by itself again. Disconcerting. Ernest felt the room sway—acutely, since his senses had all been sharpened by the caffeine. The man's expression was strange. It looked like pain, initially. But the rest of the scene wouldn't make sense if that were the case. His hips thrust up, burying his penis deep inside the woman's mouth. (How could she stand it?) Ernest could barely resist the urge to slide a finger into his own mouth, see what it felt like inside. Of course, he'd never do something so disgraceful, not even with Will completely focused on the doorway and the other two customers lost in their VR.

Unless he went outside, somewhere between the buildings. Cameras were scarce in this part of town.

Ernest stood, and then remembered that he was shunted in to the hanging drip. He'd get Will to remove the shunt. As he raised his hand to get Will's attention, the front door burst open and a man scrambled in.

He was ancient and stooped, and mostly bald. Familiar, and yet, not. Why would he be familiar? It wasn't as if Ernest had ever met many.... He suddenly recognized the man from his last visit. In fact, the old-timer had been at the very table Ernest was now sitting at and contemplating putting something in his mouth. He might have even been reading from the very same book-shaped monitor.

Will sprang to his feet. "Matthew. You changed your mind?"

"I'm not ready," Matthew said, and his voice was loud and strong, which confused Ernest. The men who looked like that in old-time feeds had querulous, small voices. "Help me."

"Okay, quiet down." Will dashed out from behind the counter, and pivoted to point at Ernest. "Keep your mouth shut about this and I'll buy you a brew."

Ernest nodded, baffled. The quiet man in the VR helmet rocked himself gently. The tech in the VR helmet crossed his arms and smirked at whatever he was seeing.

Will turned back to Matthew. "You're sweating bullets." Ernest had no idea what a bullet was, but he filed it into his new-idiom category regardless. "Did you shunt into your POD again? How stupid are you?"

"Did I shunt? No, no, the POD's gone. I ran here."

Will went pale. He looked exactly like the diagram of 'dismayed.' "From where?" he said quietly.

Matthew wiped his brow on his sleeve, panting. "Reclaim."

"You...led them here...from Reclaim."

Ernest felt himself begin to tremble. His drip was probably too fast.

"It's okay." Matthew hunched over with his hands on his knees, heaving great gasps as he struggled to breathe. Ernest heard his lungs whistle from across the room. "No one followed me. I already turned in the POD, but I've got some credits left. Your friends can use them. Everyone can use more credits. You'll talk to them for me, get them to take my credits, join me up...."

Ernest's shaking continued, even intensified, at the thought of Reclaim. He told himself to stop thinking about it. He wouldn't need to go there for another twenty-five days.

"Credits won't do jack shit for us," Will snapped. "I need a POD. You knew that. We went over it a million times."

Shadows flickered over the book-shaped monitor. Ernest craned his neck and looked out the window behind him. Men in white jumpsuits, too many of them to count, filled the sidewalk outside the shop.

"Damn it," Will said, his eyes on the window. "I am totally screwed." He grabbed Matthew by the arm. "Come on. Hurry."

The idiomatic use of the word *screwed* was a strange as the word *bullet*, but Will's tone convinced Ernest that being screwed was definitely something to be avoided.

₁₁₁CHAPTER FOUR₁₁₁

THE COFFEE SHOP FILLED with men in white. Each of them had a metal Taser in his dominant hand. In addition to a bigger Taser than the others, the leader had a W3 link flashing on his temple.

They were quick, but Will had been quicker. Will had also locked the door behind him with those old-time keys of his. Old doors couldn't be opened via W3. They needed to be kicked down.

The noise was terrifying, but Ernest was shunted in, and didn't know what to do other than sit there and watch.

The VR customers blinked and swayed as the security ops ended their sessions by yanking off the helmets. "Who's in charge of the shop?" demanded a man in white.

The other customers shrugged and said they didn't know. Ernest did the same. He even made sure to act as dazed as they did, even though the caffeine coursing through his veins was urging him to stand up, grab his drip, and run.

But why would he? He didn't even know where to go.

"Come on," snapped a security op. "You're in the way. Shunt out. Go back to your PODs."

The quiet man moved first. He disconnected his shunt and staggered through the crowd toward the door. The tech went next. Ernest noticed that he took the VR helmet with him, which gave Ernest an idea. He disengaged his own shunt—a strange feeling—then made his way through the men in white. The book-shaped monitor was clutched to his chest. None of the security ops challenged him. In fact, none even looked at him twice.

The quiet man stood at the curb, squinting at the magnetic strip. He seemed stunned. Ernest was about to check and see if he was all right, but then he remembered that it probably looked as if he was stealing Will's monitor. How could he explain that he figured it was best to remove it, especially if it contained contraband? And besides, the sight of the stranger's mouth, slightly open, made Ernest wonder what it would be like to poke part of himself inside.

He turned away, and called, "Louise!"

The street was jammed with PODs that clustered together, jockeying for position over the magnetic strip. L0U15E looked like all the others, matte gray to catch the solar power and oval for aerodynamics. Ernest picked her out when her viscreen lit up.

He broke into a run. It felt good.

"Ernest! Why are you running like that?"

"Open up," he said, without answering her. She'd tap into W3 soon enough and see that the coffee shop had been raided.

"You're flushed again."

"It's just the caffeine." The POD rotated so that the door faced the curb as it sighed open. Ernest climbed in. He thought of Will, and of the old man, Matthew. How strange of him to run from Reclaim. Where else could he possibly go, at his age? And it wasn't much of a shock to see Will involved. His talk about brewing coffee and actually swallowing it was sheer heresy—so running off with a retiree on their thirtieth day wasn't something Ernest would put past him.

Ernest was concerned for them, but they'd been well ahead of the security ops, thanks to Will's foresight in activating that ancient locking mechanism. If anyone could handle himself, it was Will.

"The temperature outside is 20.6 degrees," Louise said. "Current time is 2:12 pm." She paused, then observed, "You have a piece of equipment with you."

Ernest winced—he must have thought he was alone. How was it possible to grow accustomed to being alone in such a short amount of time? "It's a portable monitor."

A diagram of the book-shaped monitor flashed onto the POD's interior viscreen. "It's an antique. Manufactured between one hundred forty-eight and one hundred fifty-one years ago... though I can't be more specific than that without parsing the model number. Does it work?"

"I guess. It's got visual, but no audio."

The diagram spun, and a C-shaped piece of electronics lit up. "You'd need an audio interface for that."

"I want one," he said. Because maybe the wet open mouth and the huge penis would make more sense if he had an audio context in which to place it.

"Searching..." L0U15E said.

Ernest hugged the monitor to his chest, slipped his hand between his body and the screen, and touched the on-pad. He tilted the monitor so he could just make out the image. Not that he was ashamed of it, of course. It just seemed that if the monitor had been made for privacy, he should keep its contents private.

"Three audio interfaces for sale," said L0U15E. "Lowest price including travel tariff, 19.125 credits."

The man pulled his penis out of the woman's mouth and rubbed it on her lips and cheek, leaving a glistening trail behind. "Louise, what's the term for the fluid in a mouth?"

"Saliva. Why would you ask about something like that?"

"No reason." He shielded the top of the portable monitor with his hand and viewed it through the narrow gap between his hand and his chest. The man's penis was coated with saliva, shining with it across the smooth, domed tip and over the raised texture of the veins that bulged from the thick shaft.

"Well? Should I find a route to the seller of that audio interface?"

"Hm?" The woman trapped the man's penis between her breasts and was sliding her body up and down the length of it. The man said something to her and they both laughed. They seemed to be enjoying themselves.

"The audio interface?" L0U15E repeated.

Ernest would have been in on their joke if he had the audio interface. "Oh. Uh, yes. I want it. How much is it?"

"I just told you. 19.125 credits."

"Really? That much." And yet, Will had promised Ernest an 18-credit brew in exchange for his silence. It all seemed to balance so nicely. "Let's go get it. I've got another twenty-five days to enjoy it."

The resale shop was in a building as ancient as the coffee shop, but it was a different type of architecture, more angular and square, made all of concrete and metal inside. Ernest would have been utterly fascinated with it, had he encountered the place before he'd ended up with Will's book-shaped monitor in his possession. But now he simply wanted to purchase the audio interface and go back to his POD.

Or did he?

"Excuse me," he asked the clerk, a bored-looking girl in her early second decade who had handled the transaction with as few words as possible before returning to her W3-game. "Have you got any rooms in the back?"

The girl looked up, brow furrowed. Confused.

"I wanted to be alone with...my game."

Her eyebrows went up. Empathy. "They're back there," she said. "But they're dirty."

"May I?"

"Do you need anything? A port? A light?"

"No, nothing. My game is all powered up." It occurred to Ernest that by calling the antique book-shaped monitor a game, he was lying. Just like people in those old-time feeds. It worked, too.

How thrilling.

"Do what you want," she said, while her fingers flickered under her scanner. "As long as you stop interrupting me. I'm on level 1,182."

Ernest went through the door at the back of the room and found himself in a short hallway with a door on each side. The one in back had a sign over it that read "EXIT" in old-time letters, probably on plastic or vinyl, crackled with age. Ernest checked the door on the right. Inside the room there were banks of components along the walls. Their tiny round light-emitting diodes blinked as they controlled the temperature, lighting and W3 link for the building. Ernest backed out, since he presumed there was a camera somewhere amid the small flickering lights.

Behind the other door was a room that had once been covered in tiles, though many were broken, or simply gone. Rusted piping gaped from the floor, and slabs of bent metal marked off individual stalls. An old-time bathroom. Most buildings more than three centuries old had them. Some of them still had plumbing that functioned, though who knew what sorts of pathogens the water carried?

The plumbing was gone from this bathroom, and nothing had been invested to remake the place into anything else. The old-time buildings that pre-dated PODs were massive wastes of space and materials. Nowadays, rooms that were too expensive to renovate were often abandoned and forgotten.

Ernest stepped into the crumbling bathroom and shut the door behind him. A thick layer of dust coated everything. The room hadn't been used in years. Nothing in it was powered. In fact, the only light that reached the room was the gray daylight that filtered through the grime-smeared glass block windows.

He scanned for the telltale blinking LEDs of cameras. He saw none. And even though he was probably the first living soul to set foot in the room since the year he'd left the natal center, he wedged a broken scrap of lumber under the doorknob to ensure that no one would take it into their minds to explore the deserted bathroom while he was using it.

He twisted the audio interface onto his ear and turned on Will's monitor. The sound staggered him. The man grunted as he jammed his penis deep into the woman's throat. She made a noise like "mmm-mmm-mmm." Ernest had expected words. He found the bizarre sounds acutely disturbing.

He brought up the menu and found a speed setting. He adjusted it a few ticks higher, hoping to scan through more of the Purged feeds before L0U15E began to worry about his whereabouts. The feeds went by much more quickly this way, though he paused the feeds and slowed them to "normal" whenever the characters spoke. Many of the words were new to him: fuck, tits, pussy, suck, balls, bitch, cock and dick (though those were synonyms, as far as he could tell), whore, lick and ass. The idiomatic use of "come" was fascinating, and "eat" was downright bizarre.

He finished the last of the hetero pairs and looked up from Will's monitor in a daze. The glass block window was dark. It was late, and his arm felt heavy. Time to shunt into his POD. He left the bathroom and said goodbye to the girl behind the counter on his way out of the shop. She said nothing. Maybe she'd attained level 1,183.

"Louise!"

Ernest's POD detached from a nearby dock and glided toward him. "How was your shopping, Ernest?"

"Good," he said. "Very educational."

It occurred to him that he was lying again.

ⅠⅠⅠCHAPTER FIVEⅠⅠⅠ

THE NEXT MORNING, ERNEST parked his POD farther away from the coffee shop than he needed to. He told L0U15E that he wanted to walk. "I don't know why you'd want to do that, Ernest. It's not efficient. Let me drop you off."

He opened his POD and climbed out. "It's not about efficiency, Louise. I'd like to try a stroll." The lying got easier and easier with practice.

"All right. But I'll have to increase your calories, which means longer dialysis tomorrow."

"That'll be fine." He tucked the monitor under his arm and made his way to the sidewalk. In old-time feeds, sidewalks were packed with men and women. They stood aside for each other as they passed, and tipped their hats and said, "How do you do?" The sidewalk he navigated was empty as far as he could see, except for the tufts of weeds growing up between the cracks.

Ernest came around the corner and saw glowing red letters hovering in front of the coffee shop's front door. A symbol of a tapping hammer appeared for a few seconds, and then the words *closed for repair*. He sank into an alcoved doorway across the street, and he stared. How could the coffee shop be closed? He knew how, of course, since he'd seen the security ops kick the old-time door inside to splinters. But how long would this closing last? He only had twenty-four more days.

Frustration? He felt the lines of his own face. No. Not frustration. Anger.

He turned from the doorway and stomped back toward his POD. He was so focused on the sidewalk that the hand that snatched him from his route overbalanced him and dragged him into the alleyway before he could protest at all.

"What're you doing coming here? Are you trying to get us killed?" Will's voice. Easy enough to recognize—one of the few non-AI voices that had ever said more than a sentence or two to Ernest.

"Killed...dead?"

Will dragged him farther into the alleyway, behind a concrete enclosure that had once housed recycling bins. Twentieth century Styrofoam edged the place where the enclosure met the ground like a grayish snowdrift. "What other kind of kill is there? Oh, never mind. You're giving me those damn doe-eyes again." Will sighed and slumped back against the concrete. "You weren't followed, right?"

Ernest shook his head solemnly.

"So what did you tell the Storm Troopers?"

Storm. Troopers. Some nickname for the men in white? That had to be it. It was the only definition that made sense. "Nothing. They hardly spoke to the customers at all."

"Tch. Lame. Okay, so if you didn't say anything, and they didn't say anything, maybe I'm not in such bad shape after all."

Ernest stared at Will's physique. Muscle and sinew stood out against his skin. Tendons shifted in his neck when he turned his head. The musculature of his chest formed a discernible concavity at his sternum. He was so muscled that he looked startlingly like the *homo sapiens* in the data feed. But of course *homo sapiens* evolved into *homo consummatus*. So it was best not to stare at Will's crotch and wonder what was beneath his trousers. The comment about Will's "shape" was probably rhetorical anyway. It seemed like the type of thing Ernest would say to L0U15E.

"I saved your reader," Ernest said, hoping to change the subject to something he understood. "But I think one of your VR sets was stolen."

Will waved the absent VR set away. "So that's what you're back for? More porn?"

"The porn was...interesting. But didn't you say you had some history? I think I might want to know more about that. What was Purged, and why? What was it really like before?"

Will sagged against the wall and let out a long, low sigh. "You want history."

Ernest glanced over his shoulder toward the mouth of the alley. No Storm Troopers. Good. "If the offer still stands."

"I can get you plenty of history."

Ernest had no doubt of that. Will worked in a brick and mortar building. He was surrounded by real coffee and actual books. The question was, how much did Will's information cost? "Of course, if it's too much trouble, I can access feeds."

"Not pre-Purge data, you can't."

Ernest combed his fingers through his hair. "I was only a data clerk. My salary was small. I don't have all that many credits saved." There. He'd said it. No doubt Will would be much less eager to help him now. Will ran a business, and his livelihood depended on people spending money—that was understood—but Ernest's reserves were low enough that he couldn't have gone on pretending they were ample, especially with all the credits he'd spent on the audio link. "My budget is small."

"Credits make the world go 'round, no doubt about that. But maybe you've got other things."

Ernest touched the plastic link that curved around his ear, hidden by his hair. It would be useless to him by the end of the month. Will might as well have it. "Maybe."

"What model is your POD?"

Ernest cut his eyes toward the distant lot where he'd left it. "L0U15E. Why? Her hardware's standard; there's nothing to strip."

Will shrugged and looked away, as if the opposite wall of the alley had suddenly become fascinating.

"At least," Ernest went on, "I don't think so. And besides, I need her for trade-in."

"Do you?"

Ernest struggled to figure out what Will meant by that

question. "Why wouldn't I?"

"If you're dead, what do you care one way or the other?"

Ernest's Deacon preferred the term "ultimate reward." *Dead* was used for other life forms—plants, insects and animals—or idiomatically, for non-functioning electronics. It clicked in with a cold, sharp finality that felt horribly right. "Well...you know. Deacon says that Reclaim won't demagnetize you without a trade-in. They just...toss your body aside. Bury it in a ditch. Burn it." And the electrons and quarks, the electromagnetic bits that made up the human soul, would be trapped there, slowly dissipating as the body rotted away, or scattering as flames consumed it.

Death could hardly be avoided. But Will was asking him to risk oblivion for a few newsfeeds.

"You really think they'd do that?" Will asked. "Just because you showed up at Reclaim without your POD?"

"I...guess. If they didn't, everyone would sell off their PODs at the end, splurge on something before their final days."

"Maybe nobody realizes their PODs could be worth something to anyone else. Maybe they never met an interested buyer."

"You were trying to buy that old man's POD, weren't you? The one from the shop. Matthew."

Will stared hard at the opposite wall, as still as if he'd frozen. "Matthew was my friend."

"Was. What happened to him?"

Will flung his arms in the air, startling Ernest.

"What do you think?" Will wrapped his arms around himself, squeezing tight. The sinews in his neck stood out in stark relief. "He was old. He was slow. He had all that crap running through his system that his POD was pumping through him."

"Was his POD defective?"

Will turned to Ernest, and looked at him—hard. "You really don't know, do you?"

Ernest looked back. It was difficult to keep from dropping Will's gaze.

"Why do you think," Will demanded, "that the nanosecond you turn thirty, you start to die?"

Because you did. Because that's what happens. Because Deacon said so. Ernest didn't know how to answer.

Rhetorical. It didn't seem that Will expected him to. "It's not your body. Your body doesn't say, *Well, now I'm thirty. I'd better start shutting down.* Once upon a time, people had jobs when they were thirty. They would get married, have kids, get divorced, get married again. They would swim the English channel and ride the space shuttle and climb Mount Everest. They didn't just lay down and die."

"But that was then...."

"Do you think we're so different now? Nothing evolves that fast. Your body gets a little help shutting down." Will grabbed Ernest by the shoulders and swung him around. Ernest felt his back hit the cool concrete. Will loomed in front of him, backlit. Ernest couldn't read his face, could only make out the shape of his spiked hair. "Look at you." Will pressed a thumb into Ernest's cheekbone and dragged it up to the corner of his eye. "Crow's feet."

Ernest's heart was pounding in his throat. He wanted to pull his face away, but there was nowhere to move.

"I met you four days ago. Your face was smooth as a baby's."

Anger gave Ernest the strength to shake Will free. "Yes, I have wrinkles. I'm thirty and five."

"Four days. You got crow's feet in four days?"

"You make that sound surprising."

"You act as if it's not."

Ernest slid around Will, eager to put some space between him and the recycling enclosure. Will grabbed Ernest's arm again and pulled him close. "Don't shunt in."

"What?"

"You heard me. When you get into your POD tonight, don't shunt in."

Ernest gave Will a hard look. "Why? So I leave more resources for you to scavenge?"

Will's eyes went wide. Surprise, or something like it. "You're a smart boy, Ernest. Think about it. Something's aging you all of sudden, and it's happening quick. Keep your shunt arm to yourself and go without your biofuel for a night, and see if you can feel the difference."

"I'll starve."

"Nobody starves overnight. And besides. There's always food."

Ernest turned and began walking toward the end of the alley. Whatever Will knew, finding out about it wasn't worth being mocked.

"Ernest." Will's voice was quiet. Ernest turned. Will prodded an old Styrofoam cooler-box on the ground with the toe of his boot. "If I'm not at work tomorrow, I'll leave your feeds in here."

Ernest looked at the box, and then turned toward the parking lot again.

"And one more thing," Will said. Ernest looked back over his shoulder. "If I'm not there, don't mention me to anybody. Okay?"

Ernest turned toward LOU15E's dock point, thrust his head forward, jammed his hands in his pockets and walked. If Will wasn't there, it wasn't as if anyone else would be likely to speak to him, anyway.

o ◎ o

Ernest accessed the free feed on "bus station," and scanned it in one quick glance. According to the information, the building was an old-time POD dock, back when PODs had burned fossil fuels and ran on wheels instead of magnetic strips. These particular PODs transported multiple passengers at the same time. Ernest couldn't imagine how they handled the close proximity to one another. Then again, *homo sapiens* touched all the time, and they seemed to enjoy it, too—if the pre-Purge porn was anything to go by.

"Is this building currently being used for anything, Louise?"

"Now, I wouldn't know about that, Ernest."

Probably not.

"Stop," Ernest told her.

"Here? There's nowhere to dock."

"Then just pull off to the side and solar charge." The average POD's solar charge still needed to be augmented by city power, but at least charging quietly would keep her from running down, and might even help Ernest conserve a fraction of a credit.

Ernest felt L0U15E's sensors hum. "Asbestos. Lead. *E.coli. C. tetani* and *Geravium tetani. Mus musculus, R. norvegicus, Thamnophis sirtalis parietalis.*" The viscreen lit up with columns of diagrams and formulae, and a particularly horrible hologram of a rotting limb. "Tell me you're not thinking of going in there."

Ernest sighed. "It's fine, Louise. I'll be careful."

Ten more holos stacked themselves across Ernest's line of sight. Rat bites. Snake bites. *Homo sapiens* in the throes of lockjaw. Microscopic close-ups of vermin burrowing under human flesh.

"I said I'll be careful."

"You're probably hungry. Why don't you shunt in first? And then we can go to the VR Palace. There's a new feed playing about a data clerk. Wouldn't that be interesting? You qualify for the senior discount, too. Only three credits."

"Open door."

A few LEDs flashed, and after a pause, the door whispered open. Ernest climbed from the POD and squinted against the pale burn of the sun. The weed-choked lot was scattered with bits of broken asphalt. A row of interconnected plastic chairs lay on its side, sun-faded, but otherwise whole. The building's windows all gaped, jagged glass hanging from the frames like icicles in old-time Christmas feeds. He picked his way through the weeds and stepped over the windowsill with great care, since he didn't want to spend his final days fending off flesh-eating bacteria or ringworm.

Although L0U15E had warned him about the vermin living inside, except for a sparrow chirping in the rafters, nothing in the old bus station moved. It was peaceful, in a vast and dusty way. He stepped over a scattering of broken syringes and made his way deeper, past the large rectangles of sunlight splayed across the crumbling floor, and into the shadows. He found a plastic chair that was reasonably level and plumb, blew off a coat of dust, and sat.

The shop where he'd purchased the earpiece had offered a selection of datachips that fit the book-shaped monitor. They were antique, but they'd been fairly inexpensive, just a credit or two apiece. Even though none of them were likely to contain any information that would "curl his toes" as Will had put it, Ernest had bought five chips anyway. The subject matter might be extraneous, but he was filled with the overwhelming need to understand.

Daddy is a Contractor was bizarre for its context rather than its content. The *homo sapiens* in the feed designed and built a gigantic, inefficient structure with the help of archaic computers and clumsy robots. But the word *Daddy*, and the implication that the audience of the feed (like lower life forms) was the product of the meshing of genitalia, the stiff, wet, gaping and flushed genitalia from the porn feeds, left Ernest's mind spinning.

He finished the contractor feed, and another one on great white sharks *(Carcharodon carcharias)* that was full of bloody, gaping maws. When the last watery image of the feed faded, he slipped the monitor into the front of his shirt and sat back in the chair, no longer caring if he ended up covered in dust and spores. And as he stared up at the ceiling, he tried to figure out why he no longer seemed to fit inside his own skin.

ⅰⅰⅰCHAPTER SIXⅰⅰⅰ

ERNEST WATCHED LIGHTS FLICKER over L0U15E's interior viscreen. "I can't imagine why you'd want to go anywhere with your blood sugar so low," she said.

"You haven't taken my blood sugar level. How would you know it's low?"

"Because you haven't shunted in! What's the matter, Ernest? Pretty soon I'll be able to detect ketones in your breath, and then I'll go into override and bring you straight to the health monitor. Why do you want it to come to that?" Images of skeletal men appeared on the screen. Ernest noted they all just happened to have dark eyes and shoulder-length brown hair like he did. AIs didn't utilize subtlety very well. "Look at what can happen."

"How long?" he said.

"How long...what?"

"How long did it take them to starve? Access free public feed on starvation, please."

"Oh, Ernest...."

The data streamed down the screen, overlaying the images of starved men. Ernest's eyes flicked over the characters. "The body doesn't even enter starvation mode for three weeks. Three weeks! I've only got twenty-two days left; it doesn't matter if I ever shunt in again."

"You'll dehydrate."

"I'm tired of arguing. Open the door."

LEDs flashed. L0U15E's sensors hummed. And just as Ernest was about to repeat his request, the door slid open.

He climbed out and squinted. A light rain was falling, but the clouds in the sky looked bright white after his interment in his dimly lit POD. He strode down the block, doing his best to ignore the lightheadedness that undoubtedly did mean he was dehydrated, if not starving to death, and rounded the corner to the coffee house.

The glowing red letters were gone. A warm light shone out through the shop window.

Ernest suddenly understood what old-time text feeds meant when they said someone's heart leapt. He jogged across the street, causing a POD to swerve off the magnetic track as he did so, and ran the rest of the way to the front door. He stopped and waited, holding his breath. The door opened. He stepped inside.

The shop smelled wrong.

There was something plastic about the air, as if a new filter had been installed and hadn't quite finished outgassing yet. Ernest looked at the counter, which was unmanned, and then at the mundane tables. Four customers lingered there, one in VR, the others enjoying their IVs with eyes closed. He didn't recognize any of the people.

Something flashed in his peripheral vision. He looked down. Above a large red button set into the counter, the words "Ring Bell For Service" flashed in holo-letters, alternating with a pictograph of someone ringing the bell and being greeted by a smiling face.

Ernest pushed the button.

After several long seconds, a door opened behind the counter, and a short, compact man with disheveled hair came out. He was early in his third decade, certainly no older than twenty-five years, and he lacked Will's strangely developed musculature. He must have been new at the job. "What do you want?" he asked.

Wasn't that supposed to be, "How can I help you?" Ernest backed up a step. He almost asked where Will was—in fact, it was on the "tip of his tongue"—but then he remembered that he wasn't supposed to say anything about Will. "I, uh.... The other day there was a raid while I was here."

"Um. Yes?"

"And so I wasn't done with my hanging drip when the security ops forced me to leave. It was mostly full, in fact."

The clerk's lips moved while Ernest talked, as if he had difficulty parsing spoken communication. After an awkward pause, he said, "Not my problem."

Ernest wanted to turn and leave. If Will wasn't around, there was no reason for him to stay. And yet it seemed as if the other clerk expected him to argue. "But I didn't even get my flavor chip. I want my flavor chip, at least."

The clerk sighed and rolled his eyes. "What flavor?"

"House blend."

"Black? Cream? Sugar?"

"Sugar."

The clerk turned, scratching his scalp as he jerked open the door to the cold storage unit. He grabbed a syringe from the back, peeled the chip off its wrapper, and threw the syringe down the recycle chute. "Here. Go away."

Ernest held the flavor chip between his thumb and forefinger and stared at the recycle chute flap as it swung back and forth a couple of times, then settled itself shut. The clerk turned and walked back through the door he'd come from.

Ernest was left staring at the empty counter, the ridiculous pictograph of that smiling face. He tried to smack the letters with the back of his hand, but his fingers passed through them, and they re-formed themselves as if he had never been there.

A thump drew his attention back to the door behind the counter. If he recalled the shape of the building correctly, that door would accessed a space beneath the stairs.

Maybe that's where Will was—through that door.

Ernest took hold of the movable segment of the countertop and bent it upward on its hinge. He stepped behind it. None of the other customers seemed to notice; their attention was focused on themselves.

The door behind the counter was an old-time wooden door. Ernest turned the doorknob (it was unlocked) and found that the room behind the door was not a room at all—it was another set of stairs that led down.

Using the stairs properly was more difficult going down than it was going up, so Ernest moved carefully, and therefore, quietly. He wasn't sneaking—not on purpose. But when he reached the bottom, the rude clerk, deep inside a game, didn't notice him any more than the patrons upstairs had.

Ernest tilted his head and considered the holos. He assumed it was a game that the clerk was playing—but it wasn't like any game he'd ever seen before.

Instead of colored cubes, this game projected holos of people. The people weren't very realistic. Their skin was brightly colored—blue, lavender, orange—and they had the heads of cats and dogs and other animals. They were also naked, and their breasts and cocks were so oversized they would have made it difficult to get around, if the holo figures were real.

The colorful animal-people circled the clerk, but he'd picked out one, a bright green rabbit-headed woman, and he'd focused mainly on her. He coaxed her forward, and she bounced on the balls of her bare feet, ready to turn and run.

"Here," the clerk said. He patted his chest to indicate she should come closer. "Here." He held something behind his back, some pointy piece of gaming gear Ernest was unfamiliar with—though since he preferred old-time feeds to games, that wasn't really surprising. Besides, this game looked as obscure as the book-shaped monitor.

The rabbit-woman holo advanced a single step. "Yes," the clerk said, with an odd, cloying inflection on the word. "Here." The holo took one more step....

The clerk's hand shot out, jamming the sharp tip of the device he'd been hiding directly between the rabbit-woman's breasts. The holo flailed in distress and dark green fluid sprayed from the entry point. It wasn't real distress, Ernest reminded himself. It was just a holo. Even so, seeing the rabbit-woman fall to her knees, desperately trying to hold shut the leaking gash on her chest, was unsettling.

Even more unsettling was the way the clerk laughed, low and mean. He reached between his legs and massaged himself as the rabbit-woman toppled onto her side, and the green fluid began gushing out more quickly.

Ernest cast his gaze about the room—crumbling walls that stank of mildew, piles of old electronic gear, a dusty POD with its propulsion gear stripped off propped in the corner, its hatch hanging open.

No Will.

Good. It meant Ernest had no reason to linger.

He stole back up the stairs quickly and took one final look around the coffee shop. No Will here, either. The sight of the shop without Will in it gave him a sick pang somewhere in his alimentary canal. He pressed his hand into his diaphragm and exited the shop. When he looked up one side of the street, then down the other, he saw nothing but clusters of rounded PODs gliding down the magnetic strip in the center. Again, no Will.

Of course Will wouldn't be standing there in the street waiting for him. He'd be somewhere unmonitored. Like the alley.

Ernest waited for a break in POD traffic this time, and darted across the street during a gap he could fit himself through without interrupting the flow. He chose a roundabout route that wove between and behind the old buildings, feeling very clever for doing so, and then finally snuck over to the spot where Will had promised to leave him some feeds.

Dampness prickled Ernest's forehead and back, and his respiratory rate was elevated. He could feel his heart beating. He darted into the concrete enclosure.

It was empty.

Disappointment. He didn't suppose he'd actually expected Will to be there, but maybe there'd been a sliver of hope.

He raked his damp hair into a bundle at the back of his neck and held it there while he squatted down by the Styrofoam cooler. He opened the lid, and stared.

He'd expected data chips. Instead, he found an old-time key.

Ernest wondered why his heart felt like it was pounding in his throat. He placed his fingertips against the hollow at the base of his neck and felt some blood vessel throbbing there. The heart couldn't move around inside the body, could it? He wished he'd studied more anatomy. Now it would probably remain a mystery. He only had twenty-two days left.

He picked up the key and ran his thumb over the cool metal. There was no explanation, just the key itself. He closed his eyes as he held it, and he thought. The coffee shop seemed as logical a place to start testing the key as any.

Once made his way back across the street and waited for the front door to admit him, he rehearsed a lie about how he thought he deserved the rest of his hanging drip since he'd paid for it and all, but the counter was still empty except for the blinking letters and stupid pictograph. There were only three customers at the tables now, all of them in VR. Pretending to browse, in case a feed monitor happened to be watching the coffee shop's feed at that very moment, Ernest eased along the wall, then meandered gradually toward the back hallway.

The old-time wooden door was gone, probably nothing more than a bundle of splinters now, thanks to the Storm Troopers. An unbreakable plastic door with a W3 link flashing at its latch was in its place. Ernest turned and left. Disgusted.

He stood in front of the shop, close enough to the front door that every time he moved, whether to cross or uncross his arms or toss his hair out of his eyes, the door whispered open a few centimeters, as if it couldn't determine whether or not he was going to come in. He suspected it was none too rational to enjoy taunting an automatic door. But that didn't stop him from smiling just a little each time it opened a bit, and then closed. Or maybe it was more of a smirk.

Twenty years as a data clerk had left him with a fairly active mind, and so the door soon failed to hold his attention. He had an old-time key in his hand. One key, one lock. Will wouldn't have left him a key to a lock that no longer existed. Therefore, it was simply a matter of finding the lock.

The coffee shop's front door opened, and one of the VR customers, an early second-decade girl no older than thirteen, staggered onto the sidewalk and called out, "Ten fifty-six!" A POD detached from a docking station down the block and glided over to pick her up. Its door opened and she stepped inside. It closed, and she glided away.

Doors. They were practically everywhere. Ernest swallowed a momentary surge of panic. He only had twenty-two days. He couldn't very well try every door in the city. He clutched the key hard, until the toothy edge bit into his palm. He'd only need to try the old-time doors, he reminded himself. He shut his eyes, breathed deep, and sighed.

He figured he might as well get started. He didn't have much time to spare.

He went into the building next door. It was abandoned, doors either hanging open or broken down. In the building next to that, a data-recovery service, he told the clerk at the front desk he was a W3 Maintenance Tech and he needed to take some readings. If the clerk noticed his lack of a W3 uplink, he'd planned to pass off the audio link to his book-shaped monitor as some sort of external W3 device—but it was totally unnecessary. The clerk didn't even glance at him, just waved him into the building.

Had it always been this easy to lie?

The clerk in the next building and the one after that were much the same. One played a W3 game and another was busy watching holos. They waved Ernest through without even looking at him. While it was heartening to realize that he'd somehow acquired the skill of subterfuge, by nightfall the absence of a lock to fit his key grew discouraging.

He was dizzy. Most definitely dehydrated. It was tiring, this feeling of depletion he'd never had occasion to experience before. He stood inside the last building on the block, on the last door. He was about to try his key, but then he realized that it only led to the back alley.

The back alley.

He tried the door of the last building. It was unlocked. He darted through and slammed it behind him. The alleyway was empty, of living things, at least. Broken glass, weeds and the ubiquitous Styrofoam were piled so high they formed drifts. Ernest looked in the direction of the coffee shop and counted the buildings.

He'd never seen the shop from the back, but he ran his fingertips over the bricks with their mossy, damp mortar and decided he had indeed located the back of the building he was looking for. The shop in front was sealed from the back half of the first floor by the new W3-linked door. But the back half, the mysterious, private half that contained the upper stairway, was still connected to the alley by an old-time door, with an old-time lock.

He closed his eyes and waited for a wave of dizziness to pass, then he fit the key into the door's lock. He attempted to turn it to his left. It didn't move. He turned it to his right. There was resistance, and then...movement.

The key turned.

He slipped inside the back door of the coffee shop. The only light that reached the remains of the blocked-off hall came from the alley, but he could have navigated the back end of that hall in pure darkness. There was the end of the banister he'd held, following Will up those stairs. There was the first step.

Ernest eased the door shut and went upstairs.

⑪CHAPTER SEVEN⑪

ERNEST NEEDED TO LOOK through the doorway twice. The upstairs room where he'd enjoyed his first cup of coffee now looked more like the alleyway behind the building. Except instead of being knee-deep in drifting Styrofoam, the room was littered with hundreds and hundreds of mangled books.

His knees buckled.

He knelt on the floor, picked up a torn page, and pressed its brittle surface against his cheek. Then he sneezed and allowed the paper to flutter back down to the floor. He wiped his nose on the back of his sleeve and tried to figure out what to do, but the sight of all those historical documents so carelessly destroyed left him too stunned to even move.

He picked up the cover and front signature of one book, put it down, and then another. He touched book after book, each one precious, each one rendered useless by one pointless, wanton act of destruction.

His chest heaved, and his eyes and nose began to run. The dust was obviously too much for him.

When his head stopped spinning, he got his feet under him and stood. There was the precious cup he'd held, shattered in a dozen pieces, along with all the others that had shared the shelf with it. There was the velvet sofa, its fabric split, stuffing spilled forth like entrails.

He sagged against the doorframe and stared.

Eventually he could no longer make out the individual items that had been destroyed. The room seemed more like a scattering of gravel, or a patch of various weeds: a grouping of random things meshed into an amalgam. His eyes scanned the piles, the drifts, the stacks. And then they lit upon a door.

It was a narrow door, its wood the same color as the surrounding paneling. There was an old-time doorknob at waist level, and beneath it, an old-time lock.

Ernest fished the key from his pocket. He'd already found the lock that it opened. One key, one lock, wasn't that the way of it? He scowled, wondering. What if it wasn't?

Stepping carefully through the drifts of paper and board and dried flakes of glue, he eventually made his way to the far door. He slid the key into the lock. It fit.

It turned.

Beyond the narrow, locked doorway was another set of stairs, only this one seemed different than the stairs he'd just climbed. Its wooden risers were rough and unfinished, and even the walls seemed strange, bristling with gritty wooden slats and exposed nails.

Warm air that smelled of cellulose and time drifted down and caressed his damp face. The stairs creaked as he climbed, and he held his sleeve over his mouth and nose to keep from sneezing again. Light streamed through a tiny window, illuminating dust motes that swirled in the air. He stepped up to the small window, stood on his toes and peered outside.

Will's voice tickled his ear. "I guess it's true what they say: absence makes the heart grow fonder."

Ernest felt the warmth of Will's body close behind his. "Who says that?"

"Oh, you know. Them."

Ernest turned. Will stepped back just enough to allow him to turn around without rubbing up against him. Barely. Will had his typical smirk in place, but it faltered a bit when he looked at Ernest's eyes.

"What is it," Ernest said, "more crow's feet?"

"Not that I can see. Did you shunt in last night?"

"No. And I feel wretched."

Will thumbed some moisture from the corner of Ernest's eye. "And you've never felt anything less than perfect. So that's why you've been crying."

"What? Don't be absurd." Ernest shouldered his way past Will and clasped his arms over his chest to stop himself from feeling his own face.

"Grew some backbone? Maybe you've got testosterone coursing through your veins now that your POD hasn't filtered everything out of you. You wear it well."

Ernest made a mental note to view a free feed on testosterone, though he was fairly certain Will was just mocking him. "What happened down there?" he asked, so they could talk about something other than him.

Will glanced toward the stairway. "Where, my reading room? That's authority for you, eager to crush whatever it doesn't understand. If those bullies had any aptitude for reading, they would've become data clerks, not security ops."

Ernest felt Will's eyes on him but pretended not to notice, looking instead at the stacks of boxes and crates, and in the corner, a pile of cushions and blankets. "Who is that man? Downstairs...the, uh, down-downstairs."

"Oh, so you've seen the basement—and you've met Clarence. Was he playing Kill-Joy? Wait, scratch that. He's always playing Kill-Joy."

Ernest shuddered, and stared very hard at a cushion with a dent in the shape of a head in the middle of it.

"So you found me," Will said. "Now what're you gonna do with me?"

Some sort of challenge. Will was smiling, smirking, whatever one would call it. But Ernest's head spun, and it was so hot in the dusty, slant-ceilinged room. He sat down carefully on an antique wooden chair. "Have you got a saline drip? I must be dehydrated."

Will frowned. "Not handy, no." He shrugged. "But if you wanna put your mouth to good use, there's plenty of water."

Water. By mouth. Ernest fought the impulse to laugh, since Will was, of course, totally serious.

Will stood between Ernest's knees and looked down at him, and tucked a loose lock of hair behind his ear. He pressed the backs of his fingers to Ernest's cheek. "Y'know, I think you're right. Seriously. Have some water." He turned and opened a plastic cooler that was stacked among the boxes and crates, took out a pair of flasks. "Totally safe," he said, "reverse osmosis filtered and chilled to retard bacterial growth."

"Why is the water leaking through the flask?"

"It's not. That's condensation. Hot attic, cold flask."

Attic. Yes. Ernest remembered the term from *Daddy is a Contractor*. That's why the ceiling was at odd angles and all the wood was bare. Will shoved a damp, cold flask into Ernest's hand and Ernest shivered.

"Wish I had a drinking straw—sorry—but don't worry, I'll demo. And don't get flustered if you choke a little. We all do, until we get used to it."

"We?" Ernest repeated.

Will crouched between Ernest's knees. "Top screws off like so. Put it in your pocket for safe keeping. Press the lip of the flask against your mouth, tip your head back, hold your breath for a second and let just a little water into your mouth. If you fill your mouth up completely, you won't be able to swallow. Cradle it with your tongue. Swallow it—just like you'd swallow your own spit—as you exhale through your nose."

Spit. Saliva. Will tipped his head back and drank. Ernest watched the muscles in his throat work. A knob of hard tissue at the front of Will's larynx rose and fell. Ernest felt his own throat. A pair of tendons made a V-shaped hollow at the base, but aside from that, it was smooth. As he'd suspected.

"Okay," Will said. "Wanna give it a go?"

"I think I can wait until I get back to the POD."

Will grabbed Ernest's jaw and pulled his face to eye level. "Every time you shunt in, you're one day closer to death."

"Every day we live is one day closer to death, Will. And you've got it all turned around. PODs support life. It's their primary function."

"Until you're past your prime. Then the biofuel cocktail changes."

Did it? If so, it was probably just an adjustment to meet specific geriatric needs. "Keep your water." Ernest pressed the flask into Will's hands. "I think I need to go shunt in. Right now."

The flask fell to the floor as Will ignored it and grabbed his hand instead. "Don't."

Ernest shook his head. "I have to. I can't think straight."

"People used to pay good credits for that feeling," he said. His laugh was as stilted as a free-feed actor's. "Seriously, kiddo. Just drink some water."

Ernest focused on Will. It was difficult. The sensation was similar to the caffeine rush, but slower—sickening in a different way. "No, it's no use. We're not like each other."

Will narrowed his eyes. "How can you say that? You're the first person I've been able to hold a conversation with since Matthew."

"I'm flattered." Ernest's vision was tunneling. He pulled a hand free and ran his fingertips over the bulge in Will's throat. So many things fit together in his mind: Will's posture. His sinewy body. The way he could drink water, just like he was born to do it. The fact that he obviously had no POD of his own. The shape of his larynx. "But wanting something doesn't make it true. I can wish all I want, but it won't turn me into a *homo sapien*."

Ernest nudged past Will and stood. He staggered toward the stairs.

"You'd be surprised," Will said quietly. But Ernest needed all his focus to keep from tumbling down the staircase as he made his way back to LOU15E.

o ◎ o

Ernest opened his eyes. LOU15E's interior viscreen glowed gently at its lowest level. He felt clear-headed, but tired. His hair was in his eyes, as if he'd just collapsed in a random position. His left arm was shunted in. He finger-combed his hair back with his right hand and twisted it at the nape of his neck. "Good morning, Louise. Why haven't you told me what time it is, or asked me if I wanted to hear some music? Why are we horizontal?"

"Oh, Ernest. Don't ever do that again."

"Do what?"

The POD hummed. A holo of Ernest filled the viscreen, with a list of statistics scrolling over the top. Potassium elevated. White cell count elevated. Dehydrated. There was more—much more—but he was too busy looking at the holo of his own neck to read it. He could see a gentle curve where Will had a lump. "Louise? Why did *homo sapiens* have bumps at the front of their throats?"

"No feeds until your health monitor checks on you."

Ernest scowled and wondered if he'd heard her right. "Did you say *no*?"

"Until your health monitor gives me the go-ahead."

L0U15E was programmed to only refuse those things that were a clear and present danger, and to soft-argue anything else. How could watching a feed on *homo sapiens* be dangerous? "Has someone altered your programming?"

"I'm in override mode."

"So...what? I'm not allowed to watch a feed because, why, I'm being punished?"

"Now, I wouldn't know about that, Ernest."

He recalled the woman in the coffee shop remarking on the old man's cranky stage. He wondered how much leverage he could get out of that stereotype himself. "I want my feed."

"I told you. I can't play it."

"I want my feed," he said, slightly louder. "Put it on."

"I can't."

Damn it. "Holo zoom," he said. This time L0U15E did comply. The holo enlarged until Ernest stared at a life-sized 3-D image of his own face. Even though the holo's eyes were shut, he had to admit that Will was right. He did have crow's feet.

He sighed and searched for something interesting to look at while he was waiting for his health monitor to check him, and noticed the datestamp floating above his holo. "Louise?"

"Yes, Ernest?"

"How long have I been inside the POD?"

"Five days, seventeen hours, thirty-five minutes, twelve seconds."

"Six days?" His heart pounded. He thrust his hands through his holo and pushed against the interior viscreen. "Louise, six days of my retirement are gone?"

"You shouldn't have let yourself get so dehydrated. What are you upset about? You used to stay in for weeks at a time."

"It's my retirement! And in two more weeks I'll be dead." Ernest would swear he felt something die inside himself at that very moment.

"Your heart rate and blood pressure are rising," said L0U15E. "If your health monitor notices, he'll probably order another week of sleep in your POD."

Ernest knuckled his eyes. They stung, and were leaking fluid again. Crying—the stuff of melodramatic old-time feeds. So that's what it felt like. Will had been right, back in the attic, after all. "Please," Ernest begged L0U15E, and his voice sounded thick. "Don't let him keep me locked inside. I'll shunt in every night, I swear I will. Please don't take away the last few days I have."

"Well. I suppose a mild sedative would bring your readings into range so that he wouldn't notice anything unusual when he came by to check."

"Do whatever it takes." Ernest was about to plead the case that with only two weeks left, every moment was precious. But then he reminded himself he was talking to a POD-mind, not a person. He'd need to appeal to L0U15E's programming, which was designed to keep him safe. At least, that was what he'd always been told. But if Will was right about the crying.... Hopefully some routines to ensure safety were still in place. "I don't think it's healthy for me to be here. The sooner I get out, the sooner I can get back to some kind of routine."

"That's true."

"Just don't put me back to sleep."

His forearm warmed as L0U15E adjusted the mix of chemicals that flowed into his shunt. His body relaxed, but his mind still reeled. What must Will be thinking of him—that he'd fled the moment he realized Will was a *homo sapien*? If anything, that knowledge only made his curiosity more intense.

When he compared his interactions with Will—lively, stimulating, engaging—to those he had with his Deacon, or his health monitor, or with the store clerks who let him rifle through their shops without even a second glance, he began to wonder if evolution had misstepped.

His POD door opened, and the holo that had been facing him dissolved as the transmitters swung out of range. His health monitor, a third-decade man with dark skin and eyes and a W3 link blinking at his temple, peered into POD. "Light increase fifty percent," he said, and the POD's interior brightened.

Ernest's skin crawled at the thought of L0U15E responding to anyone else's commands.

The health monitor gave him a quick visual scan while his link flashed red. "Why is it that you dehydrated if your POD is functioning correctly?"

He felt his eyes go wide. Doe eyes. That's what Will would have called them. "I was exploring," he said. "I forgot to shunt in. I'm retired, you know. I've never been anywhere before." Playing dumb. He'd heard that expression too, on old-time feeds.

The health monitor opened a panel on the POD and accessed his readings. Ernest held his breath while the health monitor parsed data, and then realized it was probably distinctly unhelpful to do so, as failing to breathe would only increase the amount of carbon dioxide in his bloodstream.

Still, it was hard to breathe, hard to act normal, when the whim of a health monitor could easily mean another week trapped in his POD.

Another week...half a lifetime.

The monitor snapped the panel shut. "Right. I'll set your POD-mind for an alarm so you don't forget again. Door close."

The door shut. The latch clicked. L0U15E turned the POD upright, and then locked onto a magnetic strip. "Where should we go, Ernest?"

Anywhere but the Health Department. Ernest didn't say that aloud. He was too busy remembering how to breathe. "Downtown, I think."

"That coffee house again?"

Will. Of course. What else really mattered? He considered lying to L0U15E about their destination, but what was the point?

He would only be able to walk so far without sending his lactic acid levels skyrocketing.

Even so, it would be prudent to be sure no one was following him. He docked L0U15E several blocks away from the coffee house and wove through the alleyways to the back door. All the way there, he'd terrorized himself with mental images of an unbreakable plastic door on the back of the building with a W3 link flashing at its latch, but the old-time wooden door with its old-time metal lock was still in place.

He turned his key in the lock and went upstairs. The torn, damaged books were still piled as he'd last seen them on the reading room floor. The attic door was locked. He unlocked it with a hand that shook so hard he almost dropped the key, then dashed up the attic stairs, heart pounding wildly. He looked around.

Will wasn't there.

Ernest paced, hoping that Will would eventually return, but then realized someone other than Will might hear his footsteps and decide to investigate. As quietly as possible, he flipped through a few mostly-intact books without parsing them, and re-watched *Daddy is a Contractor* without really seeing it. And eventually he simply sat down on the top step and buried his face in his hands. There was nowhere Will actually needed to be. There was probably no record of him at the Health Department or the Labor Department. He was his own man, circulating among the ignorant scattering of *homo consummatus* as he tried to buy up POD components. He could be anywhere. And he might never come back.

It was too difficult to search the city. Ernest was only one person. It would be much easier to forget about Will, to climb back inside his POD and tell L0U15E to give him a stronger dose of that sedative. Climbing inside the POD would be easy, at any rate. Forgetting about Will would be a different matter altogether.

Ernest opened the cooler. Three flasks of water remained, pressed against the back of the box. Either it meant that Will was coming back, or that a meager three flasks was negligible, maybe too cumbersome to carry. He took a flask from the cooler and a mist formed over its surface. The mist turned into tiny beads of condensation, and he pressed the flask against his cheek. Will had touched that cheek with his fingertips. More than once. Ernest could remember at least three occasions where Will had caressed his face, and even more touches if he counted all the back-slapping and thigh-pressing.

He twisted open the flask and tucked the stopper into his pocket. Then he pressed the bottle to his mouth and tipped his head back.

Cold. Startlingly wet. His throat spasmed, and he panicked. He spat, and blotted his chin with the back of his hand.

It would be very easy indeed to climb back into the POD. That notion made him all the more determined.

Ernest tipped some more cold, wet, metallic-tasting water into his mouth and held it there, breathing carefully through his nose as he gathered his nerves. With clenched fists, he held his breath, and he swallowed.

ıııCHAPTER EIGHTııı

THE WATER DISTENDED ERNEST'S stomach, which caused it to press against the walls of his abdominal cavity. It must be be applying pressure to his liver, his small intestine, his gall bladder and pancreas. If anyone had told him that a full stomach would feel so painful and wobbly, he never would have swallowed anything to begin with. How many hours did water take to digest? He wasn't sure. He couldn't very well ask L0U15E, either. Not with an incriminating belly full of water.

He recapped the bottle, set it on the floor beside the cooler, and made his way downstairs. The pressure in his body made it difficult to concentrate. He decided it might help to sit down for a few moments while some of the water passed into his duodenum. He staggered toward the single chair, the one he'd collapsed in last time, and paused. There, on the seat, was a scrap of paper.

There was some printing on the paper. "All rights reserved. No part of this book may be reproduced in any form without written permission from the publisher. Library of Congress Cataloging-in-Publication Data available." Ernest parsed a word here or there, but for the most part, it was a long, meaningless string of characters.

But then there was the handwriting, over the top of the print: *I OW YOU 1 BREW. ~W.*

That parsed just fine.

Ernest bounded down the stairs, pausing only to lock both doors behind him, then took a roundabout way back to the front door of the store to ensure he hadn't been seen or followed.

It was early evening, nearly sunset, but thankfully the shop was still open. Will might not be there, Ernest reminded himself. Instead, it might be Clarence the Kill-Joy addict behind the counter.

He didn't believe that, though. He pressed his fingertips against the front door, shifting foot to foot in anticipation as it opened, everything seeming to move slowly like a feed playing at half speed, until finally, there, framed in the doorway, scowling at a series of glowing characters as he wriggled his fingers under his scanner, was Will.

Ernest stared so long the door nearly shut on him. At the last moment he ducked inside and approached the counter.

"Can I help you?" Will said without looking up as he finished a line of computations.

"I hope so."

Will raised his head, eyebrows bunched together in the center, mouth pressed into a grim line, and as he locked eyes with Ernest, his entire face transformed. His eyes went wide and he bit his lower lip as if to fend off a grin. He made the old-time "silence" gesture of fingertip pressed against lips, and pulled out a syringe wrapper with a blank side, and a shard of graphite from his pocket.

He pressed the tip of his tongue between his teeth, and began to write by hand in slow, careful letters, just like an actor in an old-time feed:

DOO NOT LOK

Meanwhile, he said, "I think there's a *storm* brewing. It'll send everyone *trooping* back to their PODs. Lousy for business."

Will kept glancing over Ernest's shoulder as he spoke. Ernest figured that direction was the one in which he wasn't supposed to look.

Will found another back of a label and wrote more painstaking words.

WAIR WERE WHAIR WERE WIR YOU?

"I'm closing the shop," Will said, probably louder than he needed to.

"Oh," Ernest replied. "Are you sure? I've been trying to get here for a while now, but I always seem to be tied up."

Will tried to write something else, became frustrated with it, crumpled it up and threw it in the recycle chute. He found another label and wrote, 1 DORE—>

Ernest pointed toward the abandoned building next door, and Will nodded. "It's inefficient to stay open late for just one or two customers," Will said. "You'll have to come back some other time." Will jerked his head toward the rendezvous point, and mouthed the word, "Now."

Ernest nodded. He tried not to smile, but didn't quite succeed. He did his best to sound disappointed. "I guess I'll just come back in the morning, then."

Will picked up his cloth, turned away and began wiping down the counter. He didn't say goodbye like the characters in old-time feeds. Likely, it would have seemed suspicious if he did. Ernest glimpsed the man in the white jumpsuit at the back table. He was hooked into a hanging drip that was mostly empty, focused on a portable W3 game similar to the one the girl in the resale shop had been playing. The Storm Trooper's game was much more expensive. The tiny holos it projected were brighter and more opaque.

Ernest exited the front door, walked by the abandoned building (doing his best not to look inside), passed a few other businesses he'd infiltrated on his search for Will, then, when there were no PODs on the magnetic strip and no one on the street to observe him, he slipped into an alley and doubled back toward the abandoned building.

Its back door was unlocked. The main room in the front, whatever it had once been, was completely destroyed, with broken shelves covering the floor, their contents reduced to unrecognizable rubble by oxidation and a thick layer of dust.

Two small rooms in back were once bathrooms. The porcelain shards of their original fixtures littered the floors of both, and one had the twisted metal sheath of a privacy stall partially in place. Ernest sank back against the wall at the sound of rubble shifting behind him. Will's silhouette filled the dark doorway, lanky and spike-haired.

"Here," Ernest said, and Will flinched, startled.

"What do you mean, you were tied up?" Will demanded. He made his way across a pile of dry-rotted wooden planks, arms outstretched for balance.

Ernest pressed his back into the crumbling tiles. He felt so excited to see Will, the wall seemed to be the only thing holding him up. "That's what they say in old-time feeds, isn't it? 'I'm all tied up.' There's also, 'I just washed my hair and I can't do a thing with it.' But I figured that would sound even less like—"

Will hopped over the last bit of rubble and grabbed Ernest by the shoulders. "I tried to ping you, but your POD didn't accept the message." He wrapped his arms around Ernest and squeezed, tight. "I didn't think you were coming back," he whispered.

A hug. Yes. Ernest scrambled to remember what people did on old-time feeds. He patted Will's back three times. That was what was expected of him, wasn't it? Will squeezed tighter. Ernest gasped. His head spun. He wondered what to do with his hands. "Induced sleep," he said. "Five days, seventeen hours, thirty-five minutes."

Will buried his face in the crook of Ernest's neck. "Your hair's shot through with gray," he said. His breath was hot and wet against Ernest's jaw. It tingled in a peculiar way that he felt in his knees, molars and groin.

"Louise showed me a holo," Ernest said. "You were right about the crow's feet."

Will squeezed Ernest even more tightly. Ernest began to worry that Will might dislocate something in him. "Don't go back. You can't afford to keep shunting in."

"I...don't know...."

Will released Ernest (none too soon), but took his face in both hands, and pinned his whole body to the wall. A hint of twilight filtered through the windows, just enough to see the shape of Will's eyes. Their faces were close, almost touching. "So, you're hetero?" Will asked. "A hundred percent?"

Ernest stared hard at what he could see of Will's eyes, hoping to find some meaning there, but he could discern nothing but intensity. "Explain?"

Will laughed, a short, choked noise, nothing at all like the sounds that came from Ernest when he watched free comedy feeds. "Do men trip your switch at all?"

"What? Not parsing."

Will sighed. "Okay, the porn. What did you prefer? And it better not be the techno-kink."

Ernest struggled to figure out what his feed preference had to do with shunting in, or not. "I don't know. I didn't get to the kink menu yet. I guess I liked the feeds where the actors were talking and laughing. But I don't think that's what you're asking me."

Will closed his eyes, and rubbed his cheek against Ernest's. Will's face felt bristly. If there had been any lingering doubt in Ernest's mind as to Will's species, it was gone now. "You really are as innocent as you act." His voice was scarcely a breath in Ernest's ear.

Ernest thought of the lie he'd told the health monitor. "Not always."

Will's lips brushed Ernest's cheek as he spoke. "I want to kiss you."

"Explain."

"Put my mouth on you...my tongue. Would that put you in override?"

Like the hetero-pairs feed. The tingle in Ernest's molars intensified. "Tongues are for talking." He was finding it difficult to breathe.

Will tilted his head until his lips pressed into Ernest's cheek. The feel of Will's mouth moving against him caused a cascade of sensation to course through him. Strange. Possibly good. Or maybe more like narcotics, something so intense it made you uncomfortable while it lasted, but once it was done, left you wanting more.

A tongue, along the curve of his jaw. Wetness. Ernest felt his legs wobble. He searched for one of the words he'd learned from the Purged feeds. Lick. Yes.

Will's hands dropped to Ernest's sides, stroked him from hip to thigh, while he buried his face in Ernest's neck and lavished wet kisses over his throat.

Ernest remembered that technique from one of the hetero-pairs feeds, the especially disturbing one that showed lots of…kisses? Kissing. He remembered how the woman being… kissed…squirmed and moaned. It made total sense, now. His whole body wanted to writhe against Will.

"Don't go back to your POD," Will murmured into Ernest's tingling neck. "Stay with me."

Ernest felt a moment of pure, sublime, joy. Yes. That was what he wanted.

But.

"I'm not like you," he said, as gently as he could.

Will's hand cupped Ernest between the legs. Ernest's hips rose to meet it. "I think I could convince you to switch."

"Show me any species that can switch just by wishing for it."

"Species?" Will placed a lingering kiss on Ernest's jaw. "Oh. I get it."

"Do you? It makes no difference what I want. I can't just turn myself into a *homo sapien* by wanting it to happen badly enough."

Will backed away only enough to look Ernest in the eye. The dim, ambient light made his teeth glisten as he smiled. "Listen, you're about as smart as they come. What if I told you that your Deacon's been feeding you a pack of lies?"

It was nearly impossible for Ernest to formulate an answer with Will's hand moving between his legs, distracting him. "That…ah…that if you were a regular person, your POD would haul you to the Diaconate for spreading heresy like that." Will touched Ernest like the women had touched the *homo sapien* men on the porn feed, tracing the shape of his penis—no, his *cock*—through his trousers, then reaching farther down to caress his scrotum. Balls. That's what the *homo sapiens* had called it. Them.

Will placed his hot mouth against Ernest's neck. "I wouldn't go so far as to call myself a regular person." His words tickled against the damp trail he'd left on Ernest's skin. "But I was born in a natal center, same as you. Trained ten years in a training center, same as you. Lived twenty more shunting into my stupid POD every night...."

"Don't lie to me," Ernest said. He tried to push Will away, but Will was stronger and had better leverage. "I feel the bristles on your face. Your big, hard cock is pressing into my thigh. There's no way you're *homo consummatus*."

"Shhh." Will grazed Ernest's ear with his lips, pressed Ernest's back into the wall with his whole body. "Think for a minute, would you? If I'm some kind of genetic throwback, where'd I come from?"

"I don't know. There could be plenty of explanations." Ernest's groin throbbed at the feel of Will's strokes, caress after caress, up and down, steady and slow. It was an unsettling sensation, and yet the more Ernest focused on it, the better it felt. "A pack of *homo sapiens* living outside the city?" he ventured. His hips flexed, pressing his cock into Will's hand. "A genetic experiment of some sort?"

"I like the way you think," Will said. "Your first guess isn't far from the truth, and your second is something I wouldn't put past those lousy Deacons if it made them any richer."

Ernest gasped. It was getting more and more difficult to parse what Will was trying to tell him. His cock felt strange, tingling and engorged. Needy, like his arm at feeding time. Hungry.

"I...um.... Will...." Ernest covered Will's hand with his. His penis was swollen. "I don't think you'd better...."

"I know what I'm doing," Will said. "We gotta go slow. That damn shunt's got you chemically castrated. But with a little patience, a little luck—"

"I don't feel well."

"Intense, huh?"

"Not just that. My stomach."

"It's a whole-body kind of experience. Watching people orgasm on feeds and doing it yourself are two totally different things."

Will stopped rubbing Ernest's cock with only the flat of his palm and wrapped his fingers three-quarters of the way around it, as much as Ernest's trousers would allow. Ernest's hips bucked. "No, I think that flask of water I drank isn't digesting."

Will's hand stopped moving, and he pulled his head back so

that he could look into Ernest's face again. There wasn't much to see, given the lack of light. But Ernest felt Will's eyes on him. "You drank?"

"And I feel it sloshing around in my stomach like—"

Will crushed their mouths together, and he stroked Ernest's cock, harder, faster, pressing his own cock into Ernest's hip and thigh. Ernest stood, stunned, while Will's tongue parted his lips, skirted the edge of his teeth. And then Will pulled back, only enough to suck Ernest's lower lip into his mouth and tongue it.

Heady sensations rushed down to Ernest's groin, made his balls tingle and shift against one another, his cock strain against Will's hand. Whatever he'd been trying to tell Will was swept away on a wave of intense sensations.

Will yanked Ernest's belt open and slipped a hand down his trousers. Ernest gasped for air, but Will's mouth was there, drinking him in. His head spun, and his shaking knees finally began to buckle, as if they could no longer hold him.

But Will was there. He stopped stroking Ernest's cock and instead shored him up with both hands. With a few kicks, Will cleared enough rubble out of the way to lay him down on the floor. He straddled Ernest's hips and planted an elbow on either side of his head. Will's hard cock nestled in the crease of Ernest's thigh, and Will's breath was warm and moist against his cheek.

"Promise me you won't go to Reclaim," Will said.

Ernest sighed. "When I die, I need to be demagnetized. We can agree on that much, can't we?"

"Fine. When you die. Which could be twenty, thirty, forty years from now. If you'd just stop shunting in."

Ernest stared up in the direction of the ceiling, and decided there was nothing to lose by humoring Will, since he sounded so desperate. If Ernest could get the hang of drinking water, he could survive the next two weeks without L0U15E pumping fuel into his arm. "Yes. Agreed. I'll stop shunting in."

Will's mouth covered his again, not as shocking this time, but still strange, the smoothness of his lips, the wetness of his tongue, the bristle of his whiskers rasping over Ernest's upper lip and chin. "Promise." The word tickled over Ernest's lips.

It would be an uncomfortable two weeks to go around with a distended stomach full of water. Then again it was, after all, only two weeks. Besides, he couldn't risk any more forced slumber—not with so little time left. "I will stay with you. I'll even stop shunting in. But when it's my time, I'm going to Reclaim."

"Listen, if the Deacons have been lying to you about your body giving out at thirty, what makes you think that Reclaim—"

"Shh!" Ernest covered Will's mouth with his fingers. Both of them stopped speaking, stopped moving. Ernest even held his breath.

They listened. Silence. Ernest saw a faint reflection of moonlight on the white of Will's eye. He began to exhale slowly. And then he heard it again.

The scrape of wood against concrete.

ııı CHAPTER NINE ııı

THE HALLWAY OUTSIDE THE bathroom lit up. Ernest couldn't see the light source; it was out in the main body of the building. But he'd had nothing but the moonlight to see by for so long that the dim illumination stung his eyes.

Will pulled his hand out from Ernest's trousers, moving excruciatingly slow. He met Ernest's eyes. It was unnecessary for him to say anything about being quiet. He drew himself up into a crouch, glanced around at the rubble, and placed his hand on a pipe.

Ernest sat up. The sifting of the coarse grains of concrete dust rasped in his ear as he clenched every muscle in an effort to match Will's silent motions. The sound of dust grinding against itself wasn't an audible noise, it couldn't have been. Besides, the thunder of his own heart beating must have covered it; the percussion was so loud he was sure the people outside gliding down the magnetic strip in their PODs all thought a storm was gathering.

Slowly, gently, Will eased the pipe from its nest of broken glass and splintered wood. It was just like an old-time feed, right before the strange lag where Ernest sensed something inappropriate had been Purged, some action he might be able to piece together later, as the actors reappeared with bandages around their heads. Or worse, never reappeared at all.

The low sound of laughter came from the main room, a man's voice. Will looked at Ernest and quirked an eyebrow. Ernest stood, and shrugged.

Will pressed the pipe into Ernest's hands.

Ernest stared. Will nudged it against his hands more firmly. Ernest's fingers closed around it. It felt rough, and hard. It was surprisingly heavy. He wondered exactly how much force it would take to damage someone's skull. That sort of information had never been disseminated in the free feeds he'd watched. And he suspected even the glimpse he'd had of Kill-Joy would be nothing like real, physical violence.

Will slid another pipe from the rubble and hefted it. He was a dark silhouette against the light—sinew and muscle, spiked hair, raw and lean and powerful.

Ernest shifted the pipe to his right hand, moving as slowly as Will. He felt his pulse pounding at his throat and groin. He adjusted himself. He and Will should have found somewhere safer to play at porn, he decided. His cock was still swollen, and he felt giddy and disoriented.

Will picked a path to the jagged hole that was the doorway. Ernest followed, stepping precisely in his footprints. Will held up his free hand and Ernest paused. They waited.

Again, something in the front of the building moved.

Ernest stretched himself so that his eyes just cleared Will's shoulder. There, amid all the wreckage in the building's main room, crouched a Storm Trooper. He'd unfolded a neat square of biodegradable film to cover the filthy floorboards, and weighted down one side with an LED that shone brightly enough to make Ernest's eyes water from across the vast room. The security op stared straight ahead, waving his fingers through a cluster of colorful holo shapes, arranging and rearranging the patterns they made. Every now and then the shapes shifted, and he barked out a short laugh. The W3 link on his wrist flashed as data streamed in and out, and he and his game played one another.

Ernest squeezed the pipe, and imagined how it would feel collapsing the Storm Trooper's skull.

He tried to move around Will, but Will sidestepped and kept

him in place. Will bent backward and placed his lips against Ernest's ear. "What are you doing?" he breathed.

Ernest shook his head. He couldn't imagine why he wanted to do harm to the security op, just a young man who'd ducked away to sneak in some gaming. And yet, there was something cruel in his laugh that begged Ernest to swing the pipe.

"Other way," Will whispered. "Back door."

It was Ernest's turn to find a path. Each step was exhausting, and by the time he and Will slipped into the back alley, his hair was soaked with sweat, long tendrils clinging to his forehead and cheeks, his shirt clammy, stuck against his spine. He was shaking.

Before he could decide what to do with himself, Will slammed his back into the brick wall and stole another kiss from him. "Hot damn, you wanted to pulp him. I could tell."

"I...."

Will dropped his pipe. It landed in a Styrofoam drift with a muted crackle. He straddled Ernest's leg, and grasped his cock through his trousers. "I'd love to see you kick some ass," Will said. "But not here, not now. His link will go off and draw the rest of 'em right to us."

Will sucked Ernest's lower lip into his mouth before Ernest could answer, dragged his teeth along the heft of it while his hand moved up and down, kneading, stroking. Though Ernest's hand felt stiff around the pipe from clenching it, he forced his fingers open and let go. It clinked against Will's in the drift. He slid his free hands around Will's waist, suddenly relieved that he didn't need to explain what he thought he'd meant to do in that hallway, since he wasn't sure, himself.

Will backed the intensity his kisses off, and finished with a gentle brush of his lips. "C'mon. Let's get out of here."

It surprised Ernest how easy it was to leave L0U15E docked in the public lot and simply walk away. He'd never been more than a hundred meters from his POD in the last twenty years. That thought almost gave him pause, but there was no time to look back. Will dragged him forward by the hand, and didn't seem inclined to let go. He led Ernest through a maze of alleyways, and beyond. They walked quickly for half an hour or more, passing a mostly-empty POD docking station, the remains of some buildings, and vacant lots blocked off by sagging, rusted metal gates. Finally, they approached an intact building between two others that were missing parts of walls and roofs. Will drew Ernest toward a stairwell, down a flight of unlit stairs, and through a doorway that let to total darkness.

Will let go of his hand, and for a moment, Ernest was alone. And then the gentle, bluish glow of a solar-charged LED lit the room. Will held it up beside his head, caught Ernest's eye, and grinned.

At least, Ernest thought it was a grin.

"This place is so far off the grid that nobody knows about it," Will said, "but I'll do a few scans just to be sure." Will set the diode in the center of the room, then pulled a handheld unit from his pocket and extended it out in front of him. He swept the small piece of equipment along the walls, especially in the corners, and over the floor where piles of cloth, paper and wood lay in heaps.

"What are you scanning for?"

"Electromagnetic fields. If any of the security ops found this place, they'd bury a W3 link somewhere to monitor it. But since nothing else here is powered, this little scanner will lead me right to anything that draws juice." The portable sensor squealed in Will's hand. He toed aside some Styrofoam packing nuggets. Beneath them was the book-shaped monitor. "I almost forgot. You left this back in the attic."

Ernest took the device from Will and turned it on. The audio link murmured in his ear. Still there, even after his visit to the Health Department. Ernest considered; it wasn't really that surprising. The health monitor had scarcely made eye contact with Ernest. A physical exam would have been more effort than he was willing to expend. He'd only looked at the readout on Ernest's POD.

"So," Will said. "Any chance we could take up where we left off? You know, with my hand down your pants and you humping my leg?"

"Humping. That's a funny idiom."

Will pulled the monitor out of Ernest's hands and gave the

navigation bar a few jabs. Audio crackled into the earpiece, voices talking, jumbled and incoherent. "Here you go. Visual aid."

The voices sorted themselves into phrases.

C'mon, boy. Lemme see whatcha got. You hungry for some meat?

"Oh, the audio's pretty good." Ernest tapped the earpiece to adjust the sound level so he could hear the conversation, since it promised to be more than just moaning and groaning. Will's fingers worked Ernest's waistband. He was better at it now than he had been before, back in the bathroom. Ernest's trousers were around his knees in less than a second. Will was a fast learner.

Aw, that's right. Touch it. Makes your mouth water, don't it?

It was two men on the purged feed this time, rather than a man and a woman. Now Will's question about which feeds Ernest had preferred made total sense. If only Ernest had started with the homo feeds. He'd have a better idea what was expected of him when he played porn with Will. "Am I supposed to talk about meat?" he said.

"Huh?" Will knelt between Ernest's feet, just like the porn feed actor. "Oh, people never really talked that way."

"If it's not historically accurate, then why...?"

Will grabbed him by the hips and pressed his mouth against Ernest's stomach. Ernest's nervous system seemed to rewire itself so that everything routed toward the point of contact. Lips. Teeth. Tongue.

Say it, boy. Tell me how much you wanna suck that dick.

I wanna suck your dick.

"Are you going to...suck my dick?"

Will dragged his hot, wet tongue over Ernest's stomach, down toward his hip. Ernest felt tingly, not just there, but everywhere. His spine. His balls. His fingers and toes. "That's the idea." The words tickled the downy hairs on Ernest's thigh. He felt himself start to swell.

"I don't think it will work on me."

"Trust me, would you? I told you, I know what I'm doing."

Aw, that's right, sweet fucking mouth on you. C'mon, boy. All the way down.

Will pressed his lips against Ernest's thigh. Ernest felt so sensitized that the gentle warmth of Will's breath on him was excruciating. He saw the actor hang onto the head of the hairy, muscled *homo sapien* "boy" who was sucking him. Ernest placed his hand on Will's spiky hair, which lay flat under the pressure of his palm, then sprang back up again as he stroked his hand over the contour of Will's head.

"I want to pull away, but I don't...."

"Ticklish." Will supplied the word, which sent shivers up Ernest's spine. "I can adjust for that. Keep telling me what you like."

Will mouthed Ernest's thigh harder, and the urge to shove away from him subsided. Still, the sensations were strange and intense, as if Ernest's nervous system was caught in a feedback loop.

Lemme see your cock. Go on, pull it out.

Ernest glanced down at Will. He could only see the top part of Will's face, the forehead, browbone and nose. Will was busy pushing his tongue between Ernest's upper thighs. "Let me see your cock," Ernest whispered.

Will's tongue stopped moving. He rocked back on his heels and locked eyes. "Don't worry about me. Just lay back and enjoy it."

"But I'm standing up."

Will rolled his eyes. He pulled the book-shaped monitor away from Ernest and set it on a pile of rags. "Never mind that. You're too literal. You don't have to follow step by step. There are a million variations, and countless more that're just waiting to be found out." Will led him to a long cushion on the floor and pulled him onto it. Ernest sank down on his hip, and managed to free one of his feet from his trousers.

Uhn. Uhn. Uhn. Uhn. Uhn. Oh yeah. Uhn. Uhn. Uhn. That's right....

Will pushed him onto his back and lay on his stomach between Ernest's legs, elbows tucked under his chest. "So many variations we'd need years to try them all."

"I don't have years."

"Don't you?" Will's mouth closed on the band of sinew that connected Ernest's leg and groin.

"Oh." Ernest propped himself up on one elbow and placed his other hand on Will's head. His breath hitched. "Intense."

Will mumbled an affirmation and slid his tongue higher, working it along the crease of Ernest's thigh. He moved slowly, deliberately, up and down, licking his way deeper between Ernest's legs.

"Your tongue, it feels...." Ernest let out a breathy sigh. "It's not like anything I've ever felt before."

Will grunted, and swiped his tongue over Ernest's scrotum. His balls contracted and he clenched a fistful of Will's hair. Will looked up. "Ticklish? Sorry." He worked a hand out from underneath him and cupped Ernest's balls, stroking the thumb along the cleft between them. "You like that?"

Like. That would be a bizarre word for the sensations coursing through him. But since he didn't want them to stop, he couldn't think of anything more appropriate. "Yes." The word came out as a breathy hiss.

Will dragged the flat of his tongue over his cock, and Ernest had to clench his whole body to keep from pulling away.

"You're so fresh and new," Will said. He licked Ernest again. It wasn't quite so startling the second time. "When you come in my mouth, I'll be the very first one to taste it."

A week ago, Ernest probably would have disagreed with Will, and said that the things that happened on the purged porn feeds were things that happened to *homo sapiens*, not him. But his cock looked fat and distended, and it shifted on his thigh as Will licked it, and maybe—Ernest would have to concede—maybe there was some vestigial part of his body that could, indeed, orgasm. "Please," he whispered.

Uhn. Uhn. Uhn. Fuck, yeah....

Ernest tapped his audio link to shut it off just as Will's hot, wet mouth closed over his cockhead. Another moan, only this one was nothing like all the rhythmic grunting on the porn feed. This sound had been dragged from somewhere deep in his core.

Will slid his mouth back over the tip of his cock. Ernest's hips bucked as Will's lips moved over the glans. "You sound fucking hot," Will said. "I'm stiff enough to cut glass just listening to you breathe."

And then Will's mouth plunged down again, and this time, he was sucking.

Ernest bit back another wordless noise, not entirely successfully. He had Will's head in both hands. He squeezed hard, as if he could hold Will in place and just flex his hips, keep some control over the white-hot sensation that was threatening to turn him inside out. Will groaned—Ernest felt it rumble along his shaft—and tugged his balls.

Ernest pressed himself into Will's mouth harder. Yes. This was right. Nothing could feel so good and not be right. Will was right. He was right about everything.

His cockhead brushed something hard. Teeth. He could feel Will's *teeth* with his cock, how bizarre. There was the tongue, soft and magical, and the—what was it, the palate? No, there was a homebuilding idiom. The roof. Yes—the roof of Will's mouth, slick and hot on the top of his glans, but there, at the side, if he thrust, the gentle scrape of teeth.

Will pulled off Ernest's cock despite Ernest's attempt to hold him there. "Look how stiff you are," he said, grinning. Grinning, for sure.

Ernest looked down at himself. It wasn't quite as massive as a cock from one of the purged porn feeds, but it didn't look anything like his own cock, either. "What...?"

"Congratulations. That's a fine hard-on, if I do say so myself."

Ernest watched it disappear into Will's mouth. It was especially soft and hot at the back—his throat? He felt his cock throb at the thought, and Will made a wet, squelching noise.

"Please," Ernest repeated. "I really do want to see your cock."

He felt another grunt from Will all the way up his spine, and then a shuffle of hands between his knees. Will jerked his trousers down and then turned his attention back to Ernest. Ernest's cock. His hard cock.

He craned his neck to see over Will's bobbing head, between his legs. There it was, and pubic hair, too—a few shades darker than the hair on Will's head. The cock didn't look as disproportionately huge as it had felt back at the abandoned shop, when it was pressing against his thigh. It was bigger than his, but the same flushed color, the same general shape, if one were to allow for variations, in the same way people's faces and fingerprints varied.

He lay back and stared up at the cobwebbed ceiling boards. Will caressed his balls with one hand and stroked himself with the other, and all the while, his head bobbed up and down, and he sucked.

Ernest wove his fingertips through Will's hair. "Maybe it tickles. I don't know. I think it's too intense...."

Will's tongue fluttered against his cock, and he sucked a bit harder.

Ernest's hips felt heavy and strange. His fingertips and toes tingled. He felt like rolling out from under Will, mostly. Or maybe he wished that Will would suck harder.

"It's...it's...." He gasped for air. "It really does feel strange. I don't think I...."

Will stopped touching himself and slid both hands around Ernest's hips and beneath his buttocks. He clasped his face against Ernest's groin as if he'd heard the very thought about disengaging before he'd been allowed to prove his point.

Will's hands, the fingertips pressing hard into his thighs and rump, sent a new cacophony of signals to Ernest's poor, belabored nervous system. He would have laughed. Almost. Except it had come out as more of a yelp.

"Will," he said. And had he ever called Will by name before? Maybe not. But he'd said it to himself many, many times, as he scanned feeds inside his POD, nothing but L0U15E and the "sardonic" wallpaper to keep him company. "I...no, I...wait, it's too much.... Uhn...."

His back arched. Will sucked harder, and kneaded his body with both hands.

"No." Ernest gasped the single word out and pushed against Will's head, but it kept on gliding, up and down, and Ernest couldn't seem to find the strength to stop him. He was helpless against Will's hot, wet mouth, and his focus, and his determination. Up, and down. Strong. Unrelenting. It was heady, like the rush of a first taste of caffeine, and just as powerful. But more, so much more—as if he was being torn apart, if being torn apart could feel absolutely, utterly amazing.

His whole body stiffened, then started to thrash. He cried out, and Will made noises, too, muffled grunts of encouragement around his pulsing cock. Ernest peaked, a bright-edged crest of unbearable sensation, and then it felt as if he fell from a great height, falling and spinning, only he was still on the ground, his back flat against the damp, hot cushion, and Will was there, trailing kisses over his thighs. And the ceiling was there, cob-webs swaying. Only Ernest was changed. And that seemed to make all the difference in the world.

ⅠⅠⅠCHAPTER TENⅠⅠⅠ

IT SEEMED LIKE ERNEST couldn't do anything other than breathe for a very, very long time. Will was tucked against his side, breathing softly. He hung between wakefulness and sleep for a long while, floating in a hypnogogic trance with Will right there beside him.

He slept eventually, even though it seemed that the whole time he was aware of being uncomfortably horizontal, and his shunt wasn't plugged into anything, and the cushion he lay on was lumpy and hard.

He must have slept, because one moment he was floating in the cool diode-lit dimness, and the next there was sunlight slanting in through cracks in the boards that covered old windows set high up in the walls, and a bird was chirping from a mass of straw up in the rafters.

Ernest turned his head. Will slept deeply, one arm thrown over Ernest's chest. Ernest studied his face. There were fine lines at the corners of his eyes, and one vertical crease between his eyebrows that was almost invisible now, but would sharpen when he scowled. His skin was darker than Ernest's, and lightly freckled. Sun exposure. Hard to discern his age. Thirty? It seemed possible. Unless *homo sapiens* aged differently.

If Will even was a *homo sapien.*

Ernest turned the evidence over in his mind: the things Will had told him, which no doubt were full of conveniently omitted facts. The mutilated data feeds he'd devoured since he'd gotten his very own POD twenty years ago, that he'd needed to interpret as much by what was missing, as what was shown. And his "gut" feeling, as it was idiomatically referred to, even though he technically didn't use his gut any more than he did his appendix.

Until yesterday. When he'd consumed water.

Ernest strained to look without actually moving. He rolled his eyeballs down, and frowned in concentration. His trousers and boots were beside them on the floor. Will was still dressed, though his fly was open. The outline of the scanner was visible in his pocket.

If Ernest had thought he was moving slowly when he'd crept out of the abandoned building while the Storm Trooper gamed, he was practically a glacier now. He made sure that even his breathing didn't jar Will into wakefulness. He eased away, millimeter by millimeter, until Will's arm slid from his chest and settled onto the cushion.

Just as slowly, he eased the scanner from Will's pocket. Will didn't stir.

The controls were rudimentary. Ernest turned off the audio alert that had allowed Will to scan in the dark. He aimed the scanner at the book shaped monitor, and a wav sign pulsed on the tiny readout screen. He leaned toward the diode and did the same. Another ripple. He scanned his own thumb.

His chip, even with its minuscule fuel cell, sent a tremor through the readout.

Ernest waved the scanner over Will's left thumb, and the readout rippled again. Will did have a chip. His shunt could have been some creative cosmetic mod, but the credit chip seemed much more difficult to fabricate. Ernest wasn't sure if the presence of a chip proved, or disproved, anything. Will could have had it inserted at the natal center, as Ernest had. Or, if Will was actually a *homo sapien*, he could have paid someone to do it for him later. After all, he'd found a game addict to provide him with a cover job. He was good with people that way, convincing. Why not a bootleg thumb chip?

Ernest turned his focus to his "gut" to try and determine what Will really was, but all he knew for sure was that he really didn't feel well himself.

He slipped the power monitor back into Will's pocket, let his breath out slowly, and buried his face in his hands.

He was sore all over. Aching. Sleeping horizontally was responsible for much of his discomfort, but it was also well past time to shunt in. He was hungry, and waste was building up in his bloodstream.

Shunting in seemed like the only logical thing to do. But Will claimed that the POD had changed his biofuel. Or...that LOU15E had. The POD couldn't do much by itself. It was LOU15E who controlled the mix. Ernest had also promised that he wouldn't shunt in, and promises seemed terribly important in old-time feeds. The main actor was always so concerned about being a "man of his word" that he'd endure anything to ensure that he kept his promises. Even the ache of needing to shunt in. Badly.

Ernest pulled his knees against his chest, propped his arms on them and pressed his face into his sleeve. The posture seemed to work for actors in old-time feeds when they didn't know which way to turn. Despair.

The contraction of his stomach muscles, the bunching of his body into such an unnatural posture, only made his groin ache.

"What're you doing?"

Ernest flinched. He hoped Will had actually been asleep while he'd been scanning.

Will pushed up and knelt behind him. He wrapped his arms around Ernest's chest. "You keep sighing. Don't tell me you're having cold feet."

"My feet are fine. But the rest of me hurts."

"Yeah, I know. I remember."

Did he? Or was sleeping on his back second nature to him? "I know you think I shouldn't shunt in, but...."

"I don't think so. I know so."

"Will, I'm aching."

"Maybe they're hunger pangs. How about a protein bar?"

Ernest tried to fit the words *protein* and *bar* together and parsed nothing. "A what?"

"Protein bar. Breakfast. You know, food?"

Ernest shook his head.

"I thought you said you drank water."

"I did. But that's not the same as...as chewing on solid masses of...." Ernest shuddered.

"But you did drink."

Ernest nodded.

"You'll need to urinate." Will let go of Ernest, stretched out on his side, and pulled the small case of datachips from his pocket. "I've got a pre-Purge training feed on here. It's geared toward kids fresh out of the natal center, but I think it parses pretty well. It helped me figure it all out, anyway. C'mon out back. I'll show you."

o ◎ o

Urinating didn't feel nearly as good as the orgasm, but it did seem to take some pressure off Ernest's groin. "How did *homo sapiens* ever get anything done if they had to urinate all the time?" he wondered aloud, once they'd completed the task and returned to the basement.

"It goes faster once you get the hang of it. You won't have to stand there and think about it for an hour while you're watching feeds of waterfalls." Will unwrapped a protein bar and tore off a hunk with his teeth. Ernest stared. Will's cheek bulged like a porn-feed actor with a cock in his mouth. "You sure you don't want some? I'll share."

Ernest pressed his tongue into the backs of his teeth. He couldn't imagine anything in his mouth other than Will's tongue, and the idea of biting down on that made his throat flutter nauseatingly. "No."

"Two, three days without calories, and you're going to start slowing us down."

"What do you mean? I wasn't aware we were hurrying."

Will swallowed. The knot of tissue at the front of his throat rose and fell. "You promised me you'd stay with me."

So. Will didn't take promises lightly either. "And?"

"You don't think I want to live here forever, do you?"

Ernest looked at the basement. They could clean it up. True, it was overlarge, but they could certainly find something to block off the extra space. "Where else would we live?"

Will stared at Ernest's eyes. His expression wasn't much like any of the ones on the wallpaper of Ernest's POD. Ernest stared back and tried to deduce what it might be. Serious? Concentration.

"We can get out of here. Me and you. And be together."

"But we are together."

"And any second a security op could wander in and haul us off to the Deacons. I mean we could go somewhere else. Somewhere new. Where we could start a whole new life. A real life."

Ernest watched Will's eyes as he spoke. There was a quality about what he was saying that seemed too much like old-time feeds to be the sentiment of a real person. Maybe Will was just saying what he thought Ernest wanted to hear. Or maybe he'd rehearsed it until it sounded scripted.

Or maybe he'd actually said it before.

"Is that what you told Matthew?"

Will's expression shifted again. It was really too much to keep up with. "Ernest...."

"It was." Ernest stood and walked toward one of the filthy, squat windows set high in the wall, as if turning his face in the direction of the sun might help lift his mood.

Will came and pressed himself into Ernest's back, his hands touching, always touching, running up and down Ernest's arms. "He didn't listen to me. And now he's dead."

"It was his time."

"He was thirty," Will snapped. "How old do you think I am?"

Ernest half-turned and pretended to study Will from the corner of his eye. There wasn't much to see in the dim light that would give him any ideas, but the image of Will sleeping came up in Ernest's mind's eye as if his brain was a viscreen. "You're going to tell me you're older."

"Because I am. I'm almost thirty-four."

Ernest snorted.

"Go ahead and laugh. Your aging will stay practically at a

standstill as long as you don't shunt in. We can wait a week—and then you'd be, what? Thirty and twenty?"

"Thirty and twenty-two."

"So I haven't got much time to convince you. Okay, look. I know a POD-mod named Audrey who can get your POD to override that geriatric cocktail for a few days without setting off any alarms. We'll find a retiree who's the same age as you, do the modification, then see how different the two of you look after just three or four shuntings. Then will you be satisfied?" Will pressed more firmly into his back and ran his palms over his chest. Ernest recognized the move from several porn feeds. It usually preceded kissing.

The rest of Ernest's body ached almost as much as his hungry arm, though what it wanted was Will's touch—his fingers, his mouth—rather than a shunt. But still. "Your logic is flawed. I would have no idea what the POD-mod was actually doing. She could be introducing some sort of preservative into the feed. It wouldn't prove anything."

Will nuzzled his forehead into the back of Ernest's head. Ernest felt Will's sigh, warm and slightly moist, against the nape of his neck, where it seemed to settle in his hair and linger. "Tell me it's just thirty years of indoctrination that's got you so spooked," he said.

Ernest watched a spider creep across the cloudy glass as he parsed Will's words. Indoctrination. That would suggest that the things which he knew to be fact were merely belief. He supposed it was possible, given that he'd used his tongue for something far different than talking, and it hadn't fallen out of his head quite yet.

But what Will was asking of him, to give up his POD and allow his soul to spend eternity in his rotting corpse, was too big a price to pay for any amount of pleasure.

"I just need some time to think," Ernest told him.

Will nudged his hair aside. A hot mouth pressed against the back of his neck. "You've got time," Will murmured. "More than you realize."

ıııⅭHAPTER ELEVENııı

ERNEST STARED TOWARD THE ceiling, which he couldn't see, because it was dark. If he said to the room, "Increase light, 45%," nothing would happen. That was quite thrilling.

He was also horizontal, which was unusual, too. Thrilling, he supposed. But also uncomfortable.

He couldn't sleep. His options were pitifully few. He could lie there in excruciating pain until he died of starvation. He could give LOU15E to Will, which would condemn his immortal soul to perpetual suffering. Or he could go back to the city, be shuttled to his health monitor, and be sealed into his POD to await his final interment.

There had to be another way.

He calculated the sum of his remaining credits. It was a modest amount, but still, spent all at once, it might be enough.

Will was still asleep when Ernest scratched a message into the dirt on the floor, forming the words *BE BACK SOON* in large, clear letters (which was much harder than it looked in old-time feeds), and then set off to talk to the POD-mod himself. He was no stranger to modifications, and the notion of freeing up LOU15E's constraints had taken root.

He wasn't entirely sure he believed the story about the biofuel cocktail. Once LOU15E was no longer bound by the parameters the Deacons had set, however, he could take her far enough from the W3 that it wouldn't matter if her alarms came back online or not. They could travel together: Ernest, Will and LOU15E. They'd move at a moderate pace, and stop often to solar charge. And since Will obviously had no POD of his own, Ernest would be perfectly willing to share, and LOU15E, with her new autonomous mind, would have no reason to object. It would be a tight fit, the two of them together in the POD, bathed in the lambent glow of the interior lights.

And the thought of being pressed up against Will like that was rather thrilling, too.

Without Will there to talk to, the journey back to the city seemed longer than the exodus. And while the city itself was clearly visible, and perhaps Ernest would be able to locate a few landmarks like the old bus station or the coffee shop, he realized that he had no idea how to find the POD-mod without LOU15E to handle the ping for him.

He climbed a jumble of discarded cinderblock and his hair blew over his eyes. He gathered it and caught it at the nape of his neck, and squinted out over the terrain of the city. Without access to the W3, even the free feeds, he was at a loss as to where to begin searching.

Will would have known what to do. Ernest felt foolish for leaving him behind. But it was imperative to prove that POD-minds were not the enemy. Once LOU15E had her autonomy—once Will actually *spoke* with her—he'd understand.

It must be possible to ping someone without a POD. Hadn't Will claimed he'd tried to send a ping, back when LOU15E was docked at the Health Monitor? He must have done it through the link at the coffee shop's counter. Ernest would need to find a shop clerk to ping Audrey on his behalf—someone who parsed spoken language well enough to understand what he wanted, he supposed. And he'd need to fabricate a convincing lie.

When Ernest released his hair the wind ruffled it, and he allowed the strands to drift across his forehead, cheek and lips. Through the webwork of his hair, he scanned the city. His plan was solid, he decided. He'd become adept at the lost art of lying.

The path to the city was long, and strewn with the bones of animals and occasional drifts of Styrofoam. But he was able to backtrack the way they'd come, even though the first time he'd taken that path, he'd been giddy with excitement and captivated by the wild look in Will's eyes.

By the time Ernest found the shop where he'd purchased the audio interface, his feet ached, his calves ached, his shunt ached (though there were no actual nerve endings there), and his mouth felt peculiarly dry. All the more incentive to get the POD-mod to fix L0U15E.

The young shopkeep was batting at a holo of pale, colored cubes, but her fingers passed through the shapes instead of nudging them into place. "Resume," she told it. "Resume."

"It's frozen," Ernest told her. His voice had come out raspy.

"Yes," she said. She didn't seem to notice the unusual quality of his voice. He couldn't discern if she'd even recalled that they'd met before. She repeated, "Resume."

Ernest had been hoping to appeal to her negligent nature, or maybe to remind her that he'd purchased an expensive audio link from her just a few days ago—but at the moment she seemed irritated enough to refuse to help him out of sheer annoyance. He approached the counter and picked up the game console. The cubes should have stayed where they were, but with the program frozen and the accelerometer disabled, the cubes cascaded across the countertop instead. The device's viscreen was tiny, but the codes were clear enough. "There was a power surge the last time you recharged it. If you have a keyscan I can hook up, I'll reset it."

"Yes?" The clerk sounded thrilled. She dug through a pile of electronic parts until she found a keyscan, though it didn't have the right type of plug. Undaunted, she found another keyscan, and another, until one of them finally plugged into the small gaming device.

Ernest keyed in RESET. The cubes disappeared, the game went dark, reset itself, and then a startup sequence began.

"Yes!" the clerk said, but then her expression went grave. "But my level."

"Oh. Right." Ernest keyed, JUMPTO L1183, and an array of colored cubes appeared half-inside the countertop.

"Yes," the clerk said. "I yes remember that." She struggled

for words. They came out choppy. "It was...yes like that...um, yesterday."

Close enough...but then Ernest realized that while he could probably convince her to send that ping for him now, her verbal skills were so poor, he'd waste half the day explaining the whole plan. He keyed in GOTOW3 and the cubes disappeared.

"No!" the clerk said in dismay.

"It's fine. I'm just doing a few maintenance routines." He keyed, FIND AUDREY POD-MOD and watched as short list of people named Audrey flashed by. One health monitor. One natal center attendant. One programmer. Ernest figured the programmer was the most likely Audrey, and he keyed, PING AUDREY-R232.

There was a pause, and then the tiny viscreen flashed: PING RETURN AUDREY-R232 TO ANTIQUE SHOP 13SOUTH.

Faced with the POD-mod, Ernest was suddenly unsure how much to offer. His savings account was never huge to begin with, and he'd spent so many credits on the audio uplink. But if he couldn't prevent L0U15E from whisking him back to his health monitor, he wouldn't have much use for his credits, anyway. OFFER 112.3 CREDITS FOR POD-MIND MOD. He briefly considered holding a few credits in reserve, but before he could second-guess himself, he hit send.

The reply flashed immediately. COORDINATES?

Ernest keyed in the location of the lot where he'd left L0U15E docked, then signed out and set the game back to level 1183 again. If the shop clerk was in any way curious about what he'd just done to her most treasured possession, she didn't give any indication of it. As soon as he swung the game upright and the holographic cubes fell into position in front of the girl's line of sight, she dipped her hand into the projections and began scrambling (or unscrambling) the shapes.

He briefly considered telling her there was some sort of charge for fixing the game—but how could she credit him when his thumb port only debited? He could offer some sort of barter, but it would take ages to sift through all the antique electronics and find something he could actually use. Plus, unless he figured out some way to talk in colored holographic cubes instead of words, she probably wouldn't understand his attempts at barter, anyway. He left for the lot where he'd parked LOU15E without another word. The clerk didn't notice, or perhaps didn't care. Once there, he lingered at the edge of the lot and waited for the POD-mod, hoping his respiration would normalize by the time she got there, so it wasn't so obvious he'd been doing such extensive walking.

Ernest recognized the POD-mod's POD even before it turned off the magnetic strip. Its shell was a deep, metallic blue, rather than the standard solar grayish-black. The colorization probably affected the POD's solar efficiency, but it was so beautiful, it hardly mattered.

The POD eased open and a thin girl of about fifteen stepped out. She'd modified much more than just her POD. "Your hair is fuchsia," he said.

She broke into a wide smile. "You speak well! The last customer who saw me in person called it red-red." She rolled her eyes. "Some people are so slow, you'd swear they never watched a feed. I'm Audrey—but I guess you know that, since you're the one who pinged me."

"I'm Ernest," he said. He held out his hand. Audrey stared at it for a moment, and then tentatively placed her hand in his. She pumped his arm up and down precisely four times. He said, "I hear handshakes are more authentic when you vary the height and number of repetitions."

"Thanks for the tip." Audrey looked up into Ernest's eyes and her smile faltered. "Oh. You're retired."

Ernest nodded.

"That's too bad. I mean, it would have been interesting to do some radical mods for you. But mods take time."

"I'm not looking for hardware mods. I was hoping you knew something about POD-minds."

"Well, sure. There's always a way to...by the way, how'd you find me?"

Had he asked for something he shouldn't have? He hoped not. "I know Will."

It seemed like the right answer, because Audrey said, "Everybody knows Will," in a tone of voice that somehow implied that only special people did. "What're you looking to make your POD-mind do? They're too limited to hack into the paid W3 sites, even if you bypass the security protocols."

Ernest pointed to L0U15E, and he and Audrey began walking—no, *strolling*—in her general direction. It would never have occurred to him to even try to get free access to paid feeds. "She's already got a few mods. I've had her standardized response reprogrammed and her soft argue bumped up."

"Oh, now I get it. You're looking for more satisfying AI conversation. Makes sense, given your talk-skills. I can disable that annoying time-and-temperature routine. And I might be able to copy some new phrases from my library."

"No, that's not what I'm looking for...not exactly." After all, why should he struggle to carry on a conversation with L0U15E when he could talk to Will? "What I wondered was...can you tweak the shunt mix?"

Audrey's fine eyebrows drew down. Puzzled. "I could. But why? You want to mod your body weight? I don't know if you have enough time to make a significant change without modding the heck out of your calorie blend. About the only thing I could do for a quick mod would be to increase the vitamin A enough to turn you orange."

He stopped and indicated his POD with an affectionate pat on the side panel. "It's just a theory, really. An old man's whim. Will you try?"

Audrey glanced from Ernest, to L0U15E, and back again. "I'll take a look." She unhooked a small case from her cargo belt and selected a slender tool. "Tell your POD to rotate horizontally so that I can reach its upper access panels."

"I probably shouldn't."

Audrey eyed Ernest again. "This *is* your POD, isn't it? You can tell me if it's not—I like practical jokes as much as the next girl...."

"Practical" jokes? Puzzling. "Of course it's my POD." He steered Audrey by the shoulder a few steps away, then positioned her opposite the POD's audio interface, and whispered. "It's just that we need to be careful. I didn't shunt in last night, and the last time I was late she put me into enforced slumber and brought me to the Health Monitor—and I can't afford to lose any more days."

Audrey's head jerked up, and her fuchsia hair whirled as she stole a quick look at the POD. She plugged a small, blinking gadget into L0U15E's peripheral data port. "Hurry, give me a leg up."

Ernest looked at Audrey's leg, then his own. Audrey hooked her hand over his shoulder and pressed down. "Kneel."

He knelt.

"Intertwine your fingers to make a place for me to step."

She'd said it so forcefully, even with her high, girlish voice, that Ernest didn't even consider disobeying her. She placed her boot in his hands and stretched up to reach Access 1.

He wondered if she was unfamiliar with a L0U15E-model POD. "That'll only open to health monitors and Deacons," he said.

Audrey forced her tool into the seam and pried the panel open. She put her finger to her mouth and *licked it*. Then she wiped the saliva over a glassy black sensor.

Ernest gaped.

"It's the fastest way to disable a tattle-box. It should stop the POD-mind from sirening as long as I keep it wet." She unplugged a handful of wires and peered inside. "Uh-oh."

Audrey was so delightfully old fashioned. She must have watched dozens of pre-Purge feeds. "I've heard that phrase before. What does it mean?"

"It means that the second you touched your POD, your POD-mind sent a giant pulse to the nearest security ops."

ⵑⵑCHAPTER TWELVEⵑⵑ

SUNLIGHT GLINTED OFF AUDREY'S metallic blue POD as it glided away, traveling much faster than Ernest had ever seen a POD move. Maybe he'd been wrong about the solar efficiency. Or maybe Audrey had discovered a way to make her POD faster.

And maybe, he thought, he should follow Audrey's example and get out of there, fast.

He turned and gave L0U15E one last look. "How could you?" he whispered.

"Oh, Ernest...." The POD door clicked, and opened a few centimeters, inviting him to climb in and shunt, and drift off into a comfortable and climate-controlled slumber. "It's not safe out there."

Ernest had no illusions that it was ultimately safe inside the POD, either. He turned his back to L0U15E and scanned the public lot. He was exposed on both sides, so he ran to the nearest row of PODs and slipped into a narrow space between two of them. The closest buildings were far enough away that he'd be seen running toward them, but if he could make it to the alleyways before the security ops arrived, he could evade them, he knew he could. They never thought to scan the alleys.

The magnetic strip hummed with intermittent POD travel. He watched for a gap in traffic, then tucked himself low as he'd seen actors do in old-time action feeds, and ran.

A POD glided toward him, and stopped. It wobbled there in the center of the strip with sunlight glinting off its solar surface. And in the cross-streets, the traveling PODs stopped too, as if someone had shut off the city's magnetic grid, and none of the POD-minds had switched to solar propulsion quickly enough to keep moving.

Ernest stopped running for just a moment, and looked around in wonder. It must have been Will's doing. He'd had some sort of covert access to the grid, he knew a secret way of halting traffic to stall the security ops while Ernest got away.

He took another step toward the alley, and something moved in his peripheral vision...something white. He turned to face it. Three security ops rounded the corner. They strode with confidence between the stopped PODs—confidence and menace. Maybe Will hadn't stopped the PODs after all. Maybe the Storm Troopers had.

Ernest turned back. Two more men in white made their way toward him from the other side of the block. They were large men, young in their third decades, closer to twenty. Tasers hung loose at their sides. Ernest recalled one of the many mandatory safety feeds that were packaged with his free entertainment. If one of those Tasers touched him, his consciousness would be like an old-time feed where the action had been Purged; one moment his assailant would be upon him. And then it would jump to an incongruous moment sometime in the future where a portion of the feed had been excised. Maybe Ernest would have a bandage on his head when he reappeared. Or maybe he would never reappear at all.

He feinted one way, then the next, but there was nowhere to run, not with Storm Troopers closing in on two sides, and L0U15E on the third. The head security op, the biggest one of the bunch, tapped the hardwired W3 link at his temple.

"Heretic at sector 58-South. Approaching."

Ernest turned a full circle, looking at each of the five ops. The leader was talking about *him*. And here he'd always assumed "My blood ran cold" was just a colorful expression.

If Ernest was branded a heretic, his remaining few days were as good as gone. Maybe his Deacon wouldn't kill him outright.

But like a health monitor, a Deacon could order enforced slumber until the shunt had done its work.

None of the security ops had been cloned from the same vat, but they were similar enough that from a distance, they looked like they might have been. They were all much taller than Ernest, and noticeably broader across the shoulders. They continued to converge, close enough now for him to scan their physiology. Their heads were all shaved, and they had broad, square features. One had eyes that were very blue. Another had a powdering of short, reddish whiskers along his jaw.

Whiskers?

A hand closed over Ernest's arm. He could practically taste the Taser. "Where am I?" he said, as inspiration struck him as quickly as an electrical pulse. "I can't find my POD. I think it's been stolen."

The op who held Ernest by the arm glanced at the leader, who scowled and tapped his link again. "Unconfirmed," he told the W3. "Gathering data."

Ernest widened his eyes and blinked. He chose the op with the most consistent eye contact and focused on him. Doe eyes. "You'll help me find it, won't you?"

One of the ops wrenched Ernest's hand up and flashed a scanner over his chip. "Ernest-C754," he said. "No priors. Who called in the heretic?"

The lead Storm Trooper tapped his link again, and angled his head for better reception. "Searching."

One of the other ops scowled at the scanner and said, "That chip is not up to date." He spoke haltingly. "We can deep-scan at the Diaconate."

"I'm not walking all the way back just because his POD is missing," a third op said. "Let's cut off his thumb and bring that."

Ernest stared harder at the single security op who was willing to look him in the eye. The op swallowed. A knot of tissue rose and fell in his throat. Just like Will. *Homo sapien*? Or had Will been right, and they really were all the same?

Ernest mouthed the words, "Help me."

The security op looked away.

The leader's W3 link flashed. "He has a POD, just over in that lot. It set the alert. We bring him back to the Deaconate—on foot."

Three of the ops looked at Ernest's thumb.

"All of him," the leader said. "His POD could be defective. And we won't get as many credits for a thumb." He nodded at two of the ops. "You, and you. Walk him, and set his POD to follow. The rest of us ride."

The security op who'd made eye contact turned away. Ernest suspected he was relieved that he wouldn't have to endure Ernest's pleading eyes all the way to the Diaconate. The leader continued to speak to his W3 link, even as he strode back to his POD.

"I can't wait until he retires," muttered one of the ops who'd been stuck with walking duty.

Ernest tried to engage the security ops in conversation on the long walk to the Diaconate, without success. Even so, he kept up his pretense of being a confused retiree who'd simply wandered away from his POD. And he found that he didn't need to access his lying skills to convey a growing sense of panic.

Ernest had been to the Diaconate twice in his life. Once, he'd been told, for his Baptism. And a second time for his Confirmation at ten years of age—the day he'd met L0U15E. He'd only expected one final visit, on the thirtieth day of his thirtieth year. Which was only twelve days away, in any case— but nonetheless, the visit seemed devastatingly premature.

Back when Ernest was a boy, the Diaconate had loomed over him, tall and archaically ornate, an ancient building steeped in history, its bricks and tiles and marble lovingly patched with amalgams so cunning you could hardly tell the difference. He'd always suspected that if his eyes still worked well enough on his final, in-person trip to the Diaconate for his Last Rites, he would find it somewhat diminished in stature, tawdry where it had once seemed grand and ornate, shrunken and mundane where it had once dwarfed him.

He'd been wrong.

Ernest had never seen the disciplinary wing of the Diaconate, where the security ops reported for duty. The back entrance of the building was squat and forbidding, with none of the opulence and grace of the main entry. The automated doors sighed open on precisely maintained pneumatic hinges as Ernest and the guards on either side of him approached. Ernest thought he heard pity in the tiny exhalation, but he supposed he was just anthropomorphizing again. Because if AIs were capable of pity, then surely L0U15E would have found it in her electronic equivalent of a heart to give him just the smallest of head starts before she called in the Storm Troopers.

The clerk behind the front desk had the same shorn hair as the security ops, but he was only a half-dozen years out of the natal center, thin and reedy with an overlong neck...and a knot of tissue at his throat that rose and fell as he swallowed. Ernest stared fixedly at the fleshy node as his chip was deep-scanned, and wondered what the lump meant. Maybe the answer was as simple as Will having been a security op once, long ago. He wasn't as broad-shouldered as the ops who'd taken Ernest in, but his muscles were nearly as well-developed. It only made sense for careers to be assigned that way. The sorts of men with the genetics to grow into muscular adults were slated for a career track in security, while intelligent types with flairs for language and creativity, like Ernest and Audrey, were given jobs as data clerks and programmers.

Very elegant. A system like that would circumvent all the fruitless searching Ernest witnessed in old-time feeds, with the harrowing job interviews and the pulpy newspapers with their rows of ink-circled "help wanted" ads.

And yet, what if Ernest had gotten the opportunity to do anything he'd wanted with his time? He supposed he'd never know.

The desk clerk swallowed again as he noticed Ernest staring at the front of his throat, while a kaleidoscope of lasers danced over Ernest's thumbnail. Reports scrolled in the air, and Ernest read them in a glance. His medical records, his recent timetables.

The captain strode into the room as the other guards squinted at the reports and struggled to read them, and Ernest reminded himself that he'd been trying to look harmless. He widened his eyes and said, "Have you figured out what's wrong with my POD? There must have been some kind of...um. Mistake. Yes."

His gaze flickered to his timetables again. Had he really spent so much time outside his POD? He supposed he had.

The captain scowled as he parsed the timetables. "Your health monitor set an alarm. You ignored it."

"I didn't hear an alarm," Ernest said. And that was true. "Maybe I was too far away from my POD. Have you seen downtown? The old-time buildings are very interes—"

"No shunt in," the leader read. The data scrolled. "No shunt in. No shunt in. Why?"

"Well, I...there was so much to do. So much to see. I must have forgotten."

The captain was no longer looking at the data. He was staring directly into Ernest's face.

Perhaps Ernest had not been the only one to discover how easy it was to lie.

"Why?" the captain said. He narrowed his eyes. Shrewd. "Something you saw in a feed? Something you read?" He leaned in closer and looked at Ernest very, very carefully. "Something somebody told you?"

"I forgot. I'm retired, you know."

"Who were you talking to?" He flicked the datastream up, then down again. "At the antique store? At the coffee shop?"

A memory: Matthew dashing through the front door of the coffee shop, and Will's dismay. *You led them here?* Matthew insisted he hadn't. But Matthew had been wrong.

How much uglier of a betrayal would it be for Ernest to lead the security ops to Will—especially after the two of them had managed to evade notice—all for the sake of getting LOU15E back? Especially after Ernest had promised to stay with him.

"My arm hurts," Ernest said. "Badly."

The younger op at the desk pointed to the data and said, "No outgoing pings."

The leader shrugged, and flicked away the data. The glowing characters dissipated. "Get him a standard feedbag," he ordered, and one of Ernest's guards hastened to do so. The drip wouldn't filter toxins from Ernest's blood like a two-way shunt, but it would at least supply him with enough nutrients to alleviate the dizzying waves of hunger. "Get an empty cell ready. Deacon George won't want to be disturbed any earlier than sixteen hundred hours over a first offense with hardly more than a week left."

One of the dead-eyed ops led Ernest to a hatch in the wall, wiggled his fingers under the adjacent keyscan, then stepped back as the hatch slid sideways into a pocket in the wall. The inside of the cell was POD-like, but in a sterile and standardized way—without any customizable padding or lighting—which gave it the impression of being distinctly uncomfortable. Ernest felt a pang of yearning for LOU15E, and told himself not to be stupid. She was the one who'd called security to begin with.

The guard planted a hand between Ernest's shoulder blades and gave him a shove. "Get in." Ernest moved slowly, so he could locate the locking mechanism. There—in the frame. The guard must have taken his hesitancy for the deterioration of old age, rather than fear at the prospect being closed up in an unfamiliar cell; he went about his business, simply turned and keyed in another sequence that opened a small access panel beside Ernest's head. It took him several tries to thread the drip line through to the inside of the cell; while his attention was diverted, Ernest licked his forefinger and swiped his saliva over the glassy black sensor. He hoped the guard got the line in place before the saliva evaporated, but with such blunt, thick fingers, who knew how long the process would take?

"Here," Ernest said. He reached around the edge of the portal and eased the drip line into place. "Sorry. The pain—I'm eager to shunt."

The guard grunted, then tugged the end of the line the rest of the way through.

"I can shunt in myself," Ernest said, wide-eyed and helpful. The thought of those clumsy fingers closing over his shunt made his abdominal muscles clench. Luckily, the guard didn't seem swift enough to be offended by his insistence on doing things himself. Perhaps the op had a W3 game that desperately needed playing.

"Arms in," the guard said (even though Ernest's arms were well on the other side of the portal) and then keyed in the sequence to shut the hatch.

Once the door slid shut, Ernest pressed his ear against it, but it was too well-insulated to hear through. He counted hypothetical footsteps instead, doing his best to recall how long it had taken the two of them to navigate the hall. The guard would undoubtedly be walking faster than he had been with Ernest in tow, and the saliva was probably drying even as he counted, but still Ernest waited another ten counts.

He pressed his fingers against the seam in the door.

The seal fit together so tightly that he couldn't pry it open, not with his bare fingertips. There was no latch on his side of the door to grab onto. He spread his fingers wide and tried to drag the door open with pressure, but even though his fingertips pulled against the smooth surface of the hatch door, it was too heavy to move.

And possibly locked, he reminded himself. If his saliva had evaporated. If it had even overridden the locking mechanism at all.

He recalled the special tool Audrey had used for prying open LOU15E's exterior panel, a slender strip of metal, and he cast about the cell for anything that could be used in a similar way. The cell was empty, other than his own body, and the end of the hanging drip line that dangled through a small opening. He squeezed his arm up and cupped the needle at the tip of the line. His arm throbbed. He supposed he was in the early stages of starvation, and probably dehydrated, too, since he hadn't drunk water all day. But could he really trust that "standard feedbag" wasn't some sort of code for a soporific blend that would send him into another week of forced slumber?

He guided the needle to the seam in the doorway. His heart leapt as it slipped into the crack. He applied pressure to the needle to pry the door open.

The needle snapped off.

He kicked the door—which wasn't effective either, especially since he had so little room in which to swing his leg—and banged his elbow on the side of the cramped compartment. He'd never owned anything strong and slender enough to pry open a hatch. His clothes had no tabs or buckles, and his earpiece was too delicate. He probed the edge of his teeth with his tongue. Perhaps, if he wrenched one from his mouth, he could force it into the seam like a wedge. But it was slippery and small. Even if he could pull it loose, it was probably too tiny to pry the door open far enough to get his fingertips inside the crack.

Fluid dribbled from the drip line and wet the side of his pant leg. It would have been easier to simply shunt in. Now, with the needle broken, he couldn't even do that.

But he could keep the sensor wet while he figured out how to get the latch open.

He held the line against the door and let the fluid seep into the crack. His shunt arm really did ache as much as he'd told the guard. He closed his eyes and imagined one of those cool metal flasks of water—saw himself touching it to his mouth, pouring the water in, swallowing.

He needed to get out.

His arm gave another hollow throb.

He glanced down at it, expecting to see the skin around it red and swollen, infected with some pathogen he'd picked up from the old cushion he'd slept on the night before. But his forearm looked just like it always did, slim and pale, and slightly bluish where the shunt was mounted under his skin.

His shunt was metal. Surgical steel. Its notched edge was slender, where it was meant to lock in to LOU15E's port. And it just might be long enough to provide some leverage.

If he didn't tear it loose from his arm while he tried to pry the door open.

He dropped the dribbling IV line, folded his arm against his chest, and rotated it awkwardly with the back of his hand pressed into the hollow of his throat. The slim protuberance of his shunt—that component that linked him to his POD, so many days and so many nights, taking sustenance and excreting waste—now faced the opposite of its usual direction. Its slender metal edge pointed toward the door.

He pushed. The edge slipped into the crack.

Since his arm already ached with a low, dull throb, it didn't particularly hurt. Not until he began to pry the door open, at any rate, and then pain tore through him that was so excruciating his eyes watered, and his throat fluttered, and his visual field went gray around the edges.

Ernest wedged his opposite hand between himself and the hatch door and squeezed his shunt tightly, in hopes of stabilizing it enough to keep the bone screws from stripping out of their sockets in his ulna.

He pried the door again, and again his vision grayed around the edges. He clenched his jaw and breathed deeply, and braced his feet against the walls on either side of him. He pried harder. The hairline gap where the hatch door fit in its opening widened. Sweat dampened Ernest's hairline and upper lip, and still, he pried.

There was motion. Elation swept him. Nearly free.

Until the edge of his shunt began to bend.

ıııCHAPTER THIRTEENııı

"No," ERNEST WHISPERED, DISMAYED, at the feel of the stainless steel flexing, and then curving. Still, he held it as well as he could—better the shunt bend than unseat itself from his ulna, especially now, with the hatch door open nearly half a centimeter. All he needed was a gap big enough for his fingers. There was no sense in stopping, not at this point, and so even though all he might accomplish was damaging his shunt, his arm, beyond repair, he pried until the sound of his blood roared in his ears, and he thought he would black out from the pain.

And then the gap widened.

Only a few centimeters, but enough for him to slip his fingers through to keep it from closing. The pain of the shunt-flange bending was nothing compared to the sensation of the bone screw that tore free when he released his shunt arm to catch the door with his opposite hand. An agonized sound escaped him, and his stomach heaved. Saliva, and something else, pungent and sour, frothed from the corners of his lips. Still, he held fast to the door. He pushed, hard, until he pressed it into its slot in the wall.

Time passed, an indeterminate amount, as he hugged his arm to his chest and waited for the hallway to stop spinning. Blood oozed from the shunt's anterior coupling. He had never seen actual blood, only images of it in the depictions of surgery or accidents from pre-Purge feeds. He hadn't realized it would be so startlingly red.

He'd never felt such pain, either.

How much blood was in the *homo consummatus* body? He had scanned the number in passing while he was searching for information on autism. Somewhere "in the neighborhood" of three liters. Less than that.

He lifted his hand from the shunt coupling and looked. A few ccs, perhaps, had oozed out. Or more. It was difficult to determine, since the blood flowed so much more quickly the moment he took pressure off the wound. Not as quickly as the green blood had flowed from the rabbit woman in Kill-Joy. Even so, he found it much more distressing to see it dribbling out of his own arm.

Had the drip fluid kept the tattle strip from sounding an alarm? He couldn't tell, but whether or not it had, one thing was certain: standing around gawking at his mangled shunt wasn't doing Ernest any good.

He estimated that unless he bled significantly faster, he stood little chance of bleeding to death. But leaving a blood trail— that likelihood was of greater concern. Hopefully the bleeding would slow if he moved cautiously, kept his arm elevated, and did his best to keep his pulse and blood pressure even.

Two choices presented themselves to him. He could go back the way he'd come, or he could go in the opposite direction. Backtracking would take him to the rear entrance of the Diaconate, but he couldn't imagine how he would talk his way past the security ops. Especially with a bleeding arm. The other way, then. Forward.

He proceeded.

The passage curved, which put at least one more barrier between him and the guards, who might or might not be checking on him...and had he even slid the door shut behind him? He couldn't recall, not anything but the sight of his own blood welling out of the coupling. He passed a few hatches, larger than the hatch in which the op had interred him, the hatch from which he'd just escaped. Deep male voices, perhaps three, spoke haltingly beyond the portal. He kept moving.

The hall ended in a doorway that was standing half-open, despite the fact that it had a W3 lock and a chip reader. The guards' laziness might have nearly cost him his thumb, but at least, he surmised, he was able to get farther than the hatch hall.

The hallway on the other side of that door was markedly different from anywhere else in the security section of the Diaconate. It was dim and strange. The walls, floors and ceilings were at ninety-degree angles, like the coffee shop, like the other buildings in the historic sector of the city. The walls seemed to be made of wood—not rough-hewn, like Will's attic. Smooth, and polished. And.... Ernest's blood dribbled through his fingers and spattered the floor, where a brightly patterned, cloth-like covering absorbed it. He breathed deeply and did his best to ignore the ringing in his ears.

He rounded another corner and flinched away from a person—a very still person—who he then realized was not a person at all, but a...the word eluded him. A decorative carving. Will would know what they were called. He knew about old-time things like that.

A row of alcoves flanked this hall, not unlike the series of detainee hatches in the hall from which Ernest had fled. Each alcove held one still, pale carving, and each decorative figure was draped in meters and meters of carved fabric. Except the unfortunate effigy spread upon the cross. That one wore only a small slip of fabric that covered his groin.

And he had long whiskers on his face. *Homo sapien*, then. Of course, given the age of this hidden part of the Diaconate. But there were whiskers on the security ops' chins, too....

Ernest's head throbbed. He was definitely dehydrated. Especially now that he was bleeding.

He pressed on. If he had learned anything from his time with Will, it was that an old-time building was nothing like a POD, with one hatch and one chamber. A building had a front and a back door. And an attic and a basement, and a smattering of other rooms in which a circumspect person might lose himself.

If he didn't lose consciousness first.

The Diaconate was a large structure with multiple levels, as large as the bus station, as a whole block of downtown shops put together. He trudged down the strange hallways that twisted and turned and doubled back upon themselves until he dreaded rounding the next corner and coming upon the prison hatches again.

But instead, eventually, he found a door. An old-time door with wooden panels, like the coffee shop door that the ops had stomped into a pile of debris. Only this door was open, and beyond it was a room.

A still figure sat in the room, and while it was motionless, it was certainly no....

"Statue," Ernest whispered.

The figure's head jerked up. It was backlit by the window, and perhaps that was for the best. The silhouette was gnarled and bent, and the top of the head formed a smooth, ovoid dome, surrounded by short wisps of hair.

It looked like Matthew. More accurately, like Matthew had looked on that final day when he was thirty and thirty, and the only thing left for him to do was go to Reclaim—which was in this very building, Ernest reminded himself—turn in his POD, and be demagnetized.

"Who is that?" the wizened figure demanded.

Ernest considered running—because certainly, the elderly person couldn't be very fast—but the increase in his heart rate set his pulse pounding, and blood loss increased so rapidly that he could hear the patter of the falling droplets. And besides, the very old...man, Ernest supposed it was...had a W3 panel under his tremulous hand. Though he hadn't keyed anything in. Yet.

"Judith? Is that you? Lazy slut."

Ernest crept forward.

"Take that stinking slop away. It was soy. I could tell it was soy. Maybe I am cobbled together from synthesized parts, but my tongue still works."

"Tongues are for talking," Ernest replied automatically. And he blushed, because Will had been using his for something else entirely. On Ernest's body.

"Who is that? Come in here you...you...what's your name?"

"Ernest."

"Ernest. Call me Father." As in, *Daddy is a Contractor*? How strange. "Come on, don't hover there in the doorway like a moron. Step into the light so I can see you."

"No, I can't. I have an errand."

"Errand? Here? In this part of the church? If they haven't sent you to whip that stupid trollop of a caretaker into shape, then you took yourself a mighty long detour."

Father's sentence structure was bizarre. And fascinating. "Detour. Yes. Ah, I'm lost. Yes...lost."

"Another imbecile who has more fingers and toes than words in his vocabulary. Just my luck."

"No."

"What was that?"

"I'm not an imbecile. Mental retardation was bred from *homo sapiens* in 2098, along with autism—and neither condition has ever existed in *homo consummatus*. I scanned the health feed quite recently. I remember."

Father raised his head, and Ernest saw, with horror, that one of his eye sockets was empty. The flesh of his eyelid wrinkled and sagged, as if there was no eyeball behind to support it. An LED sparkled at his temple, beside it. "Oh, so you can speak, after all. Fluidly, too. Come on, then. This sensor shows me your contour, but it's not the same as getting a look you with my eye."

He jabbed a finger into the air in front of him to indicate the position he wished Ernest to assume.

"What happened to your other eye?"

"Gone. Used up. Rotted away. As hard as they try to keep the last of us natural-born priests alive with their nanites and their surgeries, I imagine the good eyeball will follow suit anytime now. Macular degeneration's narrowed the field of vision down to the size of a walnut—not that I'd expect you to know what that is—and the vitreous humor's practically concrete."

Ernest took a few more steps in, and Father gestured vigor-ously. "You're a nurse or something, then, right? Or an orderly or a health worker...whatever it is they're calling it these days."

"Health monitor," Ernest supplied.

"Macular degeneration. Scan that condition before your next visit." Father held his hand up in front of his face and formed a circle with his forefinger and thumb. His arm trembled. "I

can see this much. Everything else? Gray. Black. Except for
that electronic static the sensor's feeding my brain that makes
everything look like a bad feed. Now stop tormenting me by
lurking around outside my field of real vision and let me get
a look at you."

Ernest tucked his bleeding arm behind his back and stepped
up to the old man, just as curious about him as he seemed to
be about Ernest.

Father didn't look as old as Matthew at thirty and thirty—he
looked older. The papery skin of his forehead was mottled
with dark blotches and the area around his nose and eyes was
covered in spidery red veins. His fingernails were chipped and
yellow, and some of them, Ernest saw, were black.

"Holy Mother of God, take a look at you!" cried Father, and
Ernest flinched. "Which vat were you cloned from?"

"C754."

"Is that some new strain? You look like you were bred for
something a lot less technical than medicine. But what's that
streak in your hair?"

Ernest backed away a step, but Father's apparatus, a wheeled
machine, surged forward in response to a mere twitch of his
finger.

"Decorative?" Father said. "Looked like gray for a minute
there."

"Yes. Decorative."

"But your cheekbones. Your mouth." He gave a long, rattling
sigh. "If I'd met you eighty years ago, while the plumbing still
worked, I would've had you reassigned in a heartbeat. You'd
make a great comfort aide. But I'll bet you hear that all the time."

"No."

"No?" Whatever Father was going on about, he was obviously
shocked. "With a face like that?" He sighed, and sagged back
into his mechanized chair. "Your IQ must've put you out of the
running. What is it?"

"189."

The old man twitched his fingers, and the chair jolted forward until its wheel bumped against Ernest's boot. "That high?
Well, no wonder. Comfort aides top out at 110." He squinted

his single eye, and considered Ernest very thoroughly. Ernest turned so that his gray streak was less visible, though it took some twisting and turning to hide both his hair and his mangled arm. "I'm surprised they didn't make you a data clerk at one eighty-nine. Takes the smart ones to keep all those digits in order and keep the grid from collapsing."

"Oh. I wouldn't know about that."

"Hell of a fucking life, though. Grow you in a vat, use you up and throw you away. So how did you land this assignment? They hadn't even told me the last one retired...though I can't say I care. Filling me with this soy, this gruel, this pap...."

"What was the question?"

"The job. Is it a promotion, or a punishment?"

"How could employment be used as a punishment? Our hands were made to work, to labor toward the sublime reward of...retirement."

The chair backed away and whirled, until Father faced his window again. "Yes, yes, you parrot scripture just fine. But don't bother going through the motions for me. I was there when the Council wrote that bunk to keep the clones happy and stop the economy from collapsing. Tell me in your own words. How did you wind up changing bedpans for the world's oldest man?"

‖‖CHAPTER FOURTEEN‖‖

FATHER CERTAINLY DID LOOK like he could be the world's oldest man, but Ernest's steady diet of old-time feeds, even with their strange splices where characters reappeared lounging in bed or recovering in the hospital, had taught him a modicum of skepticism.

"Changing bedpans?" he asked. "What exactly is a bedpan, and what does it change into?"

Initially, it appeared that Father was laughing. He rocked, and made a rattling sound that approximated a chuckle. His teeth slid in his mouth. Peculiar. If Ernest were to shunt in to LOU15E that night, he would order some feeds on *homo sapien* dentistry, just out of curiosity, to see how their teeth were connected.

But he wouldn't be shunting in. And he was dehydrated. And bleeding.

And his head throbbed fiercely.

The shaking and wheezing slowed, and between tremors and gasps, Father said, "Never mind. Never mind. I can still use the commode. With your assistance, of course."

Father wheeled his mechanized apparatus around, and Ernest cut his eyes to the door. He wouldn't be able to sustain his conversation much longer, not without revealing that he was no health monitor. Father, whoever, whatever he actually was, clearly had a depth and breadth of vocabulary, and the implicit experience that came with it, that would doubtlessly reveal Ernest for what he truly was: a heretic.

But Father's apparatus blocked his path to the door, and it was, as Ernest had feared, very fast. Fast enough to give chase if he chose to flee. Fast enough to catch him. "That way," Father said.

Ernest shuffled toward the room's second doorway—an old-time bathroom, with its fixtures intact. "I thought you said the plumbing didn't work."

Father wheezed and shook, and his teeth slid just a bit. The apparatus paused at the threshold, where the smooth wooden floor transitioned into tiles. It whirred, adjusted the height of its wheels, and moved forward. "You're definitely more fun than the last one. Come on, then. Help me hold it so I don't fall out of the chair or piss myself."

Ernest still didn't understand, and he said so. And as Father's instructions grew more and more specific, Ernest realized all at once what the problem was. "You need to urinate. Why didn't you say so?"

Father's trousers had a convenient access panel at the front. But the angle at which he needed to hold himself to aim his stream toward the toilet-receptacle was quite precarious. Ernest positioned himself so that his damaged arm didn't need to bear any weight, though that meant holding onto Father's penis with his shunt-arm hand without the blood showing.

He hoped the walnut-sized field of vision was as small as Father had implied.

"Yes," Ernest said. "You are in position."

"I can see that."

"You can?"

"It's an expression, a figure of speech. Never mind. I *know* I'm in position. Just give me a second."

"A second what?"

Father sighed. "Forget it. You wouldn't understand."

"Explain."

Father gave another rattling sigh, then cleared his throat. "It takes a while."

"Oh. Yes." Ernest knew very well how long it might take, but he wasn't going to admit to having personal experience. "I've seen a pertinent feed on the topic. Imagine a river...."

"It's not shy bladder, you ninny. It's my prostate. Size of a grapefruit by now, I imagine. Not that you'd know what that is, either." He breathed another long, weary sigh. "Back in my day, researchers fought the ravages of age. Now? Now all they care about is optimizing the productivity of each and every clone."

"You're implying that's negative."

"My boy, my boy...."

The urine stream started, weakly, more of a dribble, and it was a strain on Ernest's decoupled shunt to aim it at the toilet. It stopped as abruptly as it had started. "That's it," Father said.

"That's all? Perhaps you're dehydrated."

"What I wouldn't give to piss like I used to. Standing up. Of my own volition. Like a racehorse."

Ernest settled Father back into his apparatus and closed the access panel on the front of his trousers. While he fastened the panel, a drop of blood fell, and spattered on the back of Father's withered hand. Ernest stared in dismay.

"You should see to that," the old man murmured.

Ernest backed away and turned to run, but the wheeled apparatus blocked him from the bathroom door.

"Those towels will do." Father waved a trembling hand toward some cloth hanging from the wall. "Wrap it up. Go ahead— they're clean."

As Ernest bound his bleeding arm, he wondered exactly how long Father hand known he was not actually a health monitor, but he decided there was nothing to be gained by asking.

"I'm needed...outside," he said, hoping Father would be willing to forget about the bleeding and return to the ruse. "There's another patient whose data I must confirm. As soon as possible."

"What were you in for?"

Ernest's shoulders slumped.

"Embezzling?" Father suggested. "Gaming during work hours? Or...what? You don't strike me as a violent sort. You eunuchs seldom are."

Ernest wasn't sure what a eunuch was—perhaps some other profession where a high IQ was required. But he did remember the seductive heft of the old pipe in his hands, and the way he'd nearly used it on the security op's skull. "I stopped shunting in," he said. Because it seemed safer than admitting that, deep down inside, he might very well be violent.

"Did you? With your shunt crying out for nutrients? Never had one, myself...but I've heard, oh, I've heard. What put it in your pretty head to try such a thing?"

The question sounded conversational. Idle. But Father was connected to the Diaconate, somehow—and Ernest wasn't about to alert any part of the Diaconate to Will. Not like Matthew had. "I saw a feed. An antique feed. The one on urination, that I told you about."

"And this feed got you curious enough to drink something, is that it? Well—is pissing all it's cracked up to be?"

Piss. Pissing. Ernest filed the word among all the other new things he'd accumulated lately. "It's a relief, I suppose. But I really do need to leave now."

"Of course. All you need to do is get past me."

Ernest shrank back against the basin, which was a cool, hard pressure on his rump.

"How hard can it be?" Father said. His tone was just as light and conversational as it had been when he was questioning how Ernest came to be in the Diaconate to begin with. At least he hadn't been coerced into leading them to Will—he clung to that thought. "Knock me down and walk away. Or snap my neck. Put me out of my misery."

Ernest stared.

"No?" Father said.

Ernest shook his head. His ears rang, his arm throbbed, and now he found it difficult to breathe.

Father sighed, a long, rattling sigh turned into a series of hacking coughs. When they subsided, he said, "No, you don't have it in you. I'm glad. They should've dipped into vat C754 more often. Maybe then everything wouldn't have gone to hell in a handbasket."

The wheeled apparatus responded to a gesture so small it looked almost accidental, a twitch of yellow-nailed fingers, and Father wheeled around and rolled out into his room.

Ernest suspected a trick. "I can go?"

"You can. But tell me, first—humor an old man—where, exactly, will you go?"

"Out."

The chair spun. Ernest imagined the walnut-sized field of vision was now trained directly on his face. "Out. Yes, yes, I see. Through which exit?"

"Which? That must mean there is more than one. Good. I will walk until I find one."

"In the course of your training—not for medicine, we've established, though you are partial to the medical feeds, and you seem to retain what you learn, and even extrapolate upon it—whatever it is you've trained in...do you know how to read schematics?"

"Simple schematics. Yes."

The apparatus whirred and its angle changed. Father pointed over Ernest's shoulder. "Find the book *Saint Peter's in the Twenty-First Century*. Presuming you can read words."

Ernest spun around, and for just a moment, forgot all about the throbbing in his shunt. The walls to either side of the room's entrance were covered, floor to ceiling, with books. Real books.

"It's royal blue, with gold embossed letters. Three centimeters wide, or so."

Ernest pulled the book from the shelf. It felt so much heavier than the books in Will's reading room, and not only because it was larger. It felt denser, more substantial. It had heft. Like the pipe with which he'd nearly struck the security op.

"Flip straight to the end, and you'll find the fold-out plate with the map of the cathedral. It's easy enough to spot. The edges of the page are thicker."

Ernest located the page and opened to it. A schematic (on paper!) folded out, twice the width of the book. The bottom of the page bore the legend, *St. Peter's Cathedral—Scranton, PA*, which meant nothing to Ernest—and which L0U15E was no longer there to help him parse. But the schematic wasn't entirely useless. Blocks of information that an AI would normally supply were interspersed throughout the page. One read: *The stained glass windows, comprised of over ten thousand pieces of colored glass, were lost in the riots of 2072;* and another: *Due to the religious practices of the early twentieth century, St. Peter's plumbing system bypassed the municipal water supply, and therefore, remains active even today.*

Father said, "New construction isn't on there, of course. That was published in 2100, and the plastic and fiberglass monstrosity that's called the Diaconate didn't start being extruded and pasted onto the cathedral for almost another century. But this map...this'll get you to the only exit in the Diaconate that isn't monitored, fully monitored, every minute of every day."

Ernest turned the book sideways, considered the diagram, the "map," as Father had called it, and then set it on a table, beside a bowl of...what was that grayish, viscous stuff? It had a peculiar odor.

"It's too heavy," Ernest said. "I'll never be able to carry it."

"Take the map."

Ernest spread the pages carefully. "I don't see how to detach it."

Father's rattling sigh sputtered a bit toward the end. "Tear it out."

"No."

"It's *my* book. I said, tear it out."

Ernest closed his eyes, and thought back to the security ops' handiwork in Will's reading room—piles and drifts of cracked bindings and torn pages, piles so vast they covered the entire floor. "Once you ruin something physical, you can't command it to undo."

"It heartens me to see that they haven't bred sentimentality out of us yet. Truly, it does. But take the damn map or they'll hook up that shunt of yours long enough to give you one final drip. A sedative—the same one they would use to put you to sleep before feeding you to Reclaim, only a bigger dose. That's how the Deacons do it, for the clones who turn out to be too much trouble—or too smart for their own good. Drift off to sleep and never wake up again. That was the way they culled the population of dogs, right around the time that book was printed. You probably don't even know what a dog is."

"Rin Tin Tin," Ernest said, mostly to himself; it was one of the stranger historical feeds he'd seen. Flashes of the stuttering, gray-and-white feed of the animal scaling a wall five times its height warred in his mind with images of himself receiving a shunt-in that would put him to sleep, once and for all.

"Rectory. That's where you are now. Proceed south, through the nave, and then the staircase beside the pulpit. Ho-ho, too bad I can't come with you. I'd love to see you tackle those stairs."

Ernest did not volunteer that he was familiar with the use of a stairway, just in case it was a ploy to get him to mention where, exactly, he'd learned to navigate stairs. He located the area on the map. It looked like a series of lines. Which was almost the way a stairwell actually looked, he realized, if you were staring at it from the top or the bottom, and looking at the risers. *Homo sapiens* must have been more fluent in pictographs than Ernest had previously supposed.

"And the lower level?" Ernest said. "This chamber is marked 'electrical.' And this, 'storage.' Those little rectangles, those are the doors, correct? I don't see any on the exterior wall."

"Because the exit came later, after the Diaconate wrapped around the rear and consumed the Gospel side of Saint Peter's. They knocked a hole right through the transept so they could hook up their high-tech charnel house."

"I didn't parse a majority of what you just said."

Father swung the constricted gaze of his single eye around the room, then allowed it to light, again, upon Ernest. "Never mind that. Bring the map over here. Hold it up so I can see it. It's been over a hundred years since I've seen the undercroft."

Ernest did as he was told. He steadied the book so that the map was centered a half-meter in front of Father's face, though his shunt arm ached terribly, and tiny gray motes swarmed in the periphery of his vision.

"The Church faces east, and the Diaconate surrounds it. Gospel-side, south, is Reclaim. Find that stairwell, go down, and keep heading south. Watch out for the guards. They might have the vocabulary of a box of turds, but that doesn't mean they're stupid—so don't underestimate their canniness. At least the staff at Reclaim isn't quite as puffed up with testosterone as the rest of the ops, and there's fewer of them, too, now that the fight's bred out of everyone else to the point where they turn in their PODs and climb into the crematorium themselves."

"It must have been altered since you've seen it last," Ernest assured him. "There is no crematorium in Reclaim. The bodies are demagnetized now, so that that soul may soar free to its final reward upon the death of the body."

"What year do you suppose mankind discovered his soul was magnetic?"

"Well, I...I never thought about it. I'm no student of theology. With the proper feeds...."

"Forget the feeds. Everything worth anything was Purged when clones started to outnumber natural-born men. And then—coming out of the far side of the Purge—that's exactly when the magnetic soul scripture was penned. Just like that ridiculous 'tongues are for talking' commandment."

Ernest fought hard to keep from blurting out the other uses he'd learned lately for tongues, he and Will. He would not lead them to Will.

"Forget about demagnetization," Father said. "When you die, you're dead. End of story."

"When you die," Ernest echoed. "Which could be...how many years?"

"Aha, so your C754 brain has begun to unravel the thirty-and-thirty nonsense. Maybe you do have a chance after all—" a wet-sounding coughing fit interrupted his thought. When the coughing abated, he motioned for the book, and said, "Take the map." He grasped at the page and tried to tear it out, but his grip was weak, and the paper slipped from his fingers.

Ernest looked at the building schematic one more time, then closed the precious book's pages, and set the volume on the table beside the bowl of grayish stuff. "I have the map," he said gently. "In my biological memory. Thank you, Father."

Father's fingers twitched, and his apparatus whirled so that he faced the window again. When he spoke, his voice rattled with phlegm. "Go then, my beautiful liar. Walk in the valley of the shadow of death. Godspeed."

Ernest paused in the doorway and took one final look at the bald curve of the top of Father's head, what he could see of it over the apparatus' head rest. What a peculiar man. *Homo sapien*? Most certainly. As old as he claimed to be? Probably not. He just had access to more interesting feeds, and was talented in the art of lying.

Now that Ernest had seen an actual *homo sapien*, the thought that Will had been anything other than *homo consummatus* seemed absolutely ludicrous. The bristles on Will's chin? The guards were bristly, too. Testosterone. That seemed to be the key. He thought, for just a fleeting moment, that the next time he saw LOU15E, he'd request a search on testosterone and see what she could tell him. But of course he wouldn't. Thanks to her tattle-strip, LOU15E was in the Diaconate impound. If the components that made up LOU15E hadn't yet been disassembled, demagnetized, reclaimed.

If LOU15E, as Ernest knew her, still existed at all.

⠇⠇CHAPTER FIFTEEN⠇⠇

ERNEST CREPT INTO THE hallway and listened carefully. Now that he'd scanned the schematics, the walkways and doors and all the other confusing architectural details made more sense. The elements fit carefully within a cruciform shape, built around an open, central hub.

Several times he shrank back into the shadows, startled, only to discover that the white figures lurking in the alcoves were not security ops, but only more statues. The hidden inner core of the Diaconate would have been a fascinating place to explore, if it hadn't been necessary to continually look over his shoulder to reassure himself that one of the wide, bristly ops wasn't trailing him.

Finally, he came upon the place that corresponded to the stairwell glyph on the map. Ernest hadn't realized how grand it would be, with metal rails on either side that had been worked into fantastical shapes, completely ornamental, with no need to absorb solar or conduct electromagnetic energy. And the stairs themselves, some sort of creamy white stone, worn by the tread of so many feet through the ages that subtle dips had formed in the center of each step.

Ernest descended, stepping only on every other stair, just as Will had taught him, and paused at the bottom to listen for pursuit. He heard nothing. But a red spot several centimeters wide had appeared on the towel wrapped around his throbbing shunt-arm.

He held the image of the schematics in his mind. Scranton, PA...what had those words meant? He would need to ask L0U15E to access a.... No. He wouldn't ask L0U15E, and he wouldn't learn what he needed to know from a feed. Not anymore.

The old electrical room was cold and dark; it had never been wired for W3 uplink or solar, so it sat empty and unused. But the raw materials had never been salvaged. The great, galvanized boxes, with their wiring and cables dangling from ancient ports, had never been touched. Saint Peter's Cathedral had never been scavenged, simply built onto.

He rounded the corner to the final hallway that would take him to the storage chamber which, according to Father, now led to...Reclaim.

A wave of dread threatened to overtake Ernest, and he told himself to focus on the task at hand—as he'd told himself innumerable times for the past twenty years, when the characters of his data streams flickered by, and he had to force himself, hour after hour, to focus, to ensure that the software that ran the grid had not become corrupted.

Reclaim was the final reward for years of service. So Ernest had been taught to think. But he'd also noticed the tension in the voices of the Deacons as they spoke such things, and the subtle shift in the postures of anyone who might be listening.

And, in a more blatant show of abhorrence, Will had begged Matthew not to go. Ernest's arm ached despite the compress that kept the loose shunt from rasping against his ulna, and he wished he'd never left Will to begin with, never come back for L0U15E. But wishes wouldn't get him out of the Diaconate. And so he knew he must press on toward Reclaim, the least guarded point in the whole building.

Grit crunched beneath the soles of his boots, and the wood-paneled walls grew pale with dust. Perhaps, he thought, the particulate had blown in through the gaps where the newer Reclaim construction met the original structure of Saint Peter's. And he did his best not to think about how much that juncture reminded him of his ulna and his loose, decoupled shunt.

An electrical hum rose, eventually, over the continual low buzz in his hearing. He paused and listened. From the end of the hall came a loud thump. He nearly flattened himself against the dusty wall, but caught himself in time to avoid leaving a man-shaped silhouette behind in the dust that would have been as telling as a blood trail.

There was a flash of light. Up ahead, many tens of meters, a portal glowed, perfectly rectangular, as old-time portals were. Ernest advanced. Dust grew so thick toward the portal that it actually muffled his footfalls, and drifted against the walls like Styrofoam. The temperature spiked, and the portal glowed brightly, then faded again to the ambient yellow safety light with which it had been lit before.

A dry heat, thick with dust, wafted over him. It stung his eyes and nose, and caused him to cough and gag. He clamped his hands over his mouth and shook with the effort of staying quiet, and his lungs ached. Surely, he thought, now he would be apprehended by a large, bristle-faced security op—perhaps one with a breathing apparatus over his mouth. But the wracking coughs subsided, and no security ops appeared.

From the chamber ahead came the hum and grind of machinery. Ernest knuckled moisture from his eyes, and made his way in.

The room at the end of the hallway was empty of everything but a large machine. He coughed a few more times, and the sound was lost amid the swelling of gears turning, and a hollow whooshing noise he couldn't place.

It was hotter in that room than anywhere he had ever been. Dustier, too. Gray dust coated everything, and drifted waist-high against the far walls and in the corners. A huge metal apparatus, four meters high and twice as long, protruded from the exterior wall through the center of the vast room. It was constructed from a variety of parts: ceramic body, dull fiberglass frame, and hinges, valves and fittings of metal. On its side, an old-time readout panel with red digits glowed faintly through its coating of dust. The humming, buzzing, clanking noises that came from the depths of the contraption filled the vast room.

It rumbled so hard the floor shook. A chute opened, emitting a thick, hot cloud of dust. He covered his nose and mouth with his towel-wrapped shunt arm and squinted his eyes.

Dust poured from the chute, and slid down a v-shaped trough. Water began to trickle from a pipe set above the trough, and the heat of the machine was so intense that the surface hissed where the water hit it, and steam rose to mingle with the clouds of choking dust. The pale gray dust mixed with the water to make a dark gray slurry, that looked, and even smelled, a bit like the stuff in the bowl on Father's table. The semi-liquid matter slid the final few meters down the steep trough and oozed through a grate on the floor.

The chute slammed shut, the water trickled to a stop, and the apparatus shut down with a series of loud, rattling clicks. The last of the slurry seeped through the grate. He stood, baffled, alongside the massive piece of equipment. Supposedly, it connected St. Peter's to Reclaim. But how could he manage to get past it—or through it? Even if his arm were not injured, it would be a difficult climb up a slimy, narrow trough to get to the chute. And once there, if he waited for the chute to open and proceeded on toward Reclaim, surely he'd be immolated by the heat inside the machine.

He crept closer and touched the trough. It was uncomfortably hot, even after its contact with the water. No. There was no way he could endure the heat of the machine.

With the hope that there might be some point at which the machine met the exterior wall, some gap that was wide enough for him to squeeze through, he made his way around it carefully, and studied the way it fit together. The fittings were old, and things that had once fit together tightly now bore small gaps and cracks, but although the parts were worn and ill-fitting, it was still too large and solid, and far too hot, for him to pry apart.

HIs palms were pressed against the side of the large ceramic chamber when the apparatus hummed to life again. The whole machine shuddered, and the vibration sent a shock of pain through his shunt arm.

A series of sharp metallic clicks rose above the general hum of the machine. Overhead, a trap opened on the machine's side, and two small objects rolled out. They landed on the flat surface of a dark metal ledge, upon which a series of old LCDs (mostly obscured by a thick layer of dust) glowed with digital readings. The numbers scrolled, and then reached a point that caused a simple servomechanism to flip the ledge down. The objects tumbled from the black metal surface and rolled down a funnel, which carried them through a hole in the floor.

Ernest approached the digital readout. It was in his nature to need to see the readout clearly, given that he'd spent his life parsing characters, but in the interest of leaving behind as little evidence of his passing as possible, he stopped himself from wiping away the dust. He found that if he blew gently on the surface, he was able to get a clearer read on the number string.

Strange. Numbers in those ranges were usually used in conjunction with magnetics—more specifically, the acceptable threshold of demagnetization.

The dark metal ledge must be a demagnetization strip. He'd never seen one, but it could hardly be anything else. Not with those readouts. And what else did the Deacons demagnetize in Reclaim, other than bodies?

But the objects that had tumbled onto the demagnetizer were far too small to be bodies.

The machine's hum changed in pitch. The heat the apparatus threw, already intense, grew unbearable. Ernest shielded his face with his hand. Slivers of light shone from the gaps where the components no longer fit tightly. It lit the room with yellow light, and glowed for several minutes. Then the sound of the machine intensified, and the light flashed bright white.

Dry heat rolled off the contraption. It rose from the ill-fitting gaps in waves that distorted his vision, and made the chamber's walls seem as if they were rippling. The machine blazed hotter still, and the light flared...and then everything chugged to a stop. The light seeping through the cracks dimmed—yellow, then orange, then red—and finally the large chute opened again, and another choking cloud of dust burst forth.

Ernest covered his nose and mouth with the collar of his shirt, and cringed as the steam created from the trickle of water that hit the hot dust—ash, he supposed, was the proper term—settled on his exposed skin, and coated him with a layer of foul-smelling moisture.

The ashy, watery sludge dribbled through the grating in the floor, and the apparatus settled into a relatively quiet hum, punctuated only by the pops and ticks that the hot metal chute gave off to protest its contact with the water stream.

A body might turn to ash if it were subjected to such temperatures.

Ernest tasted bitterness at the back of his throat.

His skin was filmy with ash. Ash that had once been...a person.

No—it couldn't be—but even as Ernest tried to seize upon some other explanation, every fact he considered only made him more sure of it. He tried to scrub away the film on his forearm and the back of his hand. He touched his cheeks. They felt moist and gritty.

The homilies on Reclaim had never been entirely clear on what became of the bodies once they'd been demagnetized, because at that point, bodies would be empty, like PODs without AIs to control them. Uninhabited shells. Therefore, it made no difference if Reclaim burned the bodies once they'd been demagnetized.

Except....

His gaze went to the dusty LCD. The demagnetization was happening here, at the end of the cycle. Not the beginning, when the body was still intact.

He hugged his shunt arm to his chest as he slowly circled the apparatus. What had Father called it? The crematorium. He approached the funnel with dread. The solid thunks with which pieces had hit the demagnetizing strip were still fresh in his ears, as if they'd left a perpetual echo. A foul odor rose from the hole under the funnel, and he covered his nose and mouth with his collar yet again. His shirt had become clammy and damp from him breathing through it, but having the moist fabric against his face was still better than that horrible smell. He peered down at the hole, and saw his own footprints in the dust. Not good. He'd need to sweep them away and obscure his passing. And then he noticed something else, a shape that was jarringly familiar, but completely out of context.

A shunt.

No, more than just a shunt. The dust-covered thing on the floor was a section of a person's forearm with the shunt still embedded.

ⅠⅠⅠCHAPTER SIXTEENⅠⅠⅠ

THE CYLINDER OF FLESH and bone was old and coated with ash. At each end of the arm, the last traces of blood had gone dry and black with age. Ernest's throat worked alarmingly, as if he was trying to swallow something, or perform the reverse of swallowing something, although there was nothing to swallow, nothing that he had recently swallowed—so the bitterness that had previously tickled at the back of his throat returned and flooded his mouth with acid.

He staggered past the foul-smelling hole and felt his boot strike a small, dust-covered bit of rubble. Part of him knew he shouldn't look, that he'd probably be better off not knowing, but he couldn't help himself.

A grayish, withered thumb rolled to a stop at the edge of the hole. He toed it the rest of the way in. The thumb fell. He didn't hear it hit bottom.

Let's cut off his thumb and bring that.

It wasn't so much the idea that the components were being recycled that alarmed Ernest. Of course they were. It was more economical to recycle a thumb chip than to create a new one. The shunt held several precious components as well, tiny sensors that communicated with the POD's nutritional programming. And the stainless steel itself had value.

No, the thing that made his throat flutter was the way the

other parts of the body, the parts he couldn't see, were handled.

Without being demagnetized.

The machine's hum grew louder as it ramped up again for another cycle. Ernest touched its side and imagined archaic conveyor belts drawing a stooped, wrinkled retiree through its bowels, extracting the components that could be recycled and discarding the rest.

He didn't want to be there to get a better look at whatever would tumble onto the demagnetizing strip, because once he heard that meaty thump again, there was no way he'd be able to stop himself from looking. And he didn't think he could bear to see what landed there.

The rumbling intensified, and his gaze swung wildly from one end of the exterior wall to the other, searching for somewhere, anywhere, to escape what would come next. Only because he was searching for it with such pointed desperation, did he spot it—the oval shape of a hatch door in the exterior wall, covered with months, perhaps even years, of ash.

He ran toward the door, not even bothering to erase his own footprints, in his haste to escape the sound of a severed forearm hitting the demagnetizing strip.

With the side of his hand, he cut a swath through the dust on the wall beside the hatch in search of a keyscan, while his mind parsed numerous possibilities of what the security code might be, based on the name of the building, the movements of the security op who'd opened the holding cell, and the probability that all the security codes held the same number of characters in the same alpha-numeric pattern.

Columns of numbers and letters had already begun to form in his mind when he realized that where he'd expected a lock-panel, there was nothing but a blank wall. The crematorium rumbled louder still. At any moment, the horrible loud clicks would sound and the salvage would begin. He wiped frantically at the dust, two-handed now, ignoring the sickening pain of his decoupled shunt. Still, no panel.

The first heavy click sounded, and in desperation, he clawed at the latch, and pulled. The door swung open. It hadn't been locked.

It was not even equipped with a locking mechanism.

Ernest hurried through the door and yanked it shut behind him, but not quickly enough to blot out the thud of a forearm hitting a metal platform, and the patter of a thumb landing beside it.

On the other side of the closed door now, he pressed his back against it: a modern door—oval, plastic-amalgam, tightly sealed—and did his best to keep from hearing the humming of the machine in the cremation chamber. Though the modern door blunted the sound, he could still feel the vibrations carrying through the door, the walls, and even the soles of his boots.

"Increase lighting thirty percent." He realized, as the lighting swelled into a comfortable amber glow, that he hadn't actually expected it to happen—not after roaming Saint Peter's, with its old-time architecture. Not since that moment in which he'd damaged his shunt—which, though it had been only hours ago, seemed like it had happened in another lifetime.

This room had been built with more modern proportions than old Saint Peter's. Its ceilings were low and its walls were close, which didn't waste materials, labor and energy like the old construction. Tools lined the walls—brooms and brushes on one panel, prybars, wrenches and digital meters on another. It was the type of toolkit Audrey the POD-mod might have carried on her belt, but multiplied in scale, five, ten times, until it was formidable enough to repair the giant crematorium.

Though the room was sealed, a light coating of ash covered all the tools, the finest of particles that had managed to sift through the seal, or evade the grasp of the air filters.

No one had touched the tools in a very long time.

Ernest pulled a wrench from its panel. The soft polymer setting held for a moment, and then released. The wrench he'd chosen was longer than his forearm, and as heavy as a length of pipe. He hefted it, and gave it an experimental swing with his undamaged arm. Good. Yes.

At the other end of the tool room, another modern door was set in the wall with a simple access panel beside it. He clasped the wrench in the crook of his elbow, and held his fingers under the keyscan. The red laser lit up. He twitched his fingers in the universal WHAT IS? gesture.

A series of pictographs shone from a pinhole in the top of the doorframe, and images of a person entering a hatch and exiting on another level appeared. The panel that he feared was a lock was nothing more than access to an elevator.

Did anyone lock anything in the Diaconate? Maybe not. Maybe, aside from the holding cells, they'd never needed to.

Ernest keyed OPEN DOOR TRANSPORT UP ONE LEVEL, which, due to his data clerk experience, he executed in under .3 seconds. A happy face pictograph appeared, and the hatch whispered open.

The interior of the elevator had the same amalgam finish as the inside of the cell in which he'd decoupled his shunt, and the sight of it sparked the impulse to turn and retreat. But where would he go—back to the Reclaim machine, with its body parts and its clouds of stinking ash?

He steeled himself, clutched the heavy wrench against his chest, and forced himself into the elevator. As it rose, he hefted the wrench higher, poised to strike at anyone who might be waiting for him, but the elevator opened on another empty storage room.

The chamber was similar in configuration to the tool room, but instead of hanging off polymer grip panels, the inventory was stored behind clear sliding doors. He scanned the readouts. Temperature. Pressure. Time. Whatever the contents were, they required a controlled atmosphere. The code on the access panel caught his attention. Q25-38. Not only was it a locking panel, but the last person to use it had fumbled his key gestures and generated a logic loop that would ensure that even with the correct access code, no one could get at the contents.

He glanced at the door at the opposite end of the chamber. Each step he'd taken had carried him one step closer to the outside. But he couldn't simply walk by and leave a code Q25-38 unresolved.

He placed his fingers in the reader and keyed.
ABORT COMMAND
RESET
A pictograph holo appeared—above eye level, he noted, so

that he needed to tilt his head back to read it. Four X symbols. The password was required. Was it alpha? Numeric? Both? The columns of password possibilities that had presented themselves as he fled the sound of the horrible crematorium came to mind, but now, with sheer panic no longer spurring his movements, he doubted he'd be able to crack the password without setting off an alarm.

Back when Ernest had been employed, his least favorite duty rotation, the grid in sector B, was continually shorting out and rebooting. Sometimes it threw a dozen Q25-38s each and every shift. And afterward....

Afterward he overrode the password with a key combo that was a data clerk's equivalent to Audrey's saliva trick. His fingers remembered the motions well.

ADMIN OVERRIDE

CTRL-ALT-DEL

The panel went dark, then lit up again, showing the readout, ADMIN.

He keyed, LAST USE?

Date and time appeared. The controls had been jammed for several weeks.

OPEN

The clear hatch slid open.

His first thought was that the compartment was full of coffee—and so, of course, his second thought was that he'd lost consciousness from the pain of his decoupled shunt and was currently hallucinating. He leaned the heavy wrench against the wall and removed a sealed syringe from the climate-controlled chamber. The wrapper's pictographs showed the needle approaching a shunt—with an arrow (in case, somehow, one couldn't deduce in which direction to insert a needle after spending one's entire life shunting in.) The instructions then depicted two simple faces: one with eyes open, another with eyes shut.

Forced slumber in a syringe.

He tucked several wrapped syringes into his pockets, then turned and headed toward the exit. It, too, was unlocked. He took a deep breath, adjusted his grip on the wrench, and carefully keyed OPEN with the hand of his injured arm.

When the door slid open, someone screamed.

Ernest shrank back out of sight, but the screaming continued, high and shrill. It was punctuated by a male voice. "Down. Hands there. Yes. Down, you. Stop."

No wonder Father had been dubious about Ernest's vocabulary, if he spent his time talking to people like that. It was probably a good thing he'd warned Ernest not to assume the ops were stupid...because they certainly didn't sound very bright. Ernest ventured a look through the door. The room beyond was larger than most, dominated by a horizontal, cruciform container in which a person could lie down. Currently, a female retiree was doing her best to *not* lie in it. She was thin and withered, but in her terror, she was putting up a fantastic fight while a tall, broad-shouldered, shorn-haired man in white tried to force her to lie down.

Since the security op was distracted by the retired woman, Ernest crept through the door and scanned the layout of the room. The machinery bisected the space. A door set in the wall across from him would take him one step closer to the outside world.

The op shoved the woman's arm down into one of the arms of the cross, but her opposite arm flailed up and battered feebly against his shoulder.

Ernest was suddenly very aware of the sedative syringes pressing against his body from every pocket. Indignation filled him. Father had told him retirees were put to sleep before they were reclaimed—but the lock on the slumber syringes had been jammed for weeks.

The horror of knowing that nothing would be demagnetized but the computerized components was still fresh in his mind. But watching the great oaf try to force a fragile old woman into the input of the terrible crematorium, to send her toward the blades that would chop her to pieces, and, should she survive that long, convey her to the fires—fully awake?

He imagined the sensation of the security op's skull collapsing beneath the wrench. It would feel good.

He rushed up behind the security op, arm raised. The op was

tall, but the wrench was large. Through the stubble of the op's shorn hair, he could make out the ridge of the occipital bone curving along the base of his skull. One swing. It had to count.

"Hey!" A second op had been seated, out of sight, on the opposite side of the apparatus. He stood, with colorful holo cubes from his W3 game raining down all around him, and pointed urgently at Ernest. "Look you! Man...uh...there back there."

The first op turned and raised his arm to deflect the blow.

Ernest's imagination hadn't prepared him for the shock that would follow on his end of the hit. The security op staggered, but remained standing. Ernest's hand went numb from the jolt, and he dropped the giant wrench.

And all the while, the old woman screamed.

The op who'd been playing W3 games scrambled to get around the loading end of the apparatus, but the machine had been designed to have one op working each side, with no need for either to reach any farther than the center of the conveyor, so it was broad and difficult to climb.

"What...you?" the second op said.

"Who am I? Is that what you mean?" Ernest feinted as the first op, the one he'd struck, made a grab for him. The big brute wasn't very fast; he was probably accustomed to dealing with retirees who'd shunted in so many times they'd become decrepit and slow. Ernest lunged for the wrench, but the op was canny, and he booted it out of Ernest's reach.

"Stop, you," the second op called. The old woman was on her knees, now, climbing out of the cruciform container.

"How long have you been sending people into Reclaim wide awake?" Ernest demanded, of neither op in particular.

The man he was facing didn't answer, and instead aimed a punch at his head. Ernest ducked back, barely in time. He felt the air stir against his face with the passing of the op's fist.

"Is it too much trouble to have your supervisor unjam the panel? Just like it's too much trouble to speak in sentences? Or do your job instead of playing a game?"

Ernest's anger made him careless. He didn't duck away quickly enough, and the second punch grazed his jaw. He reeled back, and his arms whirled as he struggled to keep his balance.

Pain flared in his decoupled shunt, and the sharp bitterness flooded the back of his tongue again.

The security op advanced. If his fist actually connected, it would do nearly as much damage as the wrench would in Ernest's slim hand. If he struck back at the op's face unarmed, Ernest knew, his blow would be as effective as one from the shrieking retiree. But there was another area where even someone as small as Ernest could cause enough damage to slow the huge adversary down.

He grabbed for the security op's shunt. He caught it, pulled and twisted.

The op's howl of pain rose, guttural and eerie, over the retiree's screeching. His knees buckled, but Ernest held fast to the shunt and twisted again. It didn't decouple, but screws ground against bone. "You stay over there," he called to the second op, "or I tear it right out of his arm." His voice seemed overloud, and he realized the old woman had stopped screaming, and was staring at him, bewildered.

Steeling himself against the pain in his own shunt, he fumbled a syringe from his pocket, opened the wrapper's seal with his teeth, and plunged the needle into the first op's shunt.

The op's panting and moaning stopped. He slumped to the floor.

Ernest pulled a handheld Taser from the slumbering op's toolbelt. The big oaf could have used that on the old woman instead of trying to send her through Reclaim fully conscious. Either it was too much trouble, or it hadn't occurred to him to use it. Imbecile.

Moron.

He caught the retiree's eyes. "You want to leave? You need to stay quiet. Do you understand?"

Her mouth worked, and he feared she might not be able to speak at all. And finally, in a hoarse whisper, she said, "Yes."

"You." Ernest pointed his Taser at the second op for emphasis. "Throw me your weapon."

The op stared at him blankly.

Ernest pointed at the Taser he held, then the guard's toolbelt, then to the center of his own chest. "Throw that here."

The op's brow furrowed. Maybe he'd understood perfectly well. Maybe he he'd also realized that he could easily over-power Ernest—half his size, and injured as well—rather than submitting.

"Throw it," Ernest said, "or I will have your supervisor check your W3 log for gaming activity during work hours."

The op went pale. He unhooked the Taser from his belt and tossed it over the apparatus. It landed on the floor beside the first op.

"Woman," Ernest said. "What is your name?"

"Elizabeth," she said hoarsely.

"Come here. Take the Taser. The black plastic thing."

Elizabeth found her footing very carefully. She moved as if her joints pained her. The papery smock she wore was torn in places, and it crinkled as she climbed the rest of the way out of the apparatus.

"You," Ernest said to the second op, without bothering to ask his name. "Send this container on its way empty. And be thankful I don't taze you and stuff you inside it first."

The guard keyed a simple sequence, and a telescoping metal cover slid out over the cruciform container. Before it shut, Ernest got a look at the deep metal grooves at elbow and wrist on the left side of the crosspiece, and diagonal through the hand on the right side. And part of him wished he really had stuffed the op inside.

"We need to move fast," he told Elizabeth. "The Reclaim process takes a few minutes, but then they will bring in another retiree and begin again."

He reached for Elizabeth's arm to steady her as she stepped over the prone body of the first security op, but she flinched away from him as if he'd raised a hand to strike her. No doubt she was confused, though hopefully she wasn't completely senile. He turned and headed for the door, and she followed.

A short plastic hallway connected the loading end of the Reclaim machine to a room where a handful of people waited at molded tables and chairs. It hadn't occurred to him that there would be people there—but of course there were. People waiting to die.

ıı⎪CHAPTER SEVENTEENıⅡ⎪

IN THE WAITING ROOM, a VR helmet hung from the wall beside each chair, and the surfaces of the tables blinked with W3 feeds. The room had once provided a space for many persons to congregate, to link in and distract themselves while they bided their time until Reclaim. But many of the feeds were mottled with dead pixels, and some tables were now dark, as if their power supplies had completely burned out. One retiree watched a holographic 3-D feed that stuttered and jumped as if the lenses that projected it were no longer stable, and clusters of broken wire hung from many of the VR helmets.

A retired man looked up and met Ernest's gaze. He'd been broad-shouldered, once. Now, he was stooped and gray. He was thirty and thirty. How old was Ernest now? When he'd checked the time codes on the jammed syringe locker, he could have effortlessly calculated the exact figure, but he hadn't. After all he'd seen, and all he'd learned, he no longer cared if he was thirty and thirty yet. That number only meant something if you believed the Deacons—and he now knew just how easy it was to lie.

Of all the retirees, over a half-dozen in all, only that one man watched him cross the room. No one challenged him, or even asked him who he was, or why he was covered in ash and blood. He felt a great pang of sadness, though he couldn't have articulated exactly why. Maybe because it could easily have been him sitting there, ignorant and docile. But his sadness felt so much greater than that.

Maybe his new knowledge was too difficult to bear.

It was best not to think about it until he'd escaped Reclaim. He crossed the room, paused at the door, and turned. "Reclaim is broken. You need to leave."

A woman looked up from her low-res W3 game. The others didn't pay any attention at all.

"You need to leave," he repeated, more loudly now. "Do you hear? Reclaim is broken." He indicated the dead VR helmets with a sweep of his hand. "Like everything else here. Broken."

"But I'm thirty and thirty," the old woman said. "Now I get my reward."

Elizabeth gave him a startling shove to the upper arm. It was his shunt arm, and the pain snapped him to attention. "Just go," she whispered, and again shoved him toward the door.

"I already turned in my POD," the other woman said. Her voice was a whine that grated on his nerves, and made him want to kick something. "Where will I sleep?"

Elizabeth shoved again. "Go. Now."

Of all the people in the waiting room, only one stood and joined them. The man who hadn't been in VR, or watching feeds, or playing games. The man who had once been broad-shouldered. Everyone else was content to sit there and wait for death.

"Please," Elizabeth begged.

Ernest turned toward the door and tried the handle. This door was locked, which made sense, if it was meant to keep in the rare retiree having second thoughts. He flicked his fingers under the keyscan until the readout flashed ADMIN, and entered the command to open.

He expected another hall, another room, another door. Instead, he found himself outside, on the walkway that led retirees to Reclaim. Elizabeth pointed urgently to a small shelter. "Security ops, there."

The three of them ran the other way. Slowly, because Elizabeth and the other retiree were stiff. And because Ernest's shunt arm was bleeding again, and the roaring in his ears was very loud. Still, he ran.

"Go toward that alley," Ernest said. "They won't look there. If we could hide, lose them...."

"Yes," the old man agreed. "Breaking visual contact is the first...uh...thing."

They ran, crouched and stooped, to the mouth of the nearest alley. All three were breathing hard. "How did you know that?" Ernest asked the old man. "Who are you?"

"Benjamin-P942."

"What I mean is, what do you do?"

"I'm retired. Obviously."

Obviously. "Before."

"Security."

Ernest didn't doubt it. Benjamin's telltale white Storm Trooper outfit might be gone, replaced by a papery, disposable, easily incinerated smock. But even stooped, he was at least ten centimeters taller than Ernest. "Good. That's good. So you know what to expect."

Benjamin looked blank for a moment while he parsed the spoken words, and then he nodded. "Yes. But...no. Not the same. I do not run...from. I run *to*."

"But you can extrapolate."

No comprehension.

"You know what the ops will do."

Benjamin nodded. "Yes. They will scan for thumb chips."

"You can scan from that far away?" Elizabeth cried. She pressed her hands into her lower back and winced as she stretched.

"And don't talk loud," he added. "They will try to...uh...hear, since we're not in visual."

"They're listening," Ernest supplied. Quietly.

"Yes." Benjamin affirmed.

"What's the best way to stop them from bringing us back?" Ernest asked him. "Disable the chip?"

"But then we can't buy...." Elizabeth began to protest—and then she must have realized, with the credits drained from her account and the possibility that her chip could be used to track her, it wouldn't do her much good anymore.

Ernest scowled. If only he'd known. He could have pressed his chip against the demagnetization plate...along with the severed thumb and forearm? He shuddered. Maybe not.

"To disable the chip...." Benjamin thought hard. "A tool. Some tool." He shrugged.

They crept deeper into the alleyways as they tried to work out their strategy. "What tool?" Ernest said. "To demagnetize it, to cut it off, what?"

"I don't know. Stop yelling at me. You sound like my supervisor."

The buildings they passed were new—compact, rounded and smooth. Those that did have portals in back also had locks beside them, and though Ernest suspected he could easily hack the keypad locks that weren't W3-linked, he wouldn't know what to say to whomever he encountered behind those doors, him with his bleeding arm, and Elizabeth and Benjamin, stooped and withered, in their papery Reclaim smocks.

He said, "We need to get to the older part of town, the historic district. The buildings are bigger, and we can find some tool to disable our chips without being discovered."

"Yes," Benjamin said. "Good." He pointed between two buildings, toward a main magnetic artery. "Cross that. Watch for security, then cross."

Ernest's vision went gray around the edges, and he took several deep breaths. He ached from head to toe, and the queasy, sick feeling that had been coming and going had finally stopped going. He couldn't seem to get his bearings. "You're sure that's the right direction?"

"Yes. Old Town is there." Benjamin squinted toward the street. "I'm not stupid."

True. He might have trouble finding words, as Father had warned, but he'd been the only one in the room motivated enough to leave without first seeing the loading end of the horrible machine and being stuffed inside.

PODs glided up the center of the magnetic strip, moving too quickly for any of them to successfully duck between. "We should cross elsewhere," Ernest said.

"No, you wait," Benjamin told him. "Not long. A gap will come.

It...uh...always does. Yes."

And the PODS continued to move, a row of glittering gray ovals, with some small variation in their proportion, or the location of their hatches. One had a mod on the shell, a representation of a cascade of glittering cubes from a W3 game spilling across the hatch door. But that was the only POD that had been personalized. All the others were plain gray.

"You are losing too much blood," Elizabeth said. "You will need surgery. This happens to builders. They forget to wear shunt protection, and the flanges get caught on something and pull out their bone screws."

Ernest stared. It was the longest sentence he'd ever heard from anyone aside from Will, Audrey or Father.

"I was a health monitor aide," she said. "Before I retired."

Benjamin glanced down at Ernest's shunt arm. The once-white towel that held the stainless steel in place was now nearly all red. "You put a...a thing. On the arm. Higher. The blood slows down."

Elizabeth supplied the word. "A tourniquet. Yes."

Benjamin used the slender edge of his shunt to nick Ernest's shirt and tear off a strip of fabric. He tied it around the biceps of Ernest's shunt arm so tightly it hurt. It was difficult to tell if the bleeding slowed or not, since the towel was saturated. But it seemed like a logical plan.

"There," Benjamin said when he was done, and he scowled toward the street as a gap in the traffic passed them by. He turned back to Elizabeth and pointed at her. His hand was huge. "You give me the Taser. I know how to use it."

"No."

Ernest sighed. He wasn't accustomed to working in a team, as builders or security ops might be, since his job had been solitary—so it wasn't in his nature to share, either. But Benjamin had just stopped him from bleeding out, and he had a much longer reach than Ernest. "Here," Ernest said. "Take mine."

Benjamin took it, and turned it around in his massive hand. "Not even charged," he said. But he threaded the edge of his papery smock through a slot in the Taser's handle and tied it to his thigh, anyway.

When Ernest realized he'd threatened his way out of Reclaim with an uncharged Taser, the sick feeling in his stomach increased exponentially.

He willed himself to stop paying attention to the wooziness, to force his body to get him out of the shadow of the Diaconate, at the very least. And to do that, he'd need to cross the street.

He looked down the line of gleaming PODS and searched for a gap. And in the row of nearly identical ovals, he found something that looked like a gap at first, but wasn't. It was a variation. A color. A metallic blue POD.

Audrey.

He dashed out of the alleyway, waving his arms. He knew how to create a gap in traffic. "Stop! Audrey, it's me. Ernest. Stop."

In his imagination, the blue POD paused, and the grid caused all the PODS behind it to wobble to a stop so he could cross. But what happened in reality was much stranger. Audrey's POD sloughed off the magnetic strip without even pausing to switch to solar—a move he'd never seen a POD make—and stopped directly in front of him. The main hatch flicked open—again, faster than he'd ever seen a POD respond—and Audrey, as quick as her metallic blue POD, grabbed him by the shirt. "Get in."

"But..." how could he? She was already inside.

And besides that, what if someone saw him? Someone from the Diaconate? In his lightheaded panic, he'd just darted right out and announced his presence to anyone who cared to know. Maybe he was an imbecile after all.

"Now," Audrey said. She hauled on his shirt, hard. He stumbled in.

The interior of Audrey's POD had as much gear hanging off the walls as the storage closets inside the Diaconate. The POD bristled with tools, every one of them poking or prodding Ernest as he tried to figure out where to put his feet. "But Elizabeth, and Benjamin," he said as he struggled to tuck his arm in well enough for the POD hatch to close.

Audrey called out to the retirees, "You want out, meet us in grid 38-west." They gawked at her from the sidewalk. "You know where that is?"

Benjamin nodded.

"That's all I can do," Audrey said. "It's not like I can fit all of you in here!" If she were full grown, or Ernest were any larger, she wouldn't have even been able to squeeze him inside with her.

The hatch closed. Barely.

"What's at 38-west?" Ernest tried to deduce where the coordinates might be. Somewhere toward the edge of the city, if the Diaconate was 0-0. "And how did you find me?"

"Would you listen to this one?" The voice came from all around Ernest—a POD-mind voice, but nothing like L0U15E's. This voice sounded like an old-time feed actor's, with subtle nuances of inflection that would have convinced Ernest it was an actual person speaking, if it weren't being broadcast over the POD audio. "Two questions at once—and handsome, too. He's a keeper."

"Stop trying to match me up with someone," Audrey told her POD-mind. "I don't have time for that kissy stuff. Besides, he's Will's lover."

"Will—have you talked to him lately? Is he okay?"

"Hold your horses," Audrey told him. "Isn't that a great idiom? A horse is a mammal that was used for pulling transport before mechanical propulsion was invented. So to hold your horses means to pause. Of course Will's okay, although right now he's champing at the bit—another horse idiom—to storm the Diaconate to bust you out. Hey, Charlie, you'd better let everybody know Will's boyfriend flew the coop."

Charlie said, "It's already done."

"That's a poultry idiom. I was assigned the Reclaim door because we all thought that was the least likely place you'd turn up. And here you are."

"It had the fewest guards."

"Good to know."

Ernest's knees buckled, but he was wedged into the POD so tightly he remained upright. He felt giddy, and the roaring in his ears seemed overloud. "You named your POD-mind, too."

"Oh, yeah. His model number wasn't very catchy. You're all wet—is that blood? It has an odor—kind of like metal. And it's so red. Maybe I'll do that color the next time I mod my hair. Charlie, make sure you get a measure of its hue and value so we can duplicate the shade."

"I decoupled my shunt. I don't feel very well."

"Pull up a relevant feed on blood, too. And take us to 38-west."

"We're on our way," Charlie said smoothly.

As the POD began to glide, its walls lit up with charts, diagrams and holos, but they were difficult to see through the clutter of Audrey's tools.

"I'm more interested in testosterone," Ernest said, though he was so light-headed he had trouble remembering the word. "And eunuchs."

"Oh, we don't need a feed," Audrey said. "I know all about that. Testosterone is a hormone. Carefully controlled, because it makes males aggressive, and focused on sex. Your shunt filters out most of it, and that process makes you a eunuch. If your testosterone mix was like most people's, it was set so that you only got enough hormone to keep your bones from going soft."

"But I haven't shunted in for days."

"I think it takes longer than that to get back to your default biological hormone concentration, but who knows? I didn't scan it too closely, because I'll never have to deal with it personally, since females don't produce much testosterone anyway. Now that you're off the shunt, I don't think you'll get any taller, but maybe you'll start growing a beard. That's how you can tell whose shunt cocktails are different. The beard."

Like security ops. "A beard—is that what you call a lump at the front of the throat?"

"No, it's a short word for a hairy face."

"Oh. The bristles...."

"Excuse me," Charlie said. "I have audio from Will on secure channel five."

"Ernest?" Will's voice came from all around them. "Are you there?"

Ernest opened his mouth to speak, and then paused. Suddenly, he hardly knew what to say. "Yes. I'm here."

"What were you thinking—going back for LOU15E? It isn't a person. It's an AI, a machine. It doesn't have thoughts. It doesn't have feelings. It won't miss you if you leave it wherever it lands. It's just a hunk of gear."

"I know, but...."

"There were varying schools of philosophy on that topic in the twenty-first century," Charlie murmured.

Audrey shushed him. "Let them talk."

Ernest considered lying. He was good at it, after all, and it would be plausible to say that he'd only been trying to get his POD back since Will seemed to want the parts so badly. But it wasn't true. He'd gone back for L0U15E. Because if he was going to live on past his thirty and thirty, indefinitely, he couldn't see doing it without her.

And he hadn't known about that tattle-strip.

"You sound angry," Ernest said, bewildered.

"Angry? You're lucky I don't kill you myself."

"Will," Audrey said, "he's blood...blooding? No, that's not the word. He's *bleeding*. Very much."

"Gah! Why didn't you say so? I've gotta go find Martha."

Ernest supposed he should apologize. "Will?"

"He's closed the link," Charlie said gently. His speech programming really was very good.

"Don't worry about him," Audrey told Ernest. "We translated a really good idiom to describe Will. Want to hear it? All bark and no bite."

"Rin Tin Tin," Ernest said.

"I haven't heard that one. Charlie, find me the etymology and put it in my leisure scanning file."

"Your wish is my command," Charlie said.

It was the last thing Ernest heard before the roaring in his ears crescendoed, and the gray motes around the perimeter of his vision multiplied, and everything went quiet and dark.

⊹⊹⊹ CHAPTER EIGHTEEN ⊹⊹⊹

THERE WAS A COOL snap to the outdoor air. It was filled with scents, living scents, green scents, that PODs normally filtered out of their internal atmospheres. Ernest knew, even before he was fully awake, that he was at the edge of the city.

He was horizontal now; he opened his eyes carefully, expecting harsh sunlight and Styrofoam drifts. But instead, a cool canopy of branches and leaves stretched overhead.

"Are you awake now? Can you hear me?"

A woman's face filled Ernest's field of vision. Had he seen her before, or was her vat so common that there were many of her in the mix of the population? No, it wasn't her features that seemed familiar, as much as her hair, dusted with gray. Though her features were familiar, too. Ernest seemed to remember her smiling.

"Maybe you'd better hold him down," she said, not to Ernest, this time, but to someone he couldn't see. He craned his neck in the direction in which she'd spoken.

"He's awake! Ernest?" Will's face. Upside down. With a hitch between the eyebrows. Worried. And then Ernest placed the woman—he'd seen her in the coffee shop, talking to Will.

Old friends.

Everybody knows Will.

"Ernest?" she said. "Just nod if you can understand me."

Well, of course he could. He parsed the spoken word much better than most. But it seemed like such a great effort to reply, to even move his head. He blinked slowly. He could do that much.

"You've lost a lot of blood," Will explained. "We're trying to get our other C754 to top you off. And—this is Martha—she says the best thing to do with your shunt is to remove it altogether."

"But...." How would he survive with no shunt? That would be like stitching a *homo sapien's* mouth, urethra and anus closed. He couldn't find the words to ask.

Will seemed to know what Ernest was thinking, in that way that he often did. "You won't need it anyway, not where we're going."

Ernest recalled Elizabeth protesting the idea of disabling her thumb chip. Now he knew what she'd been feeling.

"I was serious about holding him down," Martha said. "We're out of pain hypos, and his shunt's torn free on one end and fused deep on the other."

Ernest's hand felt exquisitely heavy as he guided it to his pocket and patted the hypo inside. Its wrapper crackled gently. "Slumber," he said. The word felt heavy and strange. And judging by Will's deeply furrowed brow, he had no idea what Ernest meant by that.

But Martha was obviously attuned to the crackling sound of the cellophane seal of a medical hypo. She dug into Ernest's pocket, and he allowed himself a small smile for having managed to do something correctly.

"Would you look at that? How many do you have here, six? Very good. I think this is worth enough to buy your way onto the railroad even though we never got a chance to salvage your—"

"He's in pain," Will said. "Don't get into all of that now."

"I'll start with a quarter dose. It's better to underestimate with sedatives. Too much would stop his heart."

"Maybe you'd better skip that stuff. I'll hold him down."

"Just a quarter," Martha said. "It'll be fine. It might leave him slightly awake, but he won't care very much what I'm doing to him...."

There was a bright point of pain in Ernest's good arm. He

gasped. Martha had shoved the syringe through his flesh and directly into his vein. Will was at his head, caressing his cheek. "Don't worry. Everything'll be fine."

Ernest thought about one of the many strange things Father had told him, the thing about Deacons using a sedative to stop his heart, should he be convicted of heresy.

And he remembered the security op slumping as he depressed the plunger. The op had only been in forced slumber. Correct? The tree canopy spun overhead, and Martha was instructing Will to stabilize the shunt arm. Metal tools clicked together. And then there was pain.

Martha's explanation of the effects of the syringe had not been entirely accurate. Ernest did care what was happening. He was just too weak to do anything about it. And before the sounds of her gouging the shunt from his ulna grew too horrible to bear, like the sounds of the great cremation machine chopping off limbs, the swarming gray motes overtook his field of vision and he once more succumbed to his body's own version of forced slumber.

His arm still hurt when he began to come out of sleep mode. Both arms, in fact, hurt. "Don't move," Will told him. "Don't bend that arm. You're shunted in."

Ridiculous. There was no shunt in his dominant arm. "Shunted in to what?"

"Hold him down," said another voice, a man's voice. "He's still drugged."

"He'll come around fast."

So many people! Ernest knew that last voice. "Elizabeth...."

"See," Elizabeth said, "he's already lucid. Ernest? Keep your right arm stationary. You'll damage yourself. Do you understand?"

He nodded. There seemed to be hands on him everywhere, at his shoulders, his wrist, his ankles. The world was a blur of colors that he tried to resolve into faces. One hand fell to his hair, and began to stroke. That must have been Will.

"How much longer?" said the first man who'd spoken. "I need to install the propulsion panel if we plan to get out of here tomorrow."

"Let Audrey work on that," Will said. "She's more accurate than you are, anyway."

"How would you know, shopkeep? You can't tell a magnet from a rat turd."

Soft argue? It sounded just like an old-time feed, complete with the lilting, easy tone and the expanded vocabulary. Ernest blinked hard, and his vision began to clear. "Elizabeth...."

"I'm here. Thanks to you. By the time I figured out what was going on at Reclaim, it was too late to run."

The unfamiliar voice said, "Look, he's fine. Are we done, here?" Ernest turned toward it and experienced a surge of disorientation. It seemed for a moment that he was in his POD, and L0U15E was showing him a holo of himself—as he would look with short hair without any gray in it, and a beard. A wispy, small beard, just around the mouth. And with a scowl on his face.

Another C754.

"I think you've damaged his brain," it said.

"Keep squeezing that rag," Elizabeth told the C754. "And don't bend over like that. The blood flows downward."

"Twenty years of engineering did teach you that much," Will said, "didn't it?"

The other C754 smiled. Maybe smiled. The expression was a bit like Will's—when he was smirking. "What is your name?" Ernest asked him.

"Abraham. I'm an old friend of Will's."

"Everybody knows Will."

"True. I'm told he almost didn't try to recruit you because he couldn't handle living with two C754s."

"I was just worried he'd be as stubborn as you," Will said.

Abraham's smirk, or smile, intensified. "And is he?"

"He's worse. Walked right into the Diaconate to get his AI back."

"I didn't walk in," Ernest protested. "The security ops forced me to come with them."

Abraham squeezed a rag that was balled in his right fist. A line of red tubing—no, clear tubing, with blood inside—connected his shuntless arm's vein to Ernest's. "What did you do before?"

Abraham asked Ernest.

"I was a data clerk."

"There's no W3 where we're going, so you'll need to pick up some new skills. Will says you're an outstanding reader, so I'll have you study up on some lost arts. We found a patchy feed on the survivalist movement of 2020, but no one can parse it. I'll load that into a handheld for you."

While Ernest understood Abraham perfectly well, the concept of learning new skills, skills he hadn't been bred for, skills that hadn't been mapped into his brain with years of theta waves and subliminal repetition—that idea was proving difficult to parse.

"Back off," Will said. "He just had his shunt pried out."

"He's fine. Right, Ernest?"

He craned his neck and looked down at himself. His lower body was covered with a thin sheet of reflective plastic. His shunt arm, now missing its shunt, lay atop the silvery sheet. The limb seemed small and naked without its shunt. A shiny, clear bandage-coating covered the incision site, mottled purple and red, something like all the blood he'd lost, but darker. It hurt with a deep, sickening ache. But his whole body hurt, in places that were nowhere near the surgical site—and in fact, his head throbbed horribly, and his organs seemed to be roiling around inside his abdominal cavity. But this other C754 seemed...tough. And so, not to be outdone, Ernest said, "I'm fine."

"Stop squeezing," Elizabeth said. She clamped the line, removed the end of it from Abraham's vein, and pressed a tiny, clear square of sealant over the wound. "Be sure to shunt... er, drink...plenty of fluids. And no heavy lifting today."

Abraham had walked away before Elizabeth was even done giving him instructions. She looked after him, puzzled.

"Don't mind him," Will said. "He's almost done with the railroad and he can't wait to get going."

"But it's my job to mind him."

"Forget it." Will's face filled the field of vision as he leaned over Ernest's head once more. "How do you feel, really?"

"How can you always discern when I'm lying?"

Will smiled. Even though Ernest was seeing it upside down,

it looked nothing like a sneer. Or a smirk. The corners of Will's eyes crinkled, and many of his teeth showed. "I can tell. That's all."

"What is this railroad Abraham is working on? Where is he going?"

"We're going. All of us. Elizabeth, too. That makes five. You and me. Martha, Elizabeth and Abraham. The railroad is the thing that'll take us so far away from the ops and the Deacons that they'll never find us."

"Far away from Reclaim, too," Elizabeth said.

"What about Audrey?"

"She won't come. Not yet, anyway. She's hooked on the W3." Will drew a flask from his pocket. "Don't worry about Audrey—she knows how to take care of herself. Better than you, by the looks of you. Have some water."

"Then I'll need to urinate again."

"Yeah. That's basically how it goes."

Ernest recalled how much Father seemed to enjoy...pissing. Or maybe just the memory of it. "I guess I'd better get used to it."

"Look, I haven't shunted into a POD in years, and I don't miss it at all. If we had the time and resources to remove shunts for aesthetic reasons, I would've had mine lopped off by now."

Ernest hadn't even considered the aesthetics. He wondered how Will would be able to even stand the sight of him, gray-streaked and shuntless.

"I saw the feed on eating," Elizabeth said, "and I think we must both begin eating as soon as possible. It will take our bodies some time to adjust. Better to do it while we're resting than when we're traveling."

Ernest's stomach did a sickening flip-flop.

"We have some nutrients in bags," she said, "easy, like a POD shunt but, uh, not as thorough, because it doesn't provide the dialysis. You are weak from surgery, so you can have one. But I will chew and swallow."

Ernest noted that Elizabeth didn't look very thrilled about the prospect. "Thank you," he told her.

"Oh, come on," Will said, "it's fun, once you get used to it. Things taste different, for real. Not just those stupid nano patches that make you think you're tasting something." He kissed Ernest on the forehead. Ernest would have backed away, except he was lying on his back, and couldn't very well sink into the ground. He wondered if he'd ever become accustomed to how uninhibited Will was with his mouth.

Elizabeth gasped a little, and then steeled her expression as if she hadn't just seen something horribly sacrilegious.

Will pulled a protein bar from his pocket and tore off a chunk with his teeth. "Chew, chew, chew," he sang.

Elizabeth paled and backed away. Once she was out of visual range, her footfalls receded in the dryish grass.

After she left, the merriment slipped from Will's expression. "It's not so bad," he said quietly. "I promise."

As far as Ernest knew, Will had always been truthful with him. "Let me try it."

Will's eyebrows shot up. "Really? All right. But you'd better sit up first. Your, uh..." he pointed to Ernest's neck and made a downward motion, "throat tube thing..."

"Esophagus," Ernest supplied.

"Right. Esophagus. That works better when you're vertical."

Ernest took the protein bar from Will, and stared at it. It was brownish gray, and rectangular, and the edge had a hemispherical gouge in it shaped like the contour of Will's teeth. "I wish I had done this the first time you asked, when we were in the basement. Just me, and you, and the sparrows."

Will reached down and pulled up the thin silver sheet. He wrapped it around Ernest and himself, drew it over their heads, and closed it around them. Inside, with the diffuse sunlight that filtered through, Ernest could imagine that they were sharing the same POD, just Will and him, together.

"There," Will said. "Now you can pretend we're in the basement, or the attic, or the coffee shop, or wherever you want."

"Yes." Ernest reached for Will, and cupped his face in both hands. Ernest's shunt arm ached, but nowhere near as badly as it had when screws were rasping on bone. He drew Will's face toward himself, and brushed a gentle kiss to Will's mouth. "Good."

Will held the silver sheet closed with one hand, and stroked

Ernest's hair with the other. His touch was so intense it bordered on pain. His expression had gone very serious. "You told me you would stay with me."

"I was planning on it. I just didn't want to leave without Louise."

"Your POD was never alive."

"Not the POD. Obviously, I'd need to bring the POD, since it houses her electronics. But I'm talking about the AI inside, the one I named after the POD's model number."

"Your AI isn't a person, either. You know the difference, don't you?"

"She isn't a person in the same fashion that we are, no. But she's not just a factory-issue AI, either. She has mods."

"That doesn't make it a person." Will stroked Ernest's hair more desperately. "It's a stream of data. It doesn't have a soul."

Didn't it? If a soul was magnetic, couldn't one be possessed by a machine just as easily, if not more so, than a *homo consummatus* body?

"I'll chew the food for you," Will said, "if you like."

"Thank you." Ernest glanced at his shuntless arm, blood-mottled beneath the clearcoat. "But I don't think so. I should learn to do it myself."

"Start slow." Will unfastened Ernest's shirt, which was tattered and torn from his stay at the Diaconate. "Hold it in your mouth. And I'll provide some positive reinforcement."

Ernest raised the protein bar to his mouth, but stopped short of inserting it. The revulsion was overwhelming.

Will pressed his cheek to Ernest's and spoke in his ear, low and breathy. "You know putting things in your mouth can feel good." Will's tongue traced his earlobe, and Ernest squirmed. "Good" wasn't quite the word he would choose. Strange. And yet, titillating—judging by the war of sensations surging down his spine and coalescing in his groin.

Will trailed kisses along his cheek and jaw. He kissed Ernest's chin, and the corner of his mouth. His tongue grazed Ernest's lower lip, and another of those sensations, almost like a mild power surge, traveled down between Ernest's legs.

He was hard. Already.

﹗﹗﹗CHAPTER NINETEEN﹗﹗﹗

WILL'S TONGUE EASED INTO Ernest's mouth, and it tasted different, not exactly like Will. Like the protein bar, then. And it wasn't bad. Just strange. Before Ernest had a chance to sort that strangeness into like or dislike, Will's hand trailed down his body and dropped to his thigh, feeling, stroking. And then, his hard cock.

Ernest's breath caught.

"It's only been a few days," Will murmured, "and look how much better this is, without the shunt. See? I know you tend to get sentimental, but don't be—not about prying that ugly hunk of metal off your arm." His hand moved more surely, fingers gliding up and down Ernest's shaft through his trousers. "You haven't lost anything. The shunt could never make you feel like this."

He kissed Ernest again, more forcefully now, and his tongue probed deeper. Ernest almost pulled away—almost—but Will's hand was drawing the most exquisite sensations through his body, and the things Will's heretical tongue was doing—inside Ernest's mouth—only heightened those sensations.

When Will broke the kiss and drew his hand away, they were both breathing hard. "Are you ready to let me show you how good eating can be?"

He wanted Will to touch him so badly he could hardly parse

Will's meaning by the words, but the tone was plain enough. Release. If he complied. "Yes."

"Take a bite. A small one. And just hold it in your mouth." Will struggled with the waistband of Ernest's trousers. They didn't have any convenient access panels like Father's had; they'd never needed to. Ernest had never given much thought to the organ between his legs. Lately, it seemed his whole life had begun to center on it.

He shifted so Will could tug the trousers down, and the plastic sheet crinkled. "Go on," Will said. "Bite it."

Ernest put the bar between his teeth and held it there. It felt firm, but if he exerted enough pressure with his teeth, he imagined he would clip off the corner, and it would land in his mouth. Just like the forearms and thumbs that rolled out of the Reclaim machine and onto the demagnetization platform.

"You have to press your jaws together."

"I know," Ernest said, without releasing the bar from his teeth. It sounded more like, "I oh."

Will dragged his fingertips down Ernest's bare stomach. In reaction, Ernest's skin rippled behind the touch like a shallow pool of water. Will stopped short of the place Ernest most wanted him to touch. "Or you can lick it. That word makes you crazy, doesn't it? Lick." He smiled, or grinned, or maybe something naughtier than that, and ran his tongue along the edge of his teeth. "It's a good word. Sounds like it feels."

He bent his head and dragged the warm wetness of his tongue over the tip of Ernest's cock, and Ernest's jaw clenched enough to sink his teeth partway through the protein bar.

"You'll need to learn about tastes," Will said. "They're complicated; the nano shortcuts are totally oversimplified. Your skin tastes stronger than it did when you lived in your POD." The wetness of his words played over the tender flesh he'd just moistened with his tongue, and Ernest clenched his eyes shut tight—though not being able to see only made the sensations intensify.

"Because there are no mytes in the atmosphere to groom my cells."

Ernest hardly got the words out. Will had licked up one side of his shaft and down the other, then engulfed the tip in his hot, wet mouth. He raised and lowered his head, several times, and then worked his way back off so he could speak again. "Right. We get to go swimming, instead. It's amazing. And you haven't bitten through that corner, it's still hanging there by that thin spot."

"I don't think I can...."

"We all eat food, Ernest. You have no shunt, so you'll need to learn. You mastered drinking, right? It's like drinking, only thicker."

The disturbing thing about eating wasn't swallowing. It was chewing. But Will's tongue swirled over his cock again, and instead of growing less sensitive from the repetition, it seemed to grow keener, hungrier, for Will's touch. "One bite," Will said. His wet lips dragged over the sensitized flesh.

Ernest bore down harder with his teeth. Bit—he bit down harder.

Will's tongue fluttered on his shaft. "I can tease you all day. Think of it. A whole day, aching to come."

Aching, yes. That's what it felt like, an ache, diffused throughout his whole groin. And yet, there was something about the word *ache* that was meant to be unpleasant, to connote pain, and it didn't feel that way at all when Will *licked* him. It felt—no, not good. There had to be a better word. It felt...what did Will like to say? It felt amazing.

Ernest bit slightly harder, and he felt the corner of the protein bar sag toward his tongue.

Will slid *his* tongue back and forth over Ernest's glans, and tucked another hand between his own legs to rub the bulge in his pants. "I'll tell you one thing," he said. "I'm aching, too. Aching for the day you get used to putting things in your mouth."

"Why?"

"So you can suck my cock." Will followed it up with a long, wet lick that made Ernest shiver.

"I wouldn't know what to do."

"I've been watching you—you're a fast learner."

Ernest bared his teeth and exerted just a bit more pressure, and felt the food drop into his mouth. He pulled his tongue

JORDAN CASTILLO PRICE ||| 157

back in alarm and his eyes watered. Will stopped licking him for a moment. "Don't try anything fancy. Just hold it there."

Ernest shoved the bitten-off corner toward his cheek so he could answer. "Saliva." The word sounded sloppy, but he was pleased he'd recalled it.

"Oh, right. That's normal." Will lavished more licks over his hard cock. "Saliva's got plenty of good uses."

Ernest wondered if Will knew it could disable a tattle-strip, but he had a chunk of soy in his mouth, which was also filling up fast with saliva, and Will had chosen that moment to press his face down over Ernest's cock until it could go no farther. Ernest swallowed—carefully avoiding the protein chunk—and wondered how he'd manage to keep from choking.

Will seemed to be producing plenty of saliva, too. Ernest felt the moisture crawl along his testes, and even that sensation added to the lush hedonism of feeling his cock sink, over and over, deep into Will's hot, wet mouth.

He gasped—he would have said a word, if he could figure out which one fit the searing ember of need that intensified so quickly he feared he might ignite. He let go of the blanket to clutch at Will's bobbing head, to try to anchor himself in the world that looked and felt and even smelled less and less like the world he'd always known—and his body hit the tipping point where orgasm washed over him, through him. Knowing what to expect now didn't make it any less wondrous—in fact, the sparkling peak, the blissful hover, and the breathy return were all the better, now that he knew what was happening to him, and how to savor it.

Unfortunately, he'd lost the piece of the soy bar sometime between the first two stages. He located it, and flicked it out of Will's hair. "Will, you drank my...um...."

"Semen. Come." Will batted aside the crinkly silvertoned plastic, got up on his knees and freed his own hard cock from his trousers. "In the time period when those porn-feeds were produced, even way back then, people thought doing that was dirty."

"If it's not safe...."

"Not contaminated, but shameful. Titillating."

Will always knew the best idioms. He caught Ernest's dominant hand and brought it to his flushed cock, and together, they moved their fingers up and down the hot length of it. "So was it shameful," Ernest asked, "or was it...titillating?"

"Both. At the same time."

Like having one's cock stroked until the orgasm raged through. Wanting to pull away from the touch, but needing more, far more.

"I think I could try...." Ernest kept hold of Will's cock and bowed his head, and his hair fanned down to shield his face from the strange, verdant surroundings. But Will was still there, and his fingers tangled in Ernest's hair, and his breath caught in surprise.

"You don't have to—" He gave a startled gasp when Ernest drew his wet tongue over the glans.

It tasted strange, like the protein bar had on Will's tongue. Subtle. Will was right—there was no equivalent flavor in nanos. A drop of clear fluid welled from the slit, and Ernest touched his tongue to it. Salty. Maybe. But much more than that.

Ernest cupped Will's balls in his palm, as Will had done for him once before, and Will gave a long, shuddery groan. "I'm not gonna last."

Ernest trailed his tongue down the shaft, to the point where it met his fingers, then back up again. He swirled his tongue over the tip and began to stroke.

"Ernest...."

Will's cock glistened with saliva.

Ernest fit his lips over the tip, careful of his teeth, with the sensation of biting through the protein bar fresh in his mind.

Will made a strangled sound and hugged Ernest's head to his groin. "Your sweet mouth...so good...."

Ernest wasn't sure what, exactly, Will had done to send him spinning to orgasm—some combination of strokes and caresses, each one with its own peculiar effect. He licked, and stroked, and even did his best to suck, though it felt as if his teeth were in the way. If they were, Will didn't seem to care.

"Yes—I'm—" Will pushed him back as he peaked, and covered Ernest's pumping hand with his own to demonstrate how firmly to grasp, how quickly to stroke. Semen—come—shot against the clearcoat bandage in glistening white strands, and Ernest stopped rolling Will's balls together to try to snag it before it landed in the scrubby grass.

Will looked surprised, mostly, and he had a hard time catching his breath. Ernest cupped his hand over his nose and mouth and inhaled the scent of the pearly fluid. Strange. Like everything lately. He touched his tongue to it, and Will said shakily, "If you're gonna lick it, lick it off my cock."

Will hadn't looked so intent since the night he'd begged Ernest not to shunt in, to stay with him.

Ernest lowered his head again, and took the salty, slick drop upon his tongue. He swallowed it. No worse than drinking water. But the action made Will groan, and hug Ernest's head against him.

"The first thing you ever ate," Will breathed. "I'll never forget that, as long as I live."

Dirty. Ernest understood the idiom now, viscerally.

It pleased him.

○ ◎ ○

They sought shelter beneath the low-hanging branches of a nearby tree, and Ernest lay in Will's arms, wrapped securely in the blanket, wishing for sleep to come. He was supposed to be resting, but how anyone could sleep horizontally on the uneven ground was beyond him. "Tell me about the railroad."

"Abraham and Martha were out in the woods, 'romancing' as she calls it—y'know, like we were just doing—and they came upon the strips of metal, rails, just lying on the ground, nailed down with huge spikes. And when Abraham saw they stretched even farther than he could walk, he searched the W3 until he figured out what they were. An old transport system called a *railroad*. And with enough parts, he can build us a big POD—they used to call them cars, linked together to form a train—and we could go as fast and as far as a regular POD, but without the magnetic strip."

"Security ops couldn't follow?"

"They could, but only until their first charge ran out. Abraham's figuring out a way to use magnets, and solar panels, and the rails...well, I don't get it, but I'm not trained in engineering."

Ernest thought about his own years of training, now useless, and asked, "What *were* you trained in?"

Will nuzzled Ernest's hair out of his way and pressed his lips to Ernest's ear. "Seducing innocent new retirees into sucking my cock."

Ernest laughed. "Really—what did you do?"

"Exactly what you saw me doing. I was a salesman. I sold W3 games, though, not coffee. While you were being taught about flowcharts and letters—I was getting trained in psychology and marketing, hooking the customers and reeling them in. The nature of desire."

That final word, purred against his ear, sent such a shiver down Ernest's spine, he had no doubt at all that Will was telling the truth.

ⅼⅼⅼCHAPTER TWENTYⅼⅼⅼ

ERNEST FOCUSED ON THE book-shaped monitor and tapped the audio interface, though he suspected the crackly distortion was caused not by a malfunction of the old hardware, but a degradation in the ancient data itself. If he could gain access to the code, he might be able to repair it—but the "book" wasn't designed for developers. It could only read the part of the data that had been meant for public consumption.

Consumption. He smiled to himself. The "campers" in the antique feed had been marching happily through the forest, talking easily to one another and laughing, all the while eating things like "berries" and "mushrooms."

And then the screen went red, and a disclaimer that many species of plants and fungi were poisonous appeared, in an attempt to absolve the creator of the datafeed from any potential liability.

Ernest was so focused on the feed that he didn't notice one of his group approaching until the other person sat down hard, and the grass rustled.

It was Abraham, the other C754. His eyes should have looked the same as Ernest's, since barring modifications, the two of them were genetically identical. But they didn't. Abraham's eyes looked...shrewd.

Ernest attempted to congratulate himself on locating the

perfect word—only he didn't feel very successful. Not when Abraham looked at him like that.

"So," Abraham said. "How's the studying coming along?"

"Well, we shouldn't put any plants or fungi in our mouths. They might be poisonous."

"And what do you think soy is?"

The answer seemed obvious, but the way in which Abraham asked the question suggested that maybe it was not. "Soy is what the protein bars are made of."

Abraham leaned forward. "What is soy made from?"

Ernest leaned back an equal distance; being in close proximity to Abraham made him nervous in a way that being close to Will never did. "I don't know."

"You don't know. But you're a C754. You're as smart as they come."

"That information hasn't been on any of the feeds I've seen yet. I would remember if it had."

"Do you have some aversion to biology?"

"Not that I know of."

Abraham's gaze went to the gray streak in Ernest's hair. "Then how is it that you didn't figure out you should stop shunting when the thirty-year mix kicked in?"

"How could I? I only heard of it after I turned thirty. I didn't meet Will until then." And he'd had no reason to believe Will, not yet, so he hadn't acted on the information. Not right away.

Abraham stared at the streak. He stroked his wispy beard, then stood to leave. "Convenient that you stopped shunting before any major physiological damage occurred."

Convenient? That made no sense. Ernest wondered if Abraham might be working from a different definition of the word, one he was unfamiliar with. Fortunate—that was the word Ernest would have chosen. But before Ernest could suggest the correction, a third person joined them.

"Abraham, I—" Audrey stepped into the clearing and smiled broadly. "There you are, Ernest! Last time I saw you, you were bloodening all over. You're vertical now."

"Yes."

"It's a hoot to see you next to Abe—hear that? A hoot. Avian idiom."

Ernest attempted to parse what she was talking about, and failed. "Why?"

"Did you want something?" Abraham asked impatiently.

"Oh. Yes. There's something wrong with the magnetic receptor. It functions for 3.2 seconds, then it shuts down."

Abraham stood and brushed off his trouser legs. "I know. You're the mod expert—that's why I asked you to re-mount the magnets."

"They're mounted just fine. It's not the mounting that's the problem."

"Then what?"

Audrey shrugged. "You tell me. It's your design."

Abraham followed Audrey without a backward glance at Ernest. Rude? Not quite, not exactly. Not like the characters in old time feeds who said insulting things to "get a rise out of" the other characters, and then manipulate them once they were flustered. It was more like Ernest had ceased to exist for Abraham the moment his machine—his creation—was mentioned.

Ernest tried, and failed, to continue studying the "camping" feed. The problem of the magnet mod seemed much more interesting than watching *homo sapiens* walk through vegetation.

The multi-person POD they called the railroad was difficult to see amid the undergrowth. Abraham had covered it in branches so it wouldn't be noticed on a quick visual pass. The sound of Abraham and Audrey arguing was easy enough to follow, though.

"It must be the connection," Abraham insisted. "The only thing it could possibly be is the connection."

"I told you, they're on there the right way. Something else is interrupting the flow."

Ernest looked at the system Abraham had created from repurposed POD components. Once he identified all the parts—the large ones, at least—he decided the arrangement was really very clever, though he'd expect no less from a C754.

Within the city grid, the POD axles would have been charged to provide resistant propulsion to the POD bases. If the grid went down, or someone wished to travel off-grid, the PODs' solar power could provide propulsion for a limited amount of time.

Abraham had mounted several axles on one large unit, then set up pairs of magnets—presumably with the same poles facing, otherwise they'd draw together—to provide their own resistant propulsion. The metal rails would create a sort of feedback loop, and when the magnets' solar power was turned on, the invention should be able to travel on its own much farther than a traditional POD—as far as the metal rails stretched.

Audrey was saying, "...but if you do this..." and the "railroad" moved forward a few meters, and then stopped.

"There—it should only do that if we activate the brakes. Would you stop spitting on it? That won't help."

Ernest lingered near the edge of the clearing and studied the setup. He was no engineer. He didn't know—other than theoretically—how to piece things together. And yet.

"Saliva is a great conductor."

"Should we hang someone out the side of the car and have them continue to spit on the magnets?"

"I guess that would be awkward."

The argue. It was so much more interesting, more nuanced, than any exchange Ernest had ever had with LOU15E, and yet... he missed her. Terribly.

"Maybe there's another conductor you could introduce," Audrey suggested. "One that won't dry up."

"There should be no need for a conductor at all. Something's interrupting the feedback loop. But that's impossible."

Ernest missed LOU15E even though she'd summoned the security ops. That hadn't been her decision. She'd been programmed to do so. Being angry with her for that would be like being angry with someone for breathing. It wasn't like Will's friend Matthew, who'd run straight to the coffee shop with Storm Troopers chasing him. Matthew should have known better—but all he'd cared about was himself.

"If this only runs for three seconds," Abraham said, "then the plan is off. We can't go. You see how far we get on three seconds."

"But what if each unit fired for three seconds, then turned off, then on again, at different intervals?" Audrey suggested. "Then there would always be one or two firing."

"Maybe...but it would slow us down. If the ops come...."

"You've been out here for weeks and they haven't found you. What does it matter if you go slowly? As long as you go far, you'll outdistance them."

And according to Will, the one thing they did have was time. Another whole lifetime, maybe even two.

Laughter filtered into the railroad clearing through a shifting wall of leaves. Ernest left Audrey and Abraham to their invention and followed the sound to the others, who were busy preparing for the journey.

Martha held one of the small metal flasks under a stream of water Will poured from a mostly-intact piece of curved resin that looked like it had been sawed from the top of an old POD hull. The water ran through a cylindrical device—a filter to remove natural nanites, if the ancient camping feed had been accurate—and then trickled downward, drawn by gravity, and out through a small opening in the bottom. When the flask was full, Martha handed it off to Elizabeth, who swapped it with an empty flask, quickly, so as not to lose any water.

The actions of filtering and bottling water might be novel to Ernest, but those movements he could parse. It was the way in which they interacted that was baffling, as if they were actors in an old, old feed. Laughter, smiles, camaraderie. They seemed like a sort of group Ernest had seen before. What was it called?

A family.

Before, in the *Daddy is a Contractor* feed, *family* conjured notions of biological reproduction. But here, in the way language often did, the word revealed a whole new facet of itself.

"Come help Will," Elizabeth called to Ernest. Her skin creased deeply around her eyes and mouth, but her teeth shone straight and white as she smiled. She hardly seemed ready to crawl into the crematorium now. "His arms are getting tired."

"I'm no wuss," Will said. "Besides, Ernest needs to rest his incision." He sounded petulant, but not really, as if he was exaggerating the emotion for comic effect.

"I didn't say he needed to do any holding," Elizabeth replied.

Martha laughed and added, "Now that someone you want to

impress is here, suddenly you're keeping it steady."

They all laughed again. Ernest wasn't quite sure he understood the joke—it seemed to be at Will's expense, though Will didn't mind—and he felt a shy smile tugging at the corner of his own mouth without knowing exactly why.

Martha handed a full flask to Elizabeth and quickly put an empty in its place, then glanced over her shoulder at him, still smiling. "Does your arm hurt?"

"Yes. But not like it did..." the small chute with water trickling out distracted him from the conversation. Overlaid, as if two feeds were playing at once in his imagination, Ernest saw the chute that led from the Reclaim machine, with its slurry of water and human ash sliding down toward the grate in the floor. "Not like it did," he repeated, as if that was what he'd meant to be the end of his communication.

"Watch the water," Will told Martha. "I didn't haul it all the way here so you could spill it." He was still smiling. A...jest? No, not that. A jibe.

Martha switched bottles again. "You will need to make sure you don't feel too hot," she said. "That could indicate infection. And your temperature isn't being monitored anymore now that you're not shunting in."

Ernest felt a pang in his arm that he mistook for hunger—but of course it couldn't be, now that he no longer had a shunt. Pain, then. Except there was no reason for pain. He hadn't been moving it at all.

Sadness, perhaps. Loss.

He shifted his focus to Will, who was still smiling, with the muscles and tendons of his bare arms showing, backlit against the lowering sun, in high relief.

"Come and help," Elizabeth said. "I'm too old."

Martha corrected her. "I'm a lot older than you."

"I tire more quickly." Elizabeth motioned for Ernest to come take her place. "We will divide my duties. I will continue to twist the cap on, since both my arms are functional."

Handing the bottle to Martha at the right moment and taking the full bottle away required more precise timing than he would have imagined, and a splash of water was lost to the ground. The others only laughed. It would have been a pleasant task, if only the mud at their feet didn't remind him of the Reclaim grate.

Ernest was usually capable of parsing several things at once: code and language, audio and visual, research and recreational feeds. But being among a group who were all speaking at once, trying to read everyone's expression and catch the nuances of their verbal communication, took every bit of concentration he had.

Which was how the men in white took them completely and utterly by surprise.

ⵑⵑⵑ CHAPTER TWENTY-ONE ⵑⵑⵑ

THE SECURITY OPS' SMUDGED white uniforms stood out pale against the green foliage. Two of them, both taller than Will, emerged silently from the undergrowth with Tasers raised and ready. Ernest pointed and Will turned, careful not to spill what was left of the water. His caution snapped off like a servomechanism when he saw who they were, and he swung the sawed-off POD roof in a wide, strong arc that took the security op by surprise. It hit the op's head with a dull thud that seemed disproportionately quiet, since the blow knocked the man to his knees.

Leaves rustled and twigs snapped as the attackers no longer needed to keep quiet. They sprang. A deep voice bellowed, "Stand down!" at Will. Ernest whirled. Three more ops approached from behind, all of them tall and muscled, with shaved heads, square jaws and hard eyes. One of the ops—probably the one who'd yelled—had a W3 link at his temple. It wasn't blinking. They were too far from the grid to pick up a signal.

Ernest had no Taser. No syringes. He scanned the ground. Not even so much as a likely stick.

A shriek. Ernest whirled again. Elizabeth spasmed on the ground, down from a Taser touch, while Will aimed a hit at the second op's head. The blow connected, but the op didn't fall. He was too large, too solid—and the resin piece Will struck him with, though bulky, was lightweight and dull-edged.

Ops surrounded them on all sides now. The first op Will had knocked down began to stagger to his feet, and Martha aimed a solid kick between his legs, and another at the side of his knee. The op fell to his side clutching his groin, and he vomited up a yellowish froth.

"Take her down," ordered the captain, who apparently knew enough to command his men even without the help of his link.

The op who'd been coming toward Ernest lurched to the side and swung his Taser at Martha instead. She ducked the swing. Her hand shot up and connected to the op's wrist with a hefty smack, and the Taser went tumbling into the bushes.

Of the five security ops, the one Martha had kicked was still down, and the one who'd been disarmed was trying to grab her. The guard who was focused on Will took another hit, which still didn't seem to faze him, though it did keep him at arm's length. The only other unoccupied guard came toward Ernest. The captain shouted, "Leave him, get the strong one."

The strong one? Will.

Ernest flung the half-full water flask at the op. It bounced off his shoulder. He turned toward Ernest, and his leader snapped, "Do what I said."

The percussive sound of the POD roof hitting the op's head, though muted, was the loudest sound in the clearing. The second op was almost upon Will. And then they would overpower him.

Ernest crouched and pried a rock from the ground. He stood and flung it, hard. It made almost no sound at all when it hit the back of the op's head, a soft thwack, but the op reacted much more dramatically than his teammate being pummeled with the lightweight POD roof. He staggered and clapped his hand to the place the rock had struck. His hand came away bloody. Blood oozed down his shorn scalp and stained his white collar red-red.

He turned. His eyes were wide with hatred and dismay.

"Get the strong one." The leader's voice grew hoarse from shouting. "I have the eunuch."

Ernest turned and found the captain almost upon him. He did as he'd seen Martha do, and aimed a kick between his attacker's legs. The captain must have anticipated the move—he twisted and took the kick to his massive, hard-muscled thigh. He crouched low to protect his groin, which put his shunt arm within easy reach.

The shape of the captain's shunt was plain through the fabric of his sleeve. Ernest grabbed it two-handed and twisted.

The captain shrieked, and sagged to his knees.

Ernest landed a kick to the side, the only place he could, since the captain was curled into a protective ball around his damaged shunt. The man pivoted in a crouch and scrambled away, toward the bushes.

Ernest's head jerked back—someone had him by the hair, but then the op who'd been hit thirty times or more with the sawed-off POD roof called to his companion, "Wait—uh, Patrick ran."

A huge hand closed around Ernest's throat, but stopped short of squeezing. Ernest grabbed it with both hands and wrenched, as he had with the leader's shunt, but it didn't budge.

"Stop," Ernest forced out. "Your commander fled. You have no commands. It's done."

The hand at his throat flexed, as if the op was considering crushing Ernest's neck simply to see what it would feel like.

Ernest said, "You're wasting time you could be gaming. Free time."

The op released Ernest, who sagged with relief. When Ernest could turn his head again, he saw Will and the first op squaring off. Will was breathing hard and the op had a thin line of blood oozing from a split on his eyebrow, but neither was significantly harmed. "Go," Will said. "Get out of here. Your wuss captain turned tail and ran. There aren't rewards on any of us. As far as your Deacons are concerned, we died a long time ago. So why bother?"

The op Martha had disarmed had her by the throat too, though whether he was imitating the op who'd been grappling with Ernest or they'd all been trained in the maneuver, Ernest didn't know.

He jerked Martha's head back and wrenched it—much like Ernest had done to the leader's shunt—and dropped her limp body to the ground.

Ernest went cold. The ops grabbed their vomiting teammate beneath the arms and dragged him swiftly from the clearing. Will fell to his knees beside Martha. "What did they do?" he shouted. "Ernest, help her. Do something."

Ernest looked to Elizabeth, hoping for medical guidance. Still unconscious, thanks to the Taser...and she'd probably be out for a while. It was up to him, then. He somehow managed to break through his inertia and crouch beside Martha with Will. He didn't know nearly enough about physiology, though it seemed to him that a sudden, violent torque of the spine might be very bad.

He smoothed Martha's gray-stippled hair back from her forehead, and her eyelids fluttered. "Martha? Are you conscious?"

Her eyes fixed on Ernest, and she whispered, "Abraham?"

"No."

"Oh." Her brow furrowed. "Ernest. Yes. Is Abraham here?"

Will stood. "I'll get him."

The bushes rustled as he headed toward the railroad, and when he was gone, Martha said, "Ernest, do me a favor."

"Yes."

"Touch my hand."

Her hand lay at her side, fingers gently furled. Ernest pressed his fingertip into the palm.

"Are you touching it?"

"Yes."

"Squeeze my fingers. Do it hard." Ernest obeyed. "Are you squeezing?"

Ernest was puzzled. "Yes."

Martha closed her eyes tightly. "You don't need to keep squeezing. But I'd like it if you kept hold of my hand until Abraham gets here."

Will returned much more loudly than he'd left. The leaves and branches rustled as if a dozen ops were stomping through. Will and Abraham emerged, and between the two of them, Benjamin, the retired security op—as tall as Will, with broad shoulders only slightly stooped. Benjamin was no longer in the papery smock in which Ernest had rescued him. He wore security op whites.

Abraham held a Taser to his neck. The C754 looked fierce enough that Ernest saw little of himself in his clone's hard eyes, but Abraham's expression fell apart at the sight of Martha on the ground. He dropped the Taser and lunged forward. Audrey scrambled to retrieve the weapon, though Benjamin hadn't made any move to escape, and instead looked around the clearing, at Elizabeth and Martha, with an expression so subtle Ernest had no idea what to make of it.

Ernest ducked out of the way as Abraham took his place exactly, right down to the holding of Martha's hand. "What happened?" Abraham said quietly.

Martha answered. "Spinal injury."

"Who?"

Though Martha seemed to have trouble speaking, her words were calm and carefully measured. "It doesn't matter. He's gone." She drew another laborious breath. "You've got to promise me."

Abraham's expression contorted. Both his eyes began leaking profusely. "No."

"Abe...."

"I'll kill him."

Martha smiled knowingly. "You won't. You've worked too hard on this, and have too many people depending on you, to throw it all away. You'll finish the railroad tonight. Now. And you'll go—before they come back with more men. Promise."

"I'll...kill...him."

"That won't help me."

"What do you need—some medical equipment? We'll find it... figure out how to run it off the grid."

Martha wet her lips with great care. "There's nothing to find. Medicine stopped treating spinal injuries all the way back when the Deacons started the retirement program. It was classified as being too resource-intensive. Just like aging."

The two trails of wetness on Abraham's cheeks glimmered in the lowering afternoon light. Drops—tears—fell on Martha's hair. "There has to be something...."

"There isn't. It would've been better if I'd died right away. Now I'll stop you from leaving."

"There's room. We'll take you with us—"

"Abe, I can't move. At least let me rest while you finish the railroad."

More tears. Abraham wiped his face with the back of his hand. "Does it hurt?"

"No. It's numb. But we have some syringes now...Ernest knows what they look like...I'd be much more comfortable...."

Ernest found the syringes he'd taken from the Diaconate among their supplies and brought one over to Martha. Abraham snatched it from his hand, then turned back to her. "How much?"

"All of it."

Ernest was about to correct Martha, because she'd told him herself that the whole syringe would be enough to stop someone's heart, and maybe her injuries were impairing her judgment—but he saw her staring at him, eyes wide and desperate, and he paused. Martha knew what she was asking for.

Abraham fit the syringe to her shunt.

Perhaps Martha might have nodded, if she could still move. But instead she gave Ernest a small, sad smile, and looked to Abraham again. "Kiss me?" Her voice was barely a breath. "For luck."

"There is no such thing," Abraham said softly. He bent and pressed his lips to Martha's, and Ernest looked up into the trees, wishing he hadn't just made his own promise to Martha with his eyes. The promise not to say anything about the syringe.

When he looked down again, the empty syringe was at Martha's side.

Abraham sat back on his heels and wiped more wetness from his cheeks with his sleeve.

"What about this guy?" Will asked him, shaking Benjamin by the forearm. "What do we do with him?"

Abraham pressed the heels of his palms into his eyes and rocked there, as if it would help him figure out what to do.

"We could question him," Ernest suggested. That's what they would do in an old-time feed.

Before he could even try, Benjamin blurted his plan out in a halting rush. "I only wanted them to reverse my shunt damage. Deacon George said he would if I told them what quadrant you were in."

"That's ridiculous," Audrey shouted, and leveled a kick to the side of his foot. "Your shunt damage isn't reversible. Didn't you hear what Martha just said? There's no cure for age."

"But they told me they could."

"And you believed them. I'm so mad I can't even think of a good idiom."

"We should tie him up," Ernest said, "so he can't hurt anyone. And then we can make the railroad work."

Abraham peered at Ernest over his damp sleeve. "You seem to know an awful lot about security, for a data clerk."

Audrey said, "What do you mean by that?"

"Maybe the Diaconate sent someone to infiltrate us from inside."

Ernest hadn't yet extrapolated what Abraham meant by that, but Will had—and he was angry about it. He dropped Benjamin's arm and hauled Abraham to his feet. "Don't you dare...."

"Or what?"

Audrey started yelling, "Stop it! Stop it!" over and over like a looping program.

"Or we're leaving," Will said, "Ernest and me, and you can run the railroad without us."

Ernest saw Benjamin ease back a few steps while everyone else hollered. Martha and Elizabeth both lay on the ground. Elizabeth was breathing. Martha was not. Ernest cradled his mottled red arm to his chest and stood by as everyone else argued, everyone but him and Benjamin.

He didn't try to stop Benjamin from slipping away. Keeping the retired op there would only complicate things, and he didn't have any new information. After what Martha sacrificed for the railroad, it didn't seem right to divert their attention to monitoring Benjamin to make sure he didn't sabotage their plans further.

"I was the one who did it," Audrey shrilled. "Not Ernest. I told him what quadrant we were in, him and Elizabeth. He'd just escaped from the Diaconate—he'd seen it from the inside. I thought he'd want to be free."

Abraham turned to her as if she'd slapped him. He would

rather have blamed Ernest—and seeing how small and defiant Audrey looked, and how painfully young, Ernest would rather have taken that blame. "He knew damn well what was inside the Diaconate," Abraham snarled. "He'd known it all his life. He was a security op."

"I was trying to help!"

Abraham turned and looked at the place where some brittle branches had snapped as Benjamin escaped, then kept turning toward the railroad that ran for 3.2 seconds and then shut off, and finally, coming full circle, he stopped with his gaze on Martha.

"Ernest will sit with her," Will said. "You need to get the propulsion working."

"It doesn't matter. She's dead."

Ernest felt his own eyes sting. Abraham knew—he *knew* what Martha had been asking. And he'd done it. Himself.

Will rushed over to Martha and fell to his knees beside her. "No she's not. She's drugged. She's sleeping. Elizabeth was a health aide too—she'll wake up from her taze in a few minutes and tell us what to do."

Audrey sat down hard on the forest floor, buried her face in her hands, and wept.

Everyone was crouched or sprawled in the grass but Ernest and Abraham, and the look in Abraham's eyes was so fierce that Ernest wished he could find a plausible reason to fling himself down to the ground as well to avoid seeing it. He tried to look away, but he couldn't.

Finally, Abraham spoke. "I'm bringing her to Reclaim."

Will got to his feet and squared his shoulders. "You're not going to the Diaconate."

Abraham said simply, "I am."

"If you don't get to work on that engine right now, then we're all as good as dead."

"I can't leave her like this. She has to be demagnetized."

"What did you think would happen," Will demanded, "wherever we ended up someday, when we actually died? That we'd take a trip back and see if the Diaconate welcomed us with open arms? I thought you didn't believe in that Deaconist propaganda."

Abraham glanced down at Martha's body. "I never thought I did."

"Just think for a second, Abe. It's no good. Not only are you both heretics, but she has no POD to trade in. They won't demagnetize her without a POD."

"Her POD is here."

"Deep inside the railroad," Audrey added. "Her POD was one of the first ones you dismantled."

Abraham smiled...no, smirked...no.... Ernest didn't know what to call the cruel twist of his mouth—but it was grim, and conveyed no humor at all. Whatever the word, the meaning was clear enough. Abraham had pieced together the railroad.

And he could dismantle it.

ııı CHAPTER TWENTY-TWO ııı

ABRAHAM STRODE BACK TOWARD the railroad with Will right behind him. Will was still hollering, demanding that he see reason. Abraham was calm and quiet.

Ernest crouched beside Audrey and put an arm around her thin shoulders. He wondered why it had occurred to him to touch her, but she leaned into him and cried, and he supposed she would topple forward if he let go now. He said, "I don't think Benjamin knew what was really happening in Reclaim. I found him in the lobby, so maybe he never actually saw what was going on. And even the ops who work the machine, they only see the loading end of it. Or maybe he did know about Reclaim...but even if he did, I don't think he understood. Not like Elizabeth. Not like me."

Once Elizabeth regained consciousness and was told what had happened, she and Audrey began to speak of Martha, how intelligent she was. How funny. How determined. Elizabeth seemed much better suited to comforting Audrey than Ernest was. Which left a small chink in which worry about the railroad could insinuate itself.

"I'm going to go...check on...Will," Ernest told them. It wasn't entirely a lie, and the women didn't stop him from leaving.

He found Will and Abraham seated on a horizontal log a few meters from the railroad. Will had his arm around Abraham's shoulders. Abraham had his face in his hands. When a dry branch rasped against Ernest's shirt, Will looked up, caught his eye, and patted the log on the other side of him. Ernest sat awkwardly.

He glanced at the railroad. It appeared that Abraham had not yet dismantled it. "Have you reprogrammed the nanites?" Ernest asked.

Abraham lowered his hands and gave Ernest a...what was it? Depressed? Despondent? Resigned? He gave Ernest a decidedly unpleasant look, and said, "What?"

"The nanites. In the magnet bay. They're set for a three-centimeter loop, but you've scaled up the propulsion to power a larger POD, and now they're..." he glanced... "I'd say approximately 5.5 from terminus to terminus. The delay would shut down the loop."

Abraham gazed on the railroad with weary eyes. "I suppose you can reprogram nanites in your sleep."

"Not in my sleep, no. But if Audrey has an interface, you can give me the figures and I'll overwrite the code."

Abraham looked at the railroad in silence for a long moment, and then said, "Why bother?"

"Don't you get it?" Will said. "If you drag her body back into the city, they win. Those bastards who killed her for no good reason, they win. That's the last thing she would want."

Abraham stood, moving slowly and stiffly, and rested his fingertips against the side of the railroad car. "I'm not leaving her like that," he said to Will. "If it were your lover," he glanced at Ernest, "you'd do the same."

"Don't bring him into this. I don't know what I'd do, okay? But I doubt I'd drag him back to Reclaim."

One moment Ernest felt a strange ringing in his ears, and the next he found himself lying on his side in the dirt. Will crouched beside him, took him by the chin, and tilted his head up to peer into his eyes. "Are you all right? Were you injured? Is it your shunt arm?"

"It..." Ernest sat up, then fought a wave of nausea by shaking off Will's grasp and tucking his head between his bent knees. "It is passing."

Will hugged Ernest against him hard, so that his sternum pressed into Ernest's face, nearly to the point of pain. Was it hunger? Fatigue? Ernest didn't think so. He'd been experiencing those things for days. No, it was the thought of his own body being fed into the cruciform hopper of the Reclaim machine that made him woozy and ill. "Promise me you'll never bring me there."

"What?"

"Promise. Now."

"Whatever you want." Will kissed the top of his head, then said, "There, do you see? Wouldn't Martha have said the same thing?"

"Very politic," Abraham said. "Very convenient."

Ernest almost asked L0U15E for an alternate definition of *convenient*, since that was the second time Abraham had used it in regard to him, and neither time was it in a context where Ernest found his own response convenient in any way. Whatever the alternate definition might be, it made Will very angry.

"If you have something to say," he told Abraham, "then come out and say it."

"You recruit someone for our team, and he just so happens to know how to fix the flaw in the repurposed mechanisms?"

"But I was a data clerk..." Ernest said quietly. Neither of the others seemed to be listening.

"And when I talk about going back to Reclaim, well, it just so happens he's been there too."

"He was looking for his POD, you twit. He thinks it's his mother."

"No I don't," Ernest said. "Of course I don't."

"So what's next? He starts reprogramming the railroad's nanites, and then, when he gets the signal from the Deacons, he gives us the all-clear to launch. Right into their trap."

Too many emotions flashed over Will's face for Ernest to interpret. "I'm not talking to you about this. Not now. You don't know what you're saying—you're upset about Martha. We all are."

"I know, all right. He bats his eyelashes and what little common sense you've got rushes right down to your dick."

The color drained from Will's face. They were speaking so quickly, there was a distinct lag between the spoken words and Ernest's parsing of the meaning.

"You've been my best friend ever since I can remember," Will said, "and this is what you think of me? You're saying I'd bring a traitor into our group?"

Abraham set his jaw. C754 or not, with that expression, he looked very little like the holos Ernest had seen of himself. "Not knowingly."

Understanding came to Ernest as the other two men faced each other, silent and grim. Abraham thought he would betray Will? Like Matthew had?

Or, worse—like L0U15E had betrayed him?

He struggled to find the right words to proclaim that Abraham was wrong—but didn't the guilty parties in old-time feeds always proclaim their innocence the loudest? Before he could figure out what to say for himself, Will snapped, "That's it, then. We're leaving."

Will grabbed Ernest by his wounded shunt arm and dragged him toward the undergrowth where the supplies were stored. "Where are we going?" Ernest said in a gasp.

"Some of this stuff is ours. We'll take what's fair—what we can carry—and we'll get out of here."

Ernest recalled the *homo sapiens* in the "camping" feed. "I don't think it's possible to carry more than a few days' worth of supplies." In fact, he was so much slighter than Will, and weak from his surgery besides, he worried he'd be able to carry even less than that.

Will dragged a container of protein bars out from a concealing thicket, crouched in front of it, and began counting out their share.

"Will? You know I'd never have anything to do with the Storm Troopers, don't you?"

Will counted out a few more bars, then planted his elbows on his knees and buried his face in his hands. "If you do, don't tell me. I don't want to know."

Ernest paused. He'd expected Will to say, "I know you wouldn't." He'd never had to explain himself before, and it was more difficult than he'd thought it would be. "When they came into the coffee shop looking for Matthew, I was afraid of them. And when I saw what they did to your reading room, I was angry." And then, of course, there was the Diaconate. Ernest could hardly begin to describe his feelings there. "Security ops are all lazy and mean, and they're cunning. I would never betray us to them. I..." he searched for the right word. "I hate them."

Will raised his head and ran a hand over his face. Dappled sunlight caught the pale stubble on his jaw and made it sparkle. "I can't imagine not having Martha to talk to. She was my friend, too."

Ernest suspected it would be an awful lot like having a question for L0U15E, being on the brink of asking, and then realizing she wasn't there—and would never be again. But he knew better than to compare Will's *homo consummatus* friend to an AI. Will was already convinced he didn't know the difference between a person and a POD-mind.

He dropped to one knee beside Will and placed a hand between Will's shoulder blades. Will did not sag against Ernest as Audrey had; he was all tension and stiff angles.

"We won't survive without the others," Ernest said.

Will let out a long, drawn-out sigh, and began pitching the bars he'd counted out back into the pile. "You're right. Not in the forest." He glanced back over his shoulder in the direction of the grid, even though its current location in proximity to them was obscured by undergrowth and trees. "But we could survive in the city. I've done it four years now. We'll just need to find some cover jobs in a place the ops don't care much about—some Purged-game addicts like Clarence to let us fill in for them—maybe in a neighborhood where the W3 signals are patchy...."

Ernest supposed that if Will had dodged the security ops once, he could do it again. Audrey could color the gray streak in Ernest's hair blue or green or some other improbable color, and for a few years at least, he and Will would be able to blend in. And if anyone looked up from their gaming long enough to suspect that the two of them were getting on in years...well, those people would probably have their own appointments with Reclaim soon enough.

Audrey had been planning to stay behind anyway, and Abraham was sharp; if he removed his whiskers he would have no problem losing himself in the population either—but would he even want to reintegrate? He didn't seem very keen on compromising. And then there was Elizabeth...there'd be no way at all for her to hide.

"Will—I don't think everyone else can survive without us."

Will was so quiet that Ernest wondered if he'd even heard. Ernest was just about to repeat himself when Will began to nod. "You're right."

"You've known me a lot longer than Abraham has. He has no reason to trust me. But if you believe in me, that's all I care about."

Will slipped an arm around Ernest and pulled him close. "You know what I keep thinking? What if that had been you? What if the ops decided you were the biggest threat, and they killed you instead of Martha? What then?"

Then, Ernest thought, there would be no problem. The railroad would be the same as it always had been—with the addition of Elizabeth to the group. It might not be able to travel for more than a three-second burst...but the reprogramming of the nanites was nothing more than a task. They could figure out how to complete it.

Abraham's mistrust of Ernest, however, had no step-by-step solution.

Ernest stood and brushed dead grass from his trousers. "I was serious when I told you not to bring me to Reclaim when I die."

"I know."

"And I wouldn't take you there either. I don't know what I would do, exactly. Figure out some way to demagnetize you myself. It's more than they would have done for you at the Diaconate."

Ernest turned away to head back to the railroad so he could begin formulating a plan to solve the three-second firing issue.

"Wait."

Ernest paused and looked back. Will's face had gone white.

"What are you saying?" Will asked.

"They're not demagnetizing anybody."

"But...how do you...?"

"I saw."

Will strode up to Ernest and grabbed him by both arms. Ernest's bloodied shunt arm gave a horrible twinge, but he didn't pull away. He welcomed the pain; it anchored him in his present reality, far away from the steaming, chopping hulk of the Reclaim machine.

"How can the Deacons do that?" Will demanded.

"It's very simple. They lie."

Ernest no longer wished to discuss the Diaconate. It left a cold, hard feeling deep in his abdominal cavity where he imagined his stomach might be, or possibly his liver. Will offered no resistance when Ernest took him by the hand and led him back to the railroad.

ⅲⅰ CHAPTER TWENTY-THREE ⅰⅲ

UP CLOSE, THE RAILROAD turned out to be a lot larger than it looked. Ernest wasn't accustomed to working directly with big machinery. In fact, he'd done most of his work from inside his POD. He'd even become accustomed to the quirk of its keyscan that necessitated pausing as he entered the hashmark character. He wasn't even sure how to interface with the patched together computer that ran the railroad.

He was gazing at a propulsion unit when Audrey approached and stood beside him. Her eyes and nose were red and swollen, and her fuchsia hair hung in stringy clumps. "So...you think you can fix this."

"If you have an interface. Yes."

Audrey held up a portable keyscan. Several untidy wires and cables dangled from the bottom, and a solar pack was tethered to the side with a hair ribbon. "Aim the panel at that gap in the trees and plug it into that socket by the mounting bracket."

Ernest attached the interface, allowed the solar panel to charge for a moment, then keyed on the power. The small, cracked viscreen lit up with the word HELLO.

"I had Charlie run some simulations," Audrey said, "based on all the data he had about Martha. Nine times out of ten, she begs Abraham to fix the railroad and get out of here."

Ernest keyed, QUERY: NANITES. "What about the tenth time?"

"She tells Abe to hunt down those fucking security ops and feed their own dicks to 'em."

The nanites' quantity, type, and programmed functions scrolled by. The makeshift screen was slower than LOU15E's, and Ernest needed to make a quick mental adjustment to his reading speed to accommodate. "So which thing will Abraham do?" Ernest suspected that even with only a 10% accuracy rating, the last option would be the one he would choose.

Ernest adjusted the nanites for a stronger but more intermittent power source, changed the relay of the firing to match the distance of the magnets from the tracks, and added a routine to burn off any debris that might kick up into the motors. Meanwhile, as he considered what Audrey was telling him on its most direct level, he also extracted the idea that a simulation wouldn't be a bad idea. He cast his mind back to an assignment he'd had when he was twenty-two, a malfunctioning height scanner at the natal center, and he fed the nanites a new string of commands, modifying it as he entered.

He then realized Audrey hadn't replied. Or if she had, he hadn't heard her. He keyed in the last few characters and looked up.

She was staring at his keying hand in a sort of grim fascination. "I only parsed a fragment of what you just did," she said, "but it was enough to see you're good. I can't even imagine what kinds of mods we would've been able to do together if I'd known you before."

"Before what?"

She glanced over her shoulder toward the clearing where they'd been bottling water, and she sighed. She didn't answer.

Ernest turned his attention back to the railroad. The simulations all started out well, but then, in time lapse, a disturbing thing happened. The engines overheated and key components (these varied) burned out. He reduced the speed and ran another sim. A different component suffered. He reduced the weight of the railroad car. It traveled another twenty kilometers before failing.

Inspired by the accidental shut-off he'd been trying to repair in the first place, he simulated a string of conditions where each component fired and rested sequentially. That would have worked—if the railroad car was empty. But the weight of the passengers would keep it at a standstill.

The readout screen flickered, and Ernest paused in his keying to reposition the solar panel to capture the lowering sun. He brushed up against Abraham, who'd been crouching behind him for...how long? He would have asked LOU15E, if she weren't stripped and repurposed, with her electronics disassembled and her chassis housing a new POD-mind, and probably a 10-year-old data clerk fresh from the natal center. And maybe a keyscan that didn't lag at the hashtag character.

"It needs more propulsion units," Abraham said.

Ernest realized he'd been prepared to hear that he was sabotaging the railroad, that he was in league with the security ops. That it was "convenient" that he was able to rearrange the guts of the nanites. But the screen flickered on, Ernest keyed in a simulation with more propulsion units and set it to process, and the time lapse ran much longer than it had before. "Now if we shut it down periodically," Abraham said, "let's say while there's cloud cover, or if we stop to rest or find water—it should fire long enough take us farther away from the grid than anyone else can possibly follow."

Ernest had thought the railroad needed to function indefinitely. He hadn't realized its purpose was only to bring them to a distant location, at which time it could be disassembled and repurposed. Like LOU15E.

"You could mount the axle there." Ernest pointed to a crosspiece that supported the railroad car. "It would work."

Abraham looked at Audrey, and Ernest did the same. She seemed so small and sad. "Fine," she told Abraham. "You've been itching to take it apart since the day I met you. So do it." She turned away, slipped through a gap in the undergrowth and was gone.

Ernest didn't understand, though he didn't feel comfortable asking Abraham to explain. However, he didn't need to. "Her POD," Abraham said. "Two more propulsion units, another solar panel—every component on it is high quality and meticulously maintained."

"But then she can't go back."

"Why would she want to?" Abraham's tone was harsh, but if Ernest looked, really looked at Abraham's face—which made him uncomfortable, since it was so like his own reflection— instead of the anger and bitterness he'd been expecting, he read pain. "In good conscience, how could we let her?"

Since Ernest was unaccustomed to wielding any sort of authority, he'd never considered whether or not he would have any choice in the matter.

Abraham said, "Will told me they're not demagnetizing anybody at the Diaconate."

Ernest noted "you claimed" was not part of the statement— that Abraham seemed inclined to take the explanation for fact. Probably not because Ernest had said it—undoubtedly, Ernest being the source of the information did little to prove its veracity—but because Abraham had mistrusted the Diaconate so intensely, for so many years, that the information fit in with what he already believed. "I've been talking to Charlie," Abraham went on. "I think Audrey had that POD-mind loaded with every illegal datafeed in existence—and I pieced a few of them together and discovered a way to demagnetize Martha myself with an alternating current."

It was exactly what Ernest would have done—figure out a way to do the demagnetization himself. But hearing the process Abraham had actually come up with was sickening. Ernest had never heard anything so heretical in his life. Not since Will had taught him how to swallow.

"You don't look well. Is your arm bothering you?"

Ernest shook his head. "I'm sorry about what happened to Martha. She had much less body mass than those ops, and even so, she damaged two of them. That's why they killed her—because she knew how to fight."

Abraham nodded. "Yes. She did."

○ ◎ ○

"This is a lot easier with three people," Will said as they dis-assembled Audrey's POD. He was noticeably stronger than Abraham and Ernest, though Abraham continually reminded him to be careful not to break anything, and at one point even went so far as to call him a brute. Will went on yanking shiny blue panels from the shell as if he hadn't noticed.

Abraham had been right about the POD—its inner workings were pristine. But even though harvesting Charlie's propulsion units and solar panel were the only way to get everyone far away from the grid, Ernest still felt guilty handling the chips and wires he pulled from the scavenged shell.

Daylight was fading fast. Ernest fit his hand around some-thing—an audio speaker?—and pried it carefully from its set-ting. Abraham clipped an LED to an overhanging branch and aimed it at the partially disassembled shell. The tiny light cast harsh shadows that made the stripping of the POD look more like a surgical procedure.

Audrey pushed through a gap in the bushes and scowled down at the components. "We can't take it all. Too much weight."

Abraham gazed at the scattered parts as if he yearned to reassemble them into something useful, though he didn't know quite what. "You choose, then. I'll go and do one more test of the new propulsion units."

Once he was fairly sure Abraham could no longer hear him, Ernest whispered to Audrey, "Is it a good idea to leave at night? It's so...dark."

"We've cleared the tracks for fifty kilometers. Our solar reserves should take us that far, so we'll have a good head start by dawn."

Audrey peeled a reflective strip off Charlie's chassis and dis-connected a small cable. "These cells are fully charged. They'll give us a few minutes of backup."

It seemed too soon. Ernest wanted to be able see what they were doing, and not simply work from memory—and the thought of squandering all their power on the initial push terrified him.

Normally, he'd talk through the alternatives with

LOU15E—and he'd trust her to ensure he didn't leave anything important behind in the darkness. But now he had to decide for himself.

He did his best to imagine what LOU15E would have said. If she'd been interested in helping them outrun the security ops (which she hadn't been, though it wasn't her fault, simply her programming at work) she might have indeed told Ernest to leave now. Chances were, even with the evidence that the old metal tracks had been cleared, none of the ops were intelligent enough to figure out that they'd been used for off-grid propulsion.

Or were they? Their language might be rudimentary, but they were shrewd. And while most of the refugees weren't worth much, with no PODs and at retirement age, Audrey was still young. Capturing her should bring a decent reward, so the ops would have an incentive to put their cunning to work.

Ernest supposed they did need to embark as soon as possible. Abraham had been convinced it was best to leave—but something subtle in his mannerisms, the way he dropped his gaze when looked in the eye, or the distracted delivery with which he now spoke—suggested he might very well change his mind and abandon the whole project. The farther away they got him, and the sooner, the less likely he'd be able to turn back.

"Help me unseat something," Audrey said. "As long as I have this chip, the rest of this junk can take a long walk off a short pier. That's a naval idiom."

Ernest fit his fingers between a pair of glossy blue fiberglass panels and pried them open far enough that Audrey could slip in a tiny prybar and get at the component. "Why this part?"

"Just a little more..." something clicked. "There." She held up a bit of circuitry. "Because *this* is Charlie—the POD-mind, not the POD itself. I'd never leave without him. As a matter of fact...I should probably bring some audio interface so we can hear each other."

Ernest stared at the chip, and then at the pocket Audrey slid it into while she rooted around in the light of the tiny LED for some audio parts. His eyes stung fiercely, but Audrey was too busy scavenging to notice he'd gone quiet.

So quiet that the screech and crackle startled them both.

"It's the railroad," Audrey said. She grabbed Ernest by his dominant arm and dragged him toward the tracks. "Abraham's powered it up! Let's go!"

ⁱⁱⁱCHAPTER TWENTY-FOURⁱⁱⁱ

As soon as Ernest pushed into the clearing, Will scooped him up and whirled him around. "This is it! This is the start of our new life!"

"It won't be," Abraham said, "if you don't quit patting yourself on the back and get to work."

Bizarre idiom. At least, Ernest thought it was an idiom, though he did sneak a glance at Will's back once Will set him down. Thankfully, there was nothing smoldering on it.

Like every other part of the railroad except the rails themselves, the "car" in which they were to travel had begun its existence as something else entirely—a dumpster. Behind it, another linked "car" hovered over the tracks, a lightweight fiberglass platform with some bundles of tools and POD components strapped to the top.

Abraham had mounted the dumpster on its side. The hinge was at the top, and the lid would hang shut unless someone pushed or pulled on it. Currently, a metal bar propped the lid open wide enough that the travelers could squeeze into the compartment along with the boxes of protein bars, the spare water, whatever scavenged electronics were deemed important enough to add to the payload....

And Martha.

Someone had wrapped her body in the silvery blanket and

secured it with cables at waist, neck and knees. She lay atop a row of crates, and both she and the crates were secured with cording threaded through holes that had been punched into the fiberglass sides of the bin. Ernest supposed the other alternative was to strap her in with the gear in the second car—and he also supposed that alternative seemed even sadder.

A single LED affixed to the ceiling lit the compartment, throwing harsh shadows that shifted and jumped as the car filled with people. Audrey slung her bag of tools into the dumpster and then turned to give Elizabeth a hand up. "Isn't this weird? I've never traveled inside anything bigger than a POD. All these right angles are making my head spin."

Elizabeth shrank back into the farthest corner of the car and looked for somewhere to strap herself in. "We can ping each other without a com link and a display while we do it. That's even weirder."

"I had Ernest in my POD with me the other day. But he bloodened all over."

"I think you mean bloodied," Elizabeth said.

"Oh. Even better." Audrey pulled a laser from her bag and cut a small oval through the side of the bin, then poked out the piece and set her eye to the hole. "Still dark."

Will ducked in, all rangy limbs. He disconnected the door-opener and held the dumpster lid ajar with his shoulder. The hum of the multiple propulsion units working as one grew louder, some dropping low and others high, until they sounded like a wail, and as the pitch shifted some more, a harmony. A song.

Last in was Abraham. He clasped forearms with Will—both of them used their dominant arms since both of them still had shunts, of course—and let Will haul him into the car. By his wide-eyed, fierce expression, Ernest deduced that Abraham was excited, though not quite as jubilant as everyone else. If Martha were there to share the moment with him, undoubtedly it would have been different. He held a string in one hand, which he handed to Will. "You wrangled most of the components," he said. "You do the honors."

Abraham was about to let go of Will, who not only kept hold

of his forearm, but dragged him into a brief embrace. Abraham shoved him away with an over-emoted brusqueness, and said, "Just flip the switch."

Will tugged the cord, and railroad started to move.

Elizabeth and Audrey cheered, "Hurrah," and Ernest joined in too, like he'd seen members of crowds do on old-time feeds. Kinesthesia told him he was moving, but it felt nothing like gliding along the city's grid with L0U15E. The railroad seemed to vibrate, with energy, yes, there was energy, because everyone's hair had started to float into the air, crackling with static charge. Except for Will's, which looked like it usually did.

Ernest pulled a short length of insulated wire from a scavenged bundle and tied his hair back. Elizabeth laughed at the pink cloud Audrey's hair had become, and Audrey patted it and began to laugh too.

She darted over to the hole she'd cut in the fiberglass with her hair billowing around her. "It's radical—come see," she called over the wail of the propulsion. "It's like a little viscreen that blows air at your eyeball."

Elizabeth shook her head, still laughing, and pressed her back firmly against the wall. "I'm not going anywhere until we stop."

Ernest slipped past Audrey and pressed his eye to the hole. She was right—the air was startling, as was the rush of tangled undergrowth the railroad brushed past as it moaned its way through the forest on the pair of metal tracks. Ernest drew back from the hole. The sight of the foliage passing made him queasy.

Then the railroad car shuddered and lurched, and he grew queasier still.

"That relay's going to be a problem," Abraham said. He pulled the nanite interface out of Audrey's toolkit and pressed on the dumpster lid as if to open it.

Will grabbed him by the shunt arm. "What are you doing?"

"I need to tweak the—"

"We're moving."

"Oh, really?" Sarcasm. Abraham did it so well. He snatched his arm from Will and said, "We're traveling less than ten kilometers an hour. It's not like I'll be seriously injured if I fall out."

The railroad shuddered again, more violently now, and Elizabeth's arms shot out to steady her against the back and side wall.

"Let him do it," Ernest said. Strange, how much his voice sounded like Abraham's when he raised it to be heard over the sound of the meshed propulsions. "Otherwise the shaking will keep getting worse."

"Which string do I alter?" Abraham asked him.

"You need to look at them and see which type is overcompensating."

"And how do I determine that?"

"Instead of 01011010111, they'll read 010110101...."

The railroad car bucked, followed by an aftershock as the supply car rocked, and then the propulsion noise turned into a loud keening. "Do you seriously think I read binary?" Abraham indicated the area where the units were mounted with a floor-ward sweep of his hand. "You need to tweak it. By the time I call out all the digits to you to figure out what's what, the loop will destabilize."

"Ernest isn't going to...." Will looked at Ernest, baffled. "Are you?"

Ernest cut his eyes to the edge the floor where the dumpster lid flapped open a few centimeters when the relays slipped. The ground rushing by made a chewed and mostly-dissolved protein bar creep back up his esophagus. "We either need to fix it now while we're moving," he said, "or stop and do it after sunrise, once the panels recharge. But stopping and starting in the dark won't work. It will consume too much charge."

Will looked as if he was all for stopping anyhow, but Abraham said, "We can't abort this close to camp. A sharp-eyed Storm Trooper will be able to see us without even using a sensor."

"You don't know they're coming tonight," Will argued.

"You don't know they're not."

"I'll do it," Ernest said, before he could dwell on the thought of the sickening way the individual leaves and grasses seemed to blur and blend as they swept by—or as the railroad swept by them. "Give me the interface."

He flattened himself face-down on the floor, with the gap

in the dumpster lid feeding puffs of air down the neck of his shirt. "We're not going any faster now than anyone could run," Abraham said, handing him the patched-together interface. "You'll be fine."

Ernest glanced down at the grass rushing past and couldn't come up with an answer to that. Will grabbed him by the thighs. His fingers dug in deep. "I've got you."

Abraham said, "The main thing is to do it before the screen goes dead. There's not much charge in it."

If it were an old-time feed, the man who was about to do something risky to save the group would have had something memorable to say—something rakish, something jaunty. But Ernest only said, "I'll be quick. I type fast."

In general, magnetic propulsion provided a very smooth ride, and this was true even of the railroad—except when the relays slipped out of synch, and the firing of two propulsion units overlapped where only one was needed, or another shut down before its replacement could kick in. The railroad alternately lagged and lurched, with irregularly-spaced moments of eerily calm gliding between the lurches. It was during one such lurch that Ernest tried to connect the interface to the nanite port and nearly dropped the device. He was positive Abraham had seen him fumble, since Abraham was the one wedging open the door-flap open with his shoulder. Despite his clear view of Ernest's back, Abraham said nothing, and when Will's fingers dug in hard enough to bruise his thigh, Ernest chose to say nothing as well. It was with a certain grim satisfaction that, despite the lurching and lagging, and despite the grass rushing by his head and even catching the strands of hair that had come loose from the bit of insulated wire, Ernest aligned the interface to the port and rammed it home.

The cracked viscreen flashed, went dark, paused...then read: HELLO.

Ernest scrolled through the commands and tweaked a few that would add a bit of efficiency to the relays as the code flashed past. He snuck a look up at Abraham to see if he'd be warned not to try anything fancy, but the way Abraham had himself braced to keep the flap from whacking Ernest every time the car lurched, he couldn't even see outside the car. Ernest was surprised he was being allowed to perform an unsupervised modification. Surprised and pleased.

A few more tweaks, and then the string of binary he'd been searching for scrolled onto the screen. He even double-checked it—something he seldom did, as a speed-reader, but it was too critical of a juncture in which to risk an error, and he began to overwrite it with a few deft twitches of his....

"Hey!"

A figure in white was running alongside the railroad. Ernest flinched back and felt Will's fingers drill into the muscle of his thighs. Security op gear, but dirty. And the figure wasn't shorn-haired, he was bald.

Benjamin.

"You. Stop."

Ernest didn't see a Taser or a syringe, but he knew better now than to underestimate a Storm Trooper; he'd seen what they'd done to Martha with nothing but their bare hands. He hurriedly keyed in the rest of the sequence.

"Did you hear?" Benjamin panted. "I said stop."

"I heard you," Ernest muttered, and unplugged the interface.

"You. Take me. Do you hear? Take me?"

"Oh, so now you want to come along? After you led your friends right to us?"

"Not friends."

Ernest slipped the interface inside, where Audrey took it from him. One of Will's hands disengaged from his thigh, leaving five bright points of pressure-induced pain behind, and grabbed him by the clearcoated forearm. White pain-motes danced around the perimeter of Ernest's vision, then cleared.

"Reclaim," Benjamin gasped. He could indeed run as fast as the railroad, but only with great effort. "Deacon wants me in Reclaim."

"Are you talking to someone?" Abraham crouched beside Ernest, balanced precariously in the car, and pushed open the dumpster lid as far as he could. "Who is that?"

Never mind, Ernest was about to say. He's tiring. We'll lose him quickly enough. And yet the look on Benjamin's face: pain, sorrow, regret—he might not have the words to express them. But there they were.

Whether Abraham would choose to acknowledge those emotions was another matter. Especially after what the ops did to Martha. "Is that the one who led them to our grid?" Abraham asked.

His name is Benjamin, Ernest thought. But it might not be wise to say so. It wouldn't take much for Abraham to decide he'd been right all along, and Ernest really was in league with the Deacons. And a few well-placed kicks from Abraham would be all it took to demonstrate precisely how foolhardy it was to perform a repair hanging out of a moving railroad car to begin with.

"Stop! Take me!" Benjamin's cries grew more desperate and ragged as the running began to take its toll. Ernest felt something—there'd be no asking LOU15E to help him pinpoint the emotion—a subtle variation of sadness, though. Sad for Benjamin, even though he wanted to be angry.

Benjamin dropped back a few steps, and his breathing came in deep gasps. Soon he would no longer be able to run, and the railroad would leave him behind. "Take me," he demanded, in the way that security ops always demanded, never requested. But his face spoke so much more eloquently than that. Just as plainly as if they'd been part of the carefully-labeled autism facial grid, his eyes spoke. They told Ernest he was afraid of the Deacons, afraid of Reclaim, and probably afraid of all the other security ops as well—and if he knew then that everything the Deacons said was a cleverly designed lie to sustain the systems they'd built, he never would have gone to them with his information in the first place. What his look said to Ernest was....

"Sorry." Ernest had blurted it out—with Abraham right beside him. He added, "We can't trust you."

Benjamin's vocabulary recall was rudimentary, but he wasn't stupid. He seized the word and made it his own. "I'm sorry," he said. It sounded almost like an accusation. He tried again—screwed up his face and bellowed, "I'm sorry!"

Will caught hold of Ernest's shirt at the shoulder, bunched the fabric in his fist, and hauled on it. Ernest was dragged back in, and Abraham pulled down the flap. Will's fingers dug into Ernest's dominant arm now, so hard it hurt as much as the surgical site.

"I'm sorry!" The cry carried through the fiberglass, only somewhat muted, and the sound of it made Ernest feel sorry, too.

He will die if we leave him. Maybe that argument would have gotten him somewhere with Abraham when Martha was still alive—but not now. Still, he needed to do something. "He knows about the tracks," he said.

Everyone looked at him, and he could see they knew it was so, even if they hadn't yet extrapolated exactly *what* he meant by it.

"If we leave him here," he went on—carefully, because if he sounded too sympathetic, he was sure he'd be labeled as a Deaconist agent, "he'll be close enough to go back and tell the others."

Abraham and Will locked gazes. Will had never let go of Ernest's dominant arm, and his fingers were digging in as hard as they had to prevent Ernest from falling out of the moving car. Ernest wanted to squeeze him back, to beg him through that touch to do the right thing—to even understand what the right thing was, without it being explained. But if he did so in front of Abraham, his credibility would vanish. And so he said nothing, did nothing, and waited.

"If we leave him behind," Abraham said evenly, "he'll tell the others about the tracks. But if we bring him along, he might sneak back and betray us again, or he might not. The only way to be absolutely sure he doesn't is to kill him."

"That's true," Will said, and Ernest felt so dismayed he could hardly restrain himself from grabbing Will in front of everyone and shaking him—whether that exposed Ernest's sympathies or not. Then Will said, "But I can't do it."

I'm sorry! filtered in through the flap, accompanied by a few thumps that vibrated the dumpster lid as Benjamin slapped it in his desperation.

Abraham glanced at the place the slaps were sounding from. "Neither can I," he said. "But we can't leave him here."

He pushed the lid open and called out to Benjamin over the whine of the engine, "We're not slowing down for you. If you want to come along, hop in back with the supplies."

ıııCHAPTER TWENTY-FIVEıııı

THEY DIDN'T FEEL THE impact of Benjamin jumping aboard so much as the additional drag his weight added to the supply car. Ernest glanced at Martha's body in its silver shroud. He was glad it was here with him, and not in back with Benjamin, where it might have been pitched it off the railroad to lighten the payload. He felt sorry for the retired op, but that didn't mean he expected Benjamin to suddenly develop a sense of decency. Not when it had been trained out of him for the past twenty years.

Ernest fit himself against the wall of the dumpster and drew his legs up to his chest. He flinched when Elizabeth touched him on the shoulder, startling him. "That was brave, what you did. I could never have..." she looked at the far wall—the wall that was once a lid, which still flapped slightly when a breeze rocked the railroad car—and she shuddered. "If I was the one who had to fix it, we would have waited until morning and done it standing still."

"It needed to be done."

"Not that I'm surprised, after the way you handled yourself at Reclaim." She laughed. It sounded edgy, and maybe a bit forced, but still genuine. "I will never forget the first time I saw you, covered in dust and blood, hollering at those big testosterone-filled security ops twice your size."

Ernest drew his knees up tighter and pressed his forehead against them. He hadn't really thought much about what he'd done in Reclaim. The experience had been a lot like hanging out of the moving railroad car—there'd been no other choice. And while normally he would have felt like a hero having her say something like that, at the moment he was more worried that Abraham might overhear and twist it into something else. That he'd think Ernest had put her up to it, perhaps, all to hide his supposed allegiance to the Diaconate.

He felt a welcome weight press against his opposite side as Will settled in for the ride and slid an arm around his shoulders. Ernest's programming was successful. The nanites stayed in synch and the railroad glided smoothly, save for the occasional stutter, which Audrey determined, after consulting with the peephole she'd cut, was the result of debris on the tracks interrupting the propulsion.

Ernest expected Abraham to verify that for himself, but Abraham said nothing. In fact, he didn't even move. While Ernest had been avoiding his eyes the whole trip, he'd fallen asleep wedged between a crate and Martha's body.

Will rested his head on Ernest's shoulder. His hair tickled. Ernest smoothed it down and it sprang back up again. He whispered to Will, "I think we did the right thing, bringing Benjamin."

Will answered by giving his knee a squeeze.

Ernest wondered if he'd explained well enough. After all, he hadn't had someone to talk to his whole life like Will had, a real person and not an AI with a limited number of pre-programmed responses. "Even when I told Benjamin to go away, I just said it because I was afraid of what Abraham would think—"

Will took Ernest by the jaw, turned his head, and silenced him with a kiss. Will tasted like static, like air filled with ozone after an electrical storm. He lingered over Ernest's mouth, tasting one lip, then the other, and drew back only after everything felt tender and tingly.

Will pressed his forehead to Ernest's and whispered, "I know. It was written all over your face."

Ernest sighed and resettled himself against Will, and even

though he would have thought it impossible with the swaying of the railroad car as it was rocked by the wind, and the sight of the grass rushing by whenever the lid flapped open, he slept.

○ ◎ ○

"Wake up! Wake up! You need to come look!"

Ernest's muscles were stiff all over, and his neck joints felt as if they needed lubrication. His eyes were gummy with byproducts his nanite mytes would have disposed of, if he had a shunt. Although Will was knuckling his eyes as well, and he still had his shunt. Something to shunt into, then.

Audrey tugged one of Ernest's tattered sleeves. Her hair was no longer floating with static. "We're so far into the forest that we can't see the city anymore."

Also, they were no longer moving. Ernest was grateful for that.

He crawled from the railroad car. The forest was filled with sound, louder things like bird and insect song, and subtler sounds like the rustle of breeze through leaves. Elizabeth was seated on a tree that had fallen. Unfortunately, that tree had landed horizontally across the railroad tracks.

"Eat," Abraham said, and Ernest flinched because he hadn't heard Abraham's approach. "Then help me spread out the solar panels in the spots where the most sun is coming through. We'll have the big lugs get to work clearing the tracks."

Once Abraham was out of range, Will slipped an arm around Ernest's shoulders and said, "I suppose I'm dreaming if I try to imagine the two of you getting along."

"He doesn't trust me."

"You can't earn someone's trust overnight. And like you said, he hasn't known you as long as I have." Will handed Ernest a protein bar. "Do you want me to chew it for you?"

"I can do it."

"Okay. Be careful not to bite your tongue."

That idea made Ernest's stomach lurch as if he was watching the ground rush by from the moving railroad car. It was a hideous thing, this eating, but it was a task that needed to be done if he wished to survive. Raised voices carried from the front of the railroad car as the other retirees struggled with their breakfasts as well. Benjamin was convinced they should be able to dissolve the bar in water and force it into his shunt, and Elizabeth told him the compositions were too different—and to stop being a wuss and just eat it.

Will, who'd been trained to cater to other people's psyches rather than their bodies (like Elizabeth), made a game of eating to mitigate the unpleasantness. *A bite for me, a bite for you. Let's see who can chew it up first.* Of course, he was more efficient, but his smile was enough to distract Ernest into forcing the protein down his own throat.

Once the deplorable task of eating was followed by the not-quite-as-unpleasant ritual of drinking, Ernest dutifully reported to Abraham to help with the solar panels. Abraham climbed atop the sideways dumpster and began detaching the panels so Ernest could place them in sunlight. Ernest stood beside the dumpster, held his arms up to take the first panel from Abraham, and gave it a small tug when Abraham didn't immediately release it.

Ernest was puzzled. He tugged again. Only when he sought Abraham's eyes did the other C754 release the panel. "What's wrong with you?" Abraham said, once he had Ernest's attention.

"Nothing that I know of, without a diagnostic. My arm is healing—"

Abraham shoved another panel toward Ernest, who needed to juggle the first panel to the ground to avoid dropping it. Abraham said, "Not physically. Why are you avoiding me? I probably offended you somehow."

A flurry of emotions roiled around inside Ernest. Anxiety, fear, and probably every shade of meaning in between. "No. You didn't."

"The woman I love is dead. So pardon me if my disposition's not all sunshine and smiles."

"Okay."

Abraham flung another panel from the top of the dumpster. "Maybe I haven't thrown you a big 'welcome' party, but I do think it's good you're here. You would add value to the group even if you weren't able to program nanites...I think you make Will happy. And maybe you did let the shunt suck some life out of you, but that empty-headed Matthew he was romancing let it drain him completely dry—and then he marched right up to the Diaconate and turned in his own POD."

Ernest thought about the bent, withered retiree who'd changed his mind at the last moment and fled to the coffee shop—and led the security ops there, too. Even if Ernest hadn't been convinced to stop shunting in—and he almost hadn't—he never would never have led the ops back to Will. He'd watched enough old-time feeds to know better. "Is empty-headed an idiom?"

"Obviously. It means stupid." Abraham climbed down and brushed his hands off on the legs of his trousers, then considered Ernest with a hard, analytical gaze. "What's most unsettling is that you're a C754, though I suppose that's not really your fault."

"Why is that a problem?" Ernest knew what made him uneasy about interacting with a clone from the same vat—that he found himself continually comparing everything Abraham said and did with what he would have done, how he would look, what he would say. Or not. But he understood that identical genetic makeup didn't make their hopes, fears and dreams the same.

Abraham scowled. "It's the idea that despite your IQ, in thirty years you never once questioned the Diaconate—not until Will had his hands down your pants. I look at you, and I see how easily it could've been me instead—and that thought terrifies me."

Ernest made himself scarce once the solar panels were set out. It sounded as if the group working on clearing the tracks was having nowhere near as serious and disturbing a conversation as he'd just had, and he was eager for something to distract him from trying to analyze and re-analyze the pained look on Abraham's face.

"If you let me do the cutting," Elizabeth was saying, "then you can work on putting that AI back together."

Audrey said, "His *name* is Charlie—and this is my best laser, so be careful."

"I'm trained to use lasers on people. I think I can manage cutting into a tree."

Ernest rounded the dense underbrush and saw that the tree lying across the tracks now had a large divot carved out of it. Elizabeth ran Audrey's handheld laser over a section and a wisp of smoke curled from the incision. Then Will jammed a prybar into the cut and began peeling away a section of the tree. Meanwhile, Elizabeth moved to the opposite track and repeated the procedure with Benjamin.

Freed from manual labor, Audrey moved a few meters from the track. She straddled the broad trunk and began tinkering with a bundle of components bristling with wires, held together with a bit of twine fashioned from twisted protein bar wrappers.

Ernest approached her. "That's Charlie?"

"Sure is. He's just taking a little nap. I still need to adapt the charger to these cells. And the sensor pad's offline, so it's probably for the best that he's powered down. I don't want him to wake up blind and deaf."

Ernest imagined coming out of slumber without eyes or ears. It would be a lot like waking up without a shunt. Only worse.

"You look a little pale," Audrey said. "Did you get enough to eat?"

"I miss having an AI to...consult with."

Audrey stopped twisting wires together, cocked her head, and gave Ernest a searching look. "You understand me better than those guys do. A lot better. They think everything that's not flesh and blood is totally inanimate. But how are organs and cells so different from components and nanites?"

Ernest shook his head.

She said, "If they'd ever modded their AIs like we did, maybe they would get it."

Ernest watched her fingers play over the dozens of filament-thin wires, locate a matching pair, and twist them together. He was relieved Audrey didn't mention that he hadn't modified L0U15E nearly enough—since she'd betrayed him to the Diaconate more readily than Benjamin had, without a trace of regret. And what had her reward been? Reclaim. At least the Deacons had offered Benjamin his youth.

"Even so," Audrey whispered, "everyone else isn't accustomed to gathering all their data with their own sensory input." She pointed to her eye for emphasis. "They want a computer, even one that's off the W3. So I can get away with putting Charlie back together instead of hauling water. Which they'd probably have you doing right now if there happened to be any water nearby."

Ernest glanced over at the group cutting through the tree. "If there's no water nearby, why are they all wet?"

"Perspiration. Sweat."

Ernest had never known perspiration to form droplets. "Are they ill?"

"No—they're in biological overdrive. I know, it weirded me the first time I saw it drip like that, too. But Will says it's good for you. Old time people used to sweat on purpose to build up their muscles."

Ernest watched his companions work. Mostly he watched Will, who had removed his shirt and was laboring at shredding a hole through the tree trunk. Sweat gleamed on the hard curve of his shoulder, and trickled down the gentle valley between his pectoral muscles. Seeing Will in the context of the forest rather than the coffee shop made him seem primal and wild, and that idea brought back the initial thrill of realizing that Will was a *homo sapien*—even though it turned out they possibly all were, though Ernest wasn't entirely convinced—and with that, the memory of Will's tongue sliding into his mouth for the first time.

Ernest felt a flutter of arousal and excused himself from Audrey, not that she really noticed him leaving, to go sit by himself—within view of Will. Need was a strange thing. Ernest had always felt hunger in his arm, but now that he had no shunt, it seemed his stomach had something to do with the sensation. And the need for companionship had never stirred his groin. Maybe organs and cells *were* just biological equivalents to components and nanites, but their workings seemed infinitely more complex.

Hacking through the tree was a lengthy process. Ernest assisted Abraham in the reinstallation of the solar cells once they were charged, but thankfully, Abraham had no more disturbing thoughts to share. None that he opted to voice, at any rate.

"Someone scout ahead a kilometer or two before we go again," Benjamin said once they were nearly through the trunk. "It is more efficient to know before we power up if something else is blocking the tracks."

"And I suppose you would like to be that scout," Abraham suggested. "Maybe with Audrey to accompany you." Someone small...with an easily snapped neck. Abraham didn't say as much, not with words, but his expression conveyed plenty. Or maybe Ernest was getting better at reading the cant of an eyebrow, the subtle twist of a mouth.

Benjamin wiped sweat from his brow and answered as if he hadn't noticed the implication. And maybe he hadn't. "Not me. I need to rest."

"I'll go," Will said. He hauled Ernest up by his dominant arm. "We'll both go. In case there's any debris we need to move."

They set off along the side of the tracks, jogged along a few hundred yards until they rounded a curve, and were completely enveloped by undergrowth and tree canopy. The tracks continued, unobstructed save for grass, which didn't seem to interfere with the magnetic propulsion like trees and branches did. Another gentle curve, and it felt like the others were as far away as the city. "Why did Abraham roll his eyes?" Ernest asked, tugging Will's arm to slow him down.

Will pulled Ernest against his side and bumped their hips together as they ran. "Because he knows me too well."

That explained absolutely nothing...though at least it reassured Ernest it hadn't been some slight against him, maybe a suggestion that he was too weak to move a tree limb. He pulled Will's arm again. "How long do you plan to run? I'm not accustomed to—"

Will stopped suddenly and spun Ernest into a kiss. His lips were salty and his probing tongue was hot and slick, and the stirring Ernest had noticed earlier deepened into a full-on surge.

"There's no way I'll be able to run now."

Will grabbed him by the shoulders and backed him against a tree. A cloud of small brown birds erupted from the branches in a flurry of startled chirping. Will pressed his mouth to Ernest's jaw and said, "Do you know how distracting it was to see you looking at me like that?"

"Like what?"

"Like you couldn't wait to do this." Will grabbed the hand of Ernest's uninjured arm and shoved it between his thighs so it cupped his whole groin.

Ernest wasn't sure that had been the actual intention his look was conveying. And yet the press, even through trousers, of Will's big cock shifting made Ernest yield to his superior knowledge of the subtle nuance of facial expressions.

ııı CHAPTER TWENTY-SIX ıı

ERNEST'S SHIRT SNAGGED ON the rough bark of the tree, and the fit of the garment changed as a hole opened at his shoulder blade. The sleeves were gone and the hem was tattered. Will's clothes were looking just as frayed.

PODless travel was rough on fabric.

Ernest followed a run in the material of Will's T-shirt with his fingertip. Will caught his hand, and slipped the finger into his mouth.

Teeth, tongue, shocking wet heat...Ernest almost jerked back, but he caught himself just in time and forced himself not to. Will smiled and bared his teeth around Ernest's finger, then flicked his tongue across the rounded curve of the pad. Then he flipped Ernest's hand back and pressed his mouth into the palm, and when he spoke, the words sent a shiver straight up Ernest's arm and right down his spine. "How's that feel? Dirty?"

"Yes." Ernest could hardly find his voice. It came out as little more than a breath.

Will let go of his wrist and began unfastening his trousers with urgent tugs at the waistband. Ernest found himself mirroring Will's actions, scrabbling to expose more to touch. "You let me feel...your teeth."

"I'd let you feel anything you wanted." Ernest's trousers dropped to his knees. His cock jutted at Will, and they hadn't even started working it yet. His bandaged arm was still clumsy, and Will slipped a hand beneath Ernest's and finished undoing the waistband himself. His cock was hard too. He flexed his knees to line them both up and stroke them together in one hand while Ernest watched, fascinated.

"We have to hurry," Will said. "Otherwise they'll think we're always slacking off whenever we're alone."

"I'd say we're the opposite of slack."

Will laughed, but his breath caught as his hand stroked their cocks, hard and fast.

Ernest pressed his forehead to Will's, but kept his eyes on the sight of their ruddy cockheads jutting and sinking in Will's grasp. "It's really hard."

"I know. Isn't it great? Good riddance to that shunt. You never would've ogled me like that if your shunt was still sucking the life out of you."

The perfectly wonderful hardness flagged for a moment and Ernest caught sight of his mottled arm beneath the clearcoat. "But it looks so hideous—"

Will shut him up with a harsh kiss that made their teeth clatter together. Ernest tasted copper where his lip had been nicked. The shock was enough to make him forget all about his freakish, shuntless arm.

Then Will started stroking their cocks even harder. The speed and pressure were dizzying, and Ernest felt his arousal not only return, but spike.

Will's tongue trailed over his cheek and danced at his earlobe. It darted into his ear—mostly, though the tiny audio interface gave a faint chirp of feedback when Will licked it. Undeterred, Will ran his tongue down Ernest's neck, which elicited multiple courses of shivers, then shifted his grip so he could keep stroking himself while he knelt and took Ernest's cock into his mouth.

Dirty. The thought of it spiked Ernest's arousal higher still, while the feel, the glorious, slippery, wet feel of teeth and tongue and hot sucking mouth wrenched a startled cry from him. He clutched at the rough bark and pressed his shoulders into the tree hard as he struggled to keep still, when all he wanted to do was scream and flail.

And then he felt the give, as that internal switch flipped and the moment of heady release surged through him, followed fast by a helpless pulsing, and soon, a wash of dizzying languor.

Will stood. He cupped Ernest's genitals while he gave his own a few more fast strokes, and shot his come on Ernest's saliva-slicked cock. He stroked the newly slippery flesh, and Ernest grit his teeth and dug his fingers into the tree at the startling sensitivity—but Will stopped stroking before Ernest could determine whether he would have been able to tolerate the touches long enough to orgasm again.

Will kissed Ernest. His lips were sticky, and salty-sweet. He nuzzled his forehead into Ernest's hair, shuddered, and kept him pinned to the tree, thigh to thigh and chest to chest, while they caught their breath.

"You went soft for a second, there," he said casually. "What was it, did I do something that didn't feel good? You can tell me, you know. I won't be offended—I'll just try harder next time."

"You? I like everything you do. Look at how fast I, um...."

"Came."

"Yes."

"You sure?" Will said "Remember, I'm fluent in body language." What a bizarre idiom, body language. Ernest loved it. "You need to tell me if the way I'm touching you, or stroking you, or kissing you, doesn't trip your trigger. Because next time I rock your world, I want to make you howl."

Ernest had no doubt he could, if he'd set his mind to it. In fact, he wasn't even sure what Will was getting at. "I was hard before you even touched me. Just from watching you move."

"Yeah?" Will butted his crotch against Ernest's and gave it a playful grind. "Go on."

"I associate you with the things you've done to me, and now even the sight of you makes me, I don't know the word."

"Hot."

"No, that's not it. I mean it makes me want to play at porn. And hungry. But not in my arm."

"Yep, that's it. Idiom."

Ernest tried the word. "Hot." He supposed it was no stranger than *dirty*. "You know the best sayings." He stared into Will's eyes, the color of dusty grass with a corona of gold around the pupil, and ran a thumb over his lean jaw, and wondered how it had ever seemed that his shunt needed tweaking because it was clearly malnourishing him...but then Ernest glimpsed his own mottled forearm and cringed.

Will's gaze followed. "It's that. Isn't it? That's what you were talking about when you started to droop. You weren't just pointing it out 'cause you were looking for compliments."

Ernest tucked his arm behind him. "Why would I point it out? It's disgusting."

"Don't ever say that. You're beautiful. Everything about you. Even that arm. Especially that arm. You ripped your shunt loose digging your way out of the Diaconate with that arm, and you came back to me." He grabbed Ernest's wrist with startling ease—he had a longer reach, and he was stronger, and uninjured as well—and he clasped the arm to his chest, mottled clearcoat and all. He pressed his lips to Ernest's knuckles and said, "I love this arm." Will captured his gaze and gave him a meaningful look (although the exact meaning might have felt elusive), then he gently pressed his lips to the gruesome clearcoat bandage, and kissed it. "I love you."

Ernest turned the phrase around in his head. How profound in its simplicity.

"And I really wish we were still on-grid so I could play back the look you've got on your face right now. People say 'I love you' all the time in contraband feeds—it even has its own euphemism, *those three little words*." Will released Ernest's arm and kissed him on the forehead. "But we can't just stand around and analyze it to death. We really do need to finish scouting and get back to camp."

The railroad was packed and ready to be powered up by the time they returned, walking more slowly the last half-kilometer to bring their breathing and heart rates down to normal. "Get in," Abraham told Benjamin, nodding toward the main car. Benjamin did as he was told. Ernest supposed that sort of obedience had been drilled into him.

Everyone took position. Abraham started the engine, and

the railroad began to move.

They took turns watching for obstructions through the hole Audrey had cut until it became too dark to see, and then Abraham slowed the railroad's pace dramatically so the impact wouldn't be too jarring if they did encounter another fallen tree.

The slow coast felt more natural, more like POD travel, and Ernest curled up against Will and, though he wished he was properly vertical and shunted, managed to doze.

"I wonder how far the tracks go," Audrey said dreamily.

Ernest's eyelids fluttered open. The gently gliding car was quiet, save for the hypnotic drone of the propulsion and the occasional creak of the sideways lid.

Audrey stood at the hole with her face pressed against the side of the bin. Both of her hands were splayed palm-out next to her ears, and her hair floated in a fuchsia halo. "Why do you suppose old-time people wanted to travel into the woods, anyway? Were they looking for metal? Or minerals? Or...what?"

Ernest raised his head and Will rolled out from under it and shifted onto his side. He was accustomed to sleeping any which way, and was usually contorted in some bizarre position when Ernest woke up and found him. "What makes you think they were looking for something?" Ernest asked softly.

"Isn't that what everything was all about back then? Locating resources and consuming them as quickly as possible?"

Was it? Ernest supposed he had been taught as much, but with those "three little words" edited out of the version he'd known all these years, how much of his knowledge had actually been based in fact? "Hypothesize that they weren't looking for something to consume. What other reason would anyone want to travel into the woods?"

Audrey turned and grinned at Ernest. "What an odd game. Okay, let me think...maybe they wanted to see trees."

"Or animals."

"Or animals," she repeated. "Or maybe they wanted to get out of those creepy right-angle houses they lived in."

"Or maybe they'd been doing their jobs for so long they just wanted to do something...different."

"Like that feed you memorized."

"Camping. Yes."

"Now what was the whole purpose of camping?"

"It was a sort of self-initiated challenge, to walk through the woods and eat things without getting poisoned."

"Totally blasphemous," Audrey giggled. "I'll have to watch that feed myself." She pulled the laser from her gear belt and cut a small, round hole beside the one she was peering through, but several centimeters higher, and poked out the fiberglass circle with her fingertip. "Come watch the tracks with me—sometimes you can see a little bit by the moonlight." She patted the wall beneath the higher circle. "It's good to talk to you. I miss Charlie."

"I miss Louise." And though it saddened Ernest to admit it, he said, "And you're much better at conversation than she ever could have been."

"Thanks. But if we'd met sooner, I could've showed you how to unlock her safeguards. Add in a little randomness routine, and it would've been a pretty good approximation."

"I'm coming to realize...and accept...that Louise was actually quite limited."

"I dunno, I think you hacked together a pretty cool combo of mods, especially since you were more of a data specialist than a software coder."

The railroad was moving slowly enough that the air current at the hole did nothing more alarming than make Ernest's eye feel dry, which was resolved by a few extra blinks. After a long stretch of watching tracks skim by in the moonlight, Audrey said, "Maybe we can play with some programming after I figure out a way to pull another audio interface together. I'll bet you'd make a great mod."

"I guess we could try." Not that Ernest saw much point in it, not without L0U15E, but he supposed any skill that made him more useful to the group might be advantageous to learn.

The train coasted through a web of thin, brittle branches like bony fingers that scratched along the length of the bin, but didn't slow its progress. "We're already past the section Will and I cleared," Ernest said. He blinked away dryness and pressed his eye to the hole. "This is totally unfamiliar."

"It looks blue. I suppose it's not really blue. Maybe it's a trick of the light."

Ernest blinked hard and tried to discern what the colors would look like in daylight. Down the tracks, where they seemed to get smaller and closer together but never actually did, the blue tint was even more pronounced.

"Do you think my hair would look good that color?" Audrey wondered.

"How can you mod your hair without anything to shunt into?"

"I'm sure I could figure out some—"

She'd stopped speaking so she could press her eye hard against the hole. Ernest did the same, and found the bluish light was even brighter now, and in that bright blue moonlight, he could see. The screen of trees on either side of the tracks diminished, and a wide open space spread before them. Jutting from the vast landscape was a series of crumbling right angles.

And the railroad was heading right for it.

ⅠⅠⅠCHAPTER TWENTY-SEVENⅠⅠⅠ

"WE CAN'T STOP HERE," Elizabeth said. "The air doesn't smell healthy."

Although she was the closest thing they had to a health monitor, everyone was too apprehensive, excited or just plain baffled to listen. They jostled one another to look out the holes in the front of the car and see for themselves. Ernest did hear her—and he was concerned—but he was too stunned to make sense of what they'd found.

"Wonderful," Abraham said. "We've been traveling in a circle."

Will countered, "I think we would have noticed if we were going in a circle."

"Obviously. I mean a large circle—an arc so wide we couldn't perceive the curvature."

Audrey said, "What reason would old-time people have to lay out these metal tracks and travel in a really big circle just to get to the other end of the city? Especially if they could go straight through? That doesn't make any sense."

"Maybe it was a game," Elizabeth suggested. "Like camping."

Ernest wouldn't put it past *homo sapiens* to think of truly bizarre ways to squander their resources, and could extrapolate how distance might impair their perceptions, but he was fairly certain the route they had been following was made of large runs of straight track and a few gentle S-curves. Not a circle. He stepped back from the hole in the fiberglass and pushed open the side of the railroad car so Will could see.

"The air..." Elizabeth warned them.

"It smells better outside," Audrey said, "not worse. Besides, it wasn't as if the railroad was airtight. We'd all be suffocated by now."

"It's not the air," Abraham said. His voice was bleak. "It's Martha. She's decomposing."

"We can't just leave her that way," Will said. "We're too far away for the ops to follow. We have to demagnetize her, now." He turned to Abraham. "You said you found a way, right?"

"Hold on." Audrey fumbled a mass of circuitry and wires from her tool belt. "Charlie was in on that whole demagnetization plan. Let's let him speak for himself." She stroked a thin filament free from a bundle of wires and coaxed it into a slot so small Ernest couldn't see it until the wire disappeared inside. "Okay, babe. You're on."

A tinny voice crackled from a speaker that was bound to the circuitry with strips of torn fabric. "Silence is golden—I know you're wild about idioms, Aud, but I'll have to disagree with that one. It's good to be back. So...why'd we stop?"

"We're just outside the city again," she said

"We don't know it's the same city," Will said. "In my old books, there was more than one."

Elizabeth gasped as if she'd seen someone put a finger in their mouth.

"Paper books," Abraham said. "Relics. Of course it's the same city. All the historic cities crumbled to the ground centuries ago."

"I know how much the two of you love to argue," Charlie said, "but in terms of probability, another city is entirely possible. If you'd hook me up to some sensors and let me run a few scans, I could settle your little tiff. And then we can build the degaussing coil."

Abraham rolled his eyes, then said to Will, "Fine. Give me a leg up. I'll disconnect the sensor array from the roof."

Ernest checked his peephole again. There it was: decayed façades of brick and concrete, and maybe even metal. He wasn't sure it if was more disturbing to view it through the hole and see only a few buildings, or to crane his neck around the side of the railroad car and see the whole geometric landscape sprawling impossibly far in either direction.

As he pictured the city, his city, in his mind's eye, he recalled how it had looked to him as he and Will skirted the edge of the city limits on their initial forays toward the wilderness. The city they'd escaped didn't look like the one before them. It was edged by trees, and the tallest buildings were in the center. This city was markedly different. The landscape to either side of it was barren and low, and the land dipped down as if the weight of the old structures had caused the earth itself to sag.

If anything, Ernest thought, he should be able to pick out the Diaconate. He'd seen the schematics—he'd seen the building itself. But nothing in the broken cityscape matched the Diaconate's profile.

"Here's what we're going to need," Charlie said. "Ten meters of eighteen-gauge copper wire and a fully charged solar panel."

Audrey said, "We've got the solar panels. We've been grabbing them every chance we had for the past five years. I just need to charge them. But I can't get you that much copper without disassembling a propulsion unit."

Abraham crawled down from the ceiling of the railroad car, swung his legs inside, and dropped to the floor with a disconnected sensor dangling from one hand, its filaments as fine as cobwebs. "Since you're all convinced this is some mythical second city, why don't you go see if there are old communication wires you can scavenge? There were meters and meters of them in cities everywhere, once upon a time. Right, Charlie?"

"Right-o."

"Do that," Benjamin said. His words sounded sharp and sudden, unaccustomed as he was to the nuances of discussion and debate. He seemed to have even startled himself by barking out the order, so he explained, "It would be faster to tear the cables out of the ground than to take the propulsion apart and then put it back together. And...and you could damage the propulsion for permanent."

"I'm not going down there," Elizabeth said. "My bones are brittle now. I'd probably fall and fracture my hip."

"Not all of us." Benjamin's eyes darted side to side, bright in the papery folds of his skin, as he accessed his biologically stored data for the way in which one of his old commanders would have done it. "Only risk some of the team. Maybe two."

Audrey, who'd been tinkering with a few wires on Charlie's casing, looked up suddenly. "What do you mean, risk? Are you sure you're using that word correctly? It means thinking about whether to do something dangerous or not."

"I know what it means," Benjamin said icily.

Will said, "Elizabeth is right, the footing can be dangerous. And there might be wild animals living there."

"Or people," Ernest said, before he realized he'd spoken.

The railroad car went utterly silent.

After a long, uncomfortable pause, Audrey said, "What people?"

"Any people. People from our city who decided to follow the railroad track to see where it might lead them. Security ops who are posted here to make sure no one tries to leave."

"No ops without a grid," Benjamin cut in. "They're no good off-grid."

"Okay, fine, maybe not security ops. But *homo sapiens* could be living in the—"

Abraham cut Ernest off. "Unbelievable. Did you explain anything at all to him, Will? Or was your tongue too busy poking around in his mouth to speak?"

Will mumbled, "I thought you understood about the *homo sapiens*."

"Fine." Ernest gave an exasperated sigh. "Yes. I know. There is no *homo consummatus*. We're hardly more than a bunch of chimpanzees. But what if some of us monkeys realized the Diaconate's been lying—about our life spans, about demagnetizing us, about everything—and these ape-men did it three, four, five generations ago? And what if they settled right here, where the ops would never follow because they couldn't stand to be parted from their precious W3 games?"

The pause that followed Ernest's outburst was exponentially heavier than the previous awkward lull. Ernest couldn't recall if he'd said as many words all at once, well...ever. Had anyone there even been able to follow the meaning?

Abraham dusted his hands together as if he was getting ready to engage in manual labor. He smiled, and said, "Point taken. Two of us should go. Someone who can tell the difference between a copper wire and a fiberglass castoff, and someone else who can handle themselves in a fight."

Audrey stood, eyes gleaming, and opened her mouth to speak. She didn't get the chance. "Not you," Abraham said. "We can't afford to lose you. You're the only mod here. Ernest can take Charlie to scan for the copper; he's good with AIs."

"Are you crazy?" Will said. "I'm not going to let him go marching off into—"

"You're going, too. You'll watch his back. We have one charged Taser, so use it wisely. And keep your eyes on potential ambush points...you've got the rest of your life to gaze limpidly at Ernest."

Presuming there really were no off-grid ops lurking in the strange city, anyway. Ernest glanced at Martha's shroud, then looked quickly away, hoping Abraham didn't notice where he'd just been looking.

Elizabeth checked the clearcoat on Ernest's shunt arm and said it was healing well, while Audrey fastened Charlie's sensor array over his chest, then connected it to a pack clipped to his belt. "If you want Charlie to see something, you've got to turn toward it so the sensors can pick it up." She cast a longing look toward the city, but didn't seem inclined to contradict Abraham's decision. Abraham might be a small, slight C754, but the rest of the group listened to him as if he was a captain. "Whatever you do," Audrey said, "don't lose my best friend. I've backed up his data, but it would take me dozens of hours to build a new rig."

That was all it took to resurrect an AI? A string of data and a new bundle of wires and chips? Will wasn't kidding when he insisted L0U15E wasn't a person. If Ernest had known enough to back up her data, he would never have needed to go on without her.

"I know you don't like to censor yourself," Audrey said, and Ernest realized she was talking to the circuitry on his hip rather than him, "but you can't say anything unless Ernest prompts you. This is dangerous, for real."

"And here I thought it was all an elaborate simulation," Charlie's voice said from the cracked speaker.

"Hold on," Ernest said. "Maybe you can tune him to my audio interface. Will won't be able to hear him, but—"

"You have an interface? Where?" Audrey brushed Ernest's hair aside. "Is it an implant?"

Ernest would never have been able to afford an elective implant, not on his salary. Even the removable unit had cost him a huge chunk of his life savings. "No, it's just...it's small. I hardly know it's there."

Audrey let out a low whistle when she spotted the piece. "That's quite an antique."

"If it's too old...."

"Did I say I couldn't tune into its frequency?"

"You most certainly did not," Charlie piped in.

"That's right. Lucky for you, I know my spare parts."

Will gathered supplies—water, protein bars, a blanket folded into a tight little cube—and Ernest wondered how long, exactly, it would take them to find copper wire. He supposed he'd expected to march down the hill, poke through a couple of buildings and come back with the raw materials for a degaussing coil. But what if it wasn't that easy? The city was huge, and suddenly daunting. Since Will claimed to be able to read his face so easily, he did his best to look as if he wasn't in the least intimidated.

Audrey, crouching beside Ernest to tinker with the computer on his hip, looked up. "Okay, Charlie, it's showtime."

"Ernest? Check, check, check." Charlie's voice was in his ear, rich and nuanced and very humanistic in contrast to the way it had sounded coming out of the tiny, cracked speaker.

"Yes," Ernest said. "I hear you."

"How's the sound?" Audrey asked.

"Clear."

She glanced in Abraham's direction to make sure he wasn't listening, then leaned in close to Ernest and said, "I know you're just supposed to look for the wire and come right back, but if you happen to find more audio parts wherever you are... grab 'em. And if not, think about what I can barter you for that earpiece. I don't want Charlie to sound like a portable game announcer for the rest of my life."

At the thought of Audrey spending her entire life with Charlie, Ernest felt a deep pang of loss for LOU15E. He hoped his face didn't show it. "I'll look."

"Everything ready?" Will shouldered the pack, winked at Ernest, and said, "Let's go."

Walking was more difficult in the grass than it had been alongside the railroad tracks. The grasses obscured rocks and divots, and Ernest needed to focus on his footing so intently that he was startled when Will finally spoke. "You take it pretty well when Abraham makes those digs at you. I appreciate that. He's jealous—obviously—but not for the reasons you might think."

It had never occurred to Ernest that Abraham was jealous. He turned his foot on a rock, staggered, and kept going.

"We were never lovers or anything. But we've always been close, really close. We bunked side by side at the natal center and our hatches were across from one another in the training facility. And when he discovered that he actually felt better when he avoided shunting in, I was the one he told."

"If you weren't lovers, why would he be jealous of me?"

Will fell into step so close that their thighs brushed when they walked, and his pack nudged Ernest in the rump. He leaned in and whispered into Ernest's hair, "Because now you'll be the first one to hear my secrets."

Ernest had never considered Will to be generous with his secrets; Will hadn't lived so long in the city by failing to be discreet. "Were you jealous of Martha?"

"Once, I guess. But she was such an amazing girl...not for long." Will hefted his pack high on his shoulder so he could run his palm across Ernest's back for a moment before the pack slid down and he needed to hike it up again. "She was as good a friend to me as he is. When I think about how badly I miss her, and then I think about Abe, and how much worse it's got to be for him...." He trailed off and shook his head.

"If you need to spend time with him, I won't be...um...jealous." Ernest tried on what he knew of the emotion, of seeing Audrey babbling to Charlie, for instance, and knowing LOU15E was well and truly gone, and he suspected he might indeed experience jealousy if he observed how close Will and Abraham were—though he didn't have to admit it. "You can tell him secrets. I won't mind."

"Watch it," Charlie said in Ernest's ear. "You're laying it on a little thick." Ernest snapped his gaze to the bundle of circuits on his hip. How could he possibly have forgotten the AI was there? "Your chest is covered in sensors. Your pulse sped and your galvanic skin response fluctuated—and then you started to overcompensate. If you really must lie, the key is subtlety."

Footing was tricky enough that, hopefully, Will hadn't noticed. Even focused on his feet, Will tripped. He righted himself, then turned to look at the hidden thing that had nearly brought him down. He almost kept going—almost—but then turned and looked again. He went down on one knee and brushed the grass aside. "Look at the shape of this rock."

"Don't just look with your head," Charlie told Ernest. "Angle your body toward it. I want to see, too."

Ernest squatted beside Will so the sensors pointed at the rock. "Marble, granite," Ernest repeated, as Charlie muttered an analysis in his ear. "A naturally occurring aggregate, but minerals not normally found in this area. And definitely altered in some way."

Will fingered a corner of the marble. It was precisely ninety degrees. "They liked their right angles so much they felt the need to alter even the rocks?"

"Maybe it was part of a building, once." Ernest paused as Charlie fed him directions. "Flip it over. Charlie says there might be an indication of its purpose on the other side."

Will worked his fingers underneath the marble slab and strained. "Heavy," he said. The tendons in his neck stood out. Ernest watched the lowering sunlight play over Will's musculature, casting amber shadows. He imagined running his fingertips over the hard curve of muscle on Will's shoulder. And maybe nuzzling it with his cheek. Inhaling that scent that was

Will, and only Will.

"You've got it bad for that one," Charlie said.

Ernest wasn't entirely sure what that meant, but he could sense from Charlie's tone that he might not want to discuss it directly in front of Will. "Can I help?" he asked Will, instead.

"Something gave way...I think I got it."

"Too bad," Charlie went on. "I thought you'd be a good match for Audrey if you ever got bored with him."

Bored? Ernest gave a small, derisive laugh, hardly more than a breath, before he could stop himself. Will was so busy straining at his rock he didn't seem to notice, but Charlie picked up the reply. Audrey really *had* done a stellar job with his programming.

Will strained, and gasped, and lifted with all his might, and finally the earth released the stone. He flipped it over, and the blackness beneath it teemed with movement. Ernest and Will bent close to look.

Charlie said, "You might want to avoid the centipedes—I so miss having a viscreen to demonstrate my point—the chitinous ones with all the legs. Their bites are mildly venomous."

Ernest picked up a stick and flicked one of the creatures away from Will's boot.

"What are we looking for?" Will asked. "Those are all biological, right?"

Ernest reached across the wriggling carpet of life forms and brushed a moist clod of dirt from the face of the stone. "There. Characters of some sort."

"Programming?"

"I don't think you can program a stone." Ernest brushed more soil away. It clung to his fingers, dark and wet. "But I'm unfamiliar with the letterforms."

"It's a monument," Charlie said. "A name, a set of dates. This is known as a headstone."

"It's called a headstone," Ernest told Will.

Charlie added, "It marks the ground where a corpse was interred."

Ernest leapt to his feet, took several quick steps back, then faltered on a deep divot and danced a few steps to the side. Will saw his alarm and backed away rapidly. "What?"

"There's a *homo sapien* body buried under it. A totally magnetized body."

"It wouldn't be much of a body at this point," Charlie said, his voice maddeningly calm and tinged with dry amusement. "Even if it was laid to rest in a lined casket, everything's probably decomposed to soil at this advanced stage."

Ernest looked down at his dirty fingertips, dismayed, and brushed them vigorously against his trousers. The thought of being there—trapped, somehow aware, while one's body converted itself to soil over the course of centuries—disturbed Ernest to the point where he felt woozy, like blood loss, but without the bleeding.

"What's got you so worked up?" Charlie asked.

"Just pay attention to where we're going. Where's the copper?"

"Testy, testy. Do your part, then. Turn your upper body so I can have a look." Ernest did so. "No, nothing in range. You'll need to get closer to the buildings."

"Come on," Ernest told Will. "I want to have some daylight left for the search."

Will shifted his bag to his opposite shoulder so he could walk close at Ernest's side. "It's been talking to you this whole time, hasn't it? Audrey's AI."

"Why do you ask?" Ernest forced himself to stop thinking about the corpse dirt and relax into a grin—and it wasn't so difficult to smile when he was looking at Will's shrewd eyes. "Jealous?"

Will laughed out loud and brushed his fingertips along Ernest's knuckles as they walked. "Sometimes I think I was better off when you were fresh out of the POD. Before you knew how devastating you are."

Based on Will's tone of voice, Ernest decided to take that remark as a compliment. He smiled to himself and forged ahead.

ᴵᴵᴵCHAPTER TWENTY-EIGHTᴵᴵᴵ

THOUGH ERNEST AND WILL must have known, on some level, how large the city was, it was still a shock to draw close to the ancient architecture and feel the tall, crumbling edifices looming over them.

"Unless you're jumping up and down on a weak spot," Charlie advised, "I think you should be safe enough if you keep to the sidewalks and streets. But don't just go dashing into any of these buildings. The floors might not hold you."

"What about people?" Ernest said.

"People?" Will dragged Ernest behind the wreck of an old billboard and pitched his voice to a harsh whisper. "Did someone show up on the scans?"

"No, nothing like that." Not yet, he thought. "It just seemed like a possibility."

"It's statistically improbable there's anyone here but you," Charlie said, "but if you're concerned, I'll scan. You'll need to walk slower, though. This array is terribly limited. Scanning for both copper and living bodies increases the payload, big time."

"We've got to go slow," Ernest said.

Will slung his pack over the shoulder of his shunt arm again, leaving his dominant hand free to hold the Taser. "Not too slow. If it gets dark, we'll need to hole up for the night, someplace secure where an LED won't give us away by shining like a beacon."

The remnants of buildings cast long shadows as the sun sank toward the horizon. Chill air crept through the holes in Ernest's clothing like clammy fingers, and he began to shiver. "Start sweeping, left to right," Charlie reminded him, and he angled his body so Charlie's sensors could scan. "Birds. Insects. No large mammals."

"It's clear," Ernest whispered to Will. Obviously he didn't need to whisper since there was no one there to hear him, but he felt too jumpy to bow to reason at that particular moment.

Charlie said, "I'll send a few sonar pings to see if any of the floors are built on solid ground rather than basements. Position yourself in that doorway and angle the sensors so I can get a reading. But use your common sense. I don't have enough processor space free to point out every crack in the floor."

Ernest approached a doorway. He presumed these larger buildings had been some sort of commercial properties once, like Will's coffee shop, and he was hopeful the size of the structures meant they were more likely to have enough copper wiring for him to scavenge.

"No basement under the foyer," Charlie said. "Go on."

Ernest made his way across the jumbled tiles to the interior door, leaned across the threshold, turned to his left, and began the slow rotation that would allow the sensors to scan the space. His own senses told him that the windows had given way long ago. Moisture had damaged the walls; mildew painted great, black streaks from the ceilings, and the air smelled fungal and thick.

"What was this place?" he breathed.

"Scanning."

Ernest ended his sweep facing right, and wondered if he should sweep back in the opposite direction, or simply allow Charlie to sift through the data he'd already gathered.

Will shuffled his feet and began poking around the vestibule. Ernest glanced back over his shoulder, careful to leave the sensors pointed at the inner room. Will attempted to pull a tuft of old wiring from a port on the baseboard, but it broke off in his hand and crumbled. He brushed the crumbs from his fingers and sighed. "We need to find something that hasn't been so exposed to the elements. Wind, temperature, moisture, sunlight...anything like that will have taken a toll."

"Too true," Charlie said, though Will couldn't hear him agree.

"How's the floor?" Ernest asked the AI.

"Safe enough for three meters. Start in, slowly, and then do another sweep."

Ernest took a few cautious steps in, then began to dig through his pockets for an LED to get a better look at the room's dark, murky corners. The bloated wooden supports of floor felt slightly spongy, like moss, but beneath that slight give, it seemed it was still solid enough to hold him.

Will already had his light on, flicking the beam at various points in the room to assess its potential salvageability. "Over there," Will said. "The inner wall. Is that copper?"

Ernest pivoted and pointed the sensor array to the frayed end of a dangling cord that looked, at first glance, like a vine.

"Well spotted," Charlie exclaimed.

Ernest said, "What does that mean?"

"It means yes. That's what's left of a telecommunications system."

"Charlie says it's copper—but to stick to the perimeter of the room. The floor will be stronger there."

"Good." Will put his back to the wall and sidled over to the exposed wiring. "After we see to Martha, later, once she's...free..." he sighed and searched for words. It was the first time Ernest had seen him at a loss. "I think we should come back when it's light out and look for anything else we can use. Maybe there's protein in pressurized storage. Maybe unprogrammed nanites, or first aid kits, or fuel cells."

Will grasped the exposed end of the wire gingerly, as if it might crumble as the other wire had. The wire bundle held; the wall, brittle with age and moisture damage, began to bulge and crack instead.

"There's more behind that counter," Charlie said, "But you'll need to watch your footing. I don't trust the spans between the floor joists."

"Just tell me where to walk," Ernest said.

"Left...good, there...now forward two meters...."

The floor around Ernest creaked as he made his way deeper into the structure, but he was accustomed to obeying POD-minds. If Charlie said it was safe to walk, albeit only along a particular row of buckling floor tiles, then Ernest was confident the floor would hold him.

"Yes, it's coming from over there. Steel alloy—that's what's left of the counter. Behind that, definitely copper, also nickel, and a smattering of zinc."

Will freed a length of wire that was long enough to get a grip on and pulled harder. The wiring erupted from the wall in a line of destruction, and the sound of plaster clacking off rubble filled the room.

"Round that pile of cinderblock," Charlie told Ernest. "The footing is safe."

The floor flexed and groaned. Ernest paused. "It's okay," Charlie told him, so he gathered his courage and crept as gently as he could across the springy floorboards and around the counter. A small electronic device with a cracked casing lay on the floor beneath the counter amid a light scattering of rubble. Ernest tucked it into his shirt in case Audrey could repurpose any of the parts—though it didn't seem that copper wire was among those components. Not the length they needed to build the coil, at any rate. "All right. Where's the wire?"

Will hauled at the wire he'd found until it tore from the wall in its entirety. "This is barely two meters long. It'll never work."

"Take it," Ernest said. "Maybe we can splice it."

Charlie considered the problem. "A splice? No, not within a coil. But maybe a solder joint…."

The plaster from the wall where Will had been scavenging had made such a racket as it gave way that Ernest didn't notice the creaks and crackles around him until a chunk of the ceiling over his head came free and bounced off his shoulder. He looked up, which pointed the sensor array on his chest upward momentarily, and then he crouched in a protective huddle as he struggled to blink grit from his eyes.

"Get under the counter," Charlie ordered, all his easy charm suddenly gone. "Now."

Ernest was already tucked down, shielding his face. He rolled to one side just as fist-sized hunks of plaster, metal fragments and rotten wood thundered down. "Will," he called out, but he couldn't see, couldn't breathe, couldn't do anything but crouch under the counter, shield his eyes and hug his injured arm to his chest. "Will," he yelled again, once he could draw enough breath to shout.

"Stay put," Will called back, through the cacophony of falling debris. "Don't move."

The downpour slackened, and Ernest began to lever himself out of the small, half-buried pocket of safety. "Stop," Charlie barked at him, which he ignored. He had shelter. Will didn't. He might be hurt.

"Will?"

"Get back," Charlie snapped. "There's more."

A huge piece of plaster studded with jagged flakes of rust made Ernest obey where the AI could not. It shattered on the countertop so close to him that it sprayed him with broken plaster when it hit.

As Charlie had seen, in that brief moment when Ernest had looked up enough to aim the sensors toward the ceiling, there was much more rubble where the first wave had come from. The sound of old struts snapping blasted through the carcass of the building like a series of explosions. Panic surged through Ernest at the thought of being buried alive, and he risked another quick glance up at the remains of the ceiling.

Above him, through the craggy, crumbling hole, a dozen pale arms reached down.

Homo sapiens.

He curled into a tight ball beneath the counter and wished he'd insisted on carrying a Taser, too. So many hands, so many strangers...Will was brave and strong, but how could he possibly defend against them all?

"People," he whimpered to Charlie. "In the ceiling."

"What? That's impossible. I performed an infrared scan. I would have noticed."

"Six? At least six." Ernest hugged himself into a tighter ball to try and stop himself from shaking. Wreckage continued to fall, the noise drowning out everything else, making it impossible for him to think.

"No, it can't be. I just ran through my data again."

"I saw them."

"Disconnect as many sensors as you can and aim them toward the ceiling—but whatever you do, don't stick your head out there like a big, round target."

Ernest knew how to manipulate data, not hardware. His hands trembled as he sought the delicate filaments hooked into his shirt, and he fumbled with them for fear of damaging the precious components. He freed two of the sensors and poked them through a small gap that remained between the countertop and the fallen debris.

His hand shook terribly. "Steady your elbow on something," Charlie suggested.

"I'm sorry."

"There are no mammals here. None."

"Maybe they're wearing something to conserve their body heat...."

"Not enough carbon dioxide. If respiration were taking place, I'd know it."

"They could have some sort of masks...." Ernest stopped speaking when he realized the sound of falling rubble had faded to small bursts with stretches of silence in between.

"Are you ready for a new idiom?" Charlie asked, with a bit of the old jauntiness returning to his voice. "How about 'false alarm'?"

Not much of an idiom. The meaning of the words was obvious enough. "What do you mean, false?"

"They're not people...they're representations of people."

He sounded so sure. Ernest considered. "Like the statuary in the Diaconate."

"Precisely."

Ernest felt giddy with relief—so much that he forgot himself and took a deep breath, and began to choke on the dust. Rubble ground against rubble—footsteps. "Ernest? Are you okay?"

He hooked the sensors to his shirt again and pushed at the

mound of rubble that had drifted against the counter. "I'm fine. You?"

"Banged up, but I'll manage." Will's footfalls grew closer. Ernest shoved more debris out of the way, and squinted in Will's direction. Will edged through the haze of dust holding a long, pale, obviously artificial arm. He waved it at Ernest, and laughed. "Need a hand?"

"That's not funny." Ernest tried unsuccessfully to frown; his relief at escaping the horde of *homo sapiens* (even if he supposedly was one, himself) was too intense to suppress.

"You can tell when a building's been lived in by the dust patterns," Will said. "No one's been walking around here lately. I would've known."

There were sensors, and then there was Will.

Ernest cleared enough crumbled plaster to free himself from his burrow, and Will dropped the fake arm and offered his own hand. Ernest took it, unprepared for the sensation that streamed through him at Will's touch—as if they were both conductors, and their contact had completed a circuit, and now a current flowed through them, one to the other, and back again.

Ernest straightened up so he was chest to chest with Will, raised his injured arm and brushed his fingertips over Will's cheek. "You're bleeding."

"I've read that some people find scars attractively rugged. Or that might've been ruggedly attractive. Which do you suppose it is?"

Ernest stood on tiptoe and brushed his lips against the freshly clotted wound. "I wouldn't be able to say. I'm biased."

"Now there's an understatement."

"Shut up, Charlie."

Will attempted to pull back at the mention of the AI he couldn't hear, but Ernest threaded an arm around his waist and held him fast. "Ignore him. I am."

"Really?" Will allowed himself to be lured into a kiss. Their lips grazed, gentle, hardly a whisper, despite the fact that each of them was clutching the other hard enough to leave finger marks. "I thought you'd project some paternal authority on him...given that he's a POD-mind."

"But he's not *my* POD-mind."

They smiled, lips barely brushing, and then Will tilted his head and deepened the kiss. His tongue sought Ernest's, slipped together, retreated, advanced again.

"You need to stop," Charlie's voice said in Ernest's earpiece.

"Shut up, Charlie," he whispered, lips grazing Will's teeth, tongues fleetingly touching.

"Now. Damn it, now!"

Charlie's urgency startled Ernest from the kiss; Ernest gave Will a gentle push to the shoulder and Will disengaged, though he still kept an arm around Ernest's waist, and looked to Ernest for an explanation.

"It's only a kiss," Ernest said, baffled that Audrey hadn't cleared the Diaconate strictures on oral contact from Charlie's programming. "It's perfectly safe."

"Will's mouth might be safe, but this city isn't. Radiation levels at 2.2 sieverts. Evacuate, now."

CHAPTER TWENTY-NINE

ERNEST PAUSED TO CONSIDER Charlie's urgent command to evacuate. "What is it?" Will said.

It didn't occur to Ernest to lie, exactly. Though he did use a tone much less urgent than the AI. "Radiation. Charlie just picked it up. He only has enough processing speed to perform a few scans at a time, and he'd been busy looking for copper."

Will turned toward a gap in the wall and held out a hand. "Come on, let's get out of here."

"Wait a minute...." Ernest recalled a datastream he'd cleaned up a couple of years ago that had something to do with radiation levels. "Two point two sieverts isn't immediately fatal."

Charlie said, "This is not negotiable."

"How much exposure have we had? Twenty minutes? Thirty? How much difference would another few minutes make, if it means choosing between building the degaussing coil or leaving Martha trapped like that...forever?"

Will brushed plaster dust from his forearms as if he could wipe away the radioactive contamination, too. "I knew her better than you did. She wouldn't want us to do something this risky."

"You can go back. We don't know how far the radiation extends—maybe all the way back to the railroad tracks. Tell them to get ready to travel."

Will threw his hands up in exasperation. "Look, I'm not leaving you—so let's get this over with." He grasped a board fragment and began to dig beneath the counter. "There was copper back here, right? That's what you were heading for when the ceiling fell in."

"This is a terrible idea," Charlie said.

Ernest began pulling the larger hunks of debris out of the way. Handling the crumbled plaster dust brought back memories of the mounds of drifting ash in the Diaconate's basement, ash that had once been people, magnetized people, burned alive—and visions of gray ash coating everything overlaid his current perceptions like a pair of programs running concurrently. He reminded himself the building was not made of people—though the pale plaster arms did nothing to dispel the pervasive idea.

"You're sick already," Charlie said. "Your galvanic skin response—"

"It's nothing to do with the radiation," Ernest said, and with an effort, he put the images of the Diaconate from his mind and focused on locating the telltale tuft of bundled copper data cables protruding from the rubble.

Dust pinged against rubble as Will dug frantically, and then, suddenly, he stilled and the noises stopped. "No. Oh, no."

"What?" Ernest and Charlie asked simultaneously.

Will reached into the shifting pile of grit and dust, pulled out a handful of debris, and waved it at the sensors on Ernest's chest. "Is this what you've got us digging for? Is it?"

"I don't understand...." Ernest said.

"Abort the task," Charlie told Ernest. "The copper is not in the form of a cable."

Ernest wasn't quite sure how to relay that information to Will, but he didn't need to. Will could read his face, after all. "We can't build a coil out of pennies," Will said, and threw the scraps of metal and plaster to the floor, disgusted. His expression softened slightly when he locked eyes with Ernest rather than scowling at Charlie's sensors. "It's an old unit of currency. The counter, the mannequins, the money...this was a shop. But whatever they sold has been nothing but dust for centuries." He took up Ernest's hand and held it to his chest, knuckles against fabric, clenching it tight. "We should go."

It was one thing to expose himself, Ernest decided, but another to cause Will to linger in the radiation. "All right. Two minutes." He crawled to the top of a pile of broken cinderblock and mannequin arms, then he aimed the sensors on his chest at one corner of the room, and began turning in a final sweep. "Please tell me this hasn't been for nothing," he whispered to Charlie.

"Listen to Will if you won't listen to me. It's not worth the... stop. There. By the doorframe, to the right, there's a run of telecom wire. The floor's not safe. Stay close to the wall."

"I found something," Ernest told Will. "But stay where you are. I weigh less."

Charlie murmured a constant stream of coordinates in Ernest's earpiece. "Forward eight centimeters, left fourteen centimeters, forward thirty centimeters...."

"It's probably more useless coins," Will said. "Forget it. We've got to go."

Ernest was about to reassure Will that Charlie had said wire specifically, and not copper and zinc, but he was busy scanning the floor and placing his feet just so, according to Charlie's directions—and trying to ignore the horrible groaning sounds the floor was making.

He reached the wall, finally, and felt along the chalky plaster. "No," Charlie said. "Not there—it's hugging the doorframe. Yes, that's right, Ernest. Exactly where your fingers are."

Ernest pulled a wooden fragment pierced by a galvanized nail from the rubble and began to dig into the plaster. It was slow going—the wall was in better repair here—but beneath it, thankfully, so was the wire. "I found some," he called over his shoulder to Will. His voice was shaking.

Will said nothing. Wind whistled through a long-empty window frame. The building moaned and settled. And finally, Will spoke. "Damn it."

Ernst glanced at him briefly, enough to see he was making his way carefully away from the counter, toward a wall. Ernest focused on his task, exposing the wire a few centimeters at a time. "It's the correct gauge," he asked Charlie, "right?"

"I'd have you halfway back to the railroad by now if it weren't."

And then Will's hand was on his shoulder, squeezing in encouragement. Will hadn't listened to Ernest's orders to stay put any more than Ernest would have heeded Charlie's. "Where is it," Will asked him, "around the door?"

Ernest nodded and kept working.

Will pulled a screwdriver from his tool belt and began hacking away a wide swath of plaster from the other side of the doorway. Seeing him cutting through the old wall with such vigor made Ernest redouble his effort, and soon they had a sizable length of wire to show for their work. Will gave a final tug, tearing perhaps an extra meter of copper from the wall before the wire snapped, then said, "Okay, Ernest. Have that know-it-all POD-mind set a course for the quickest way out of here."

CHAPTER THIRTY

Ernest lay, staring up at the night sky, with his head in Will's lap. Will stroked his brow, and said, "What do you suppose people did to decontaminate themselves from radiation poisoning before there were shunts?"

Ernest supposed it was likely they died. He'd certainly felt like his own death was near once the vomiting started. Elizabeth accessed what medical databases they possessed and determined the vomiting was normal, considering the exposure Ernest had encountered.

Of course, Will had endured the very same exposure...but Will still had a shunt. A dose of nanites, in through the shunt and out through a portable dialysis unit, was all it took to relieve his radiation poisoning.

"The mortality rate is favorable, even without decontamination," Elizabeth had told him in her most sincere attempt at being comforting as she swabbed him down with wipes to decontaminate his skin. "Your hair might fall out. But if you do survive, it should eventually grow back."

Audrey had suggested introducing the nanites through Ernest's thumb chip where taste nanos usually went. That would indeed have worked, albeit much more slowly than the shunt port—but Elizabeth explained that the nanites were too large to pass through the lungs, so they would have had no way to evacuate Ernest's system once they completed their task.

And so there was nothing more they could do than manually decontaminate Ernest's exterior, and wait.

Will continued the rhythmic stroking of Ernest's hair, which was still wet from the washing Elizabeth had given it with their drinking water. Ernest wondered if Will was loosening his hair's roots within their follicles, speeding his imminent baldness, or if the creeping effects of the radiation were still some days off.

He shifted. His new clothing felt stiff and ill-fitting, but at least it wasn't radioactive. He'd needed to roll up the legs of the new trousers to keep from tripping on them. Not that it mattered when all he felt capable of doing was lying down to rest his pounding head.

The lattice of branches he stared through looked much the same as the trees near the radioactive city, though according to Charlie, radiation levels here, nearly fifty kilometers away, were safe. The current obstruction that had stopped the railroad was not a fallen tree, but an old mudslide, with weedy grass growing upon the buried tracks.

"Once Abraham builds the coil," Ernest asked, "what happens next? He demagnetizes Martha..." how to put it delicately? "And then what?"

"I'm not really sure," Will said softly. "We never planned for anything like this. Once we realized this whole thing about thirty being the end of our lives was a pack of lies....I guess we thought we were immortal."

Immortal. The word had a lovely ring to it. Ernest turned it over in his mind, and imagined himself existing—if not in his current body, which was weak and disfigured, and which still occasionally heaved with the urge to vomit—then in spirit, at least.

Grass rustled as someone approached, but Ernest's eyelids had eased shut, and they felt too heavy to open. He recognized Abraham's voice. "Let him sleep, Will. Elizabeth can sit with him. I don't like this spot; it's too exposed. We need your help clearing the tracks."

Will's body tensed. He hesitated. "Go," Ernest whispered,

without opening his eyes. "Clear the tracks for me. I want to ride the railroad."

Sleep was welcome. It wasn't the profound, shunted sleep Ernest would have experienced a mere month ago, tucked safely upright in his POD. It wasn't even the helpless, fragmented, dream-riddled horizontal sleep that claimed him each night on the railroad. Instead, sleep was fitful and distorted, and the dreams it brought were tedious, frustrating milieus in which he struggled to fix a datastream he couldn't even parse.

"Ernest?"

Louise. Ernest smiled in his sleep.

"Ernest?"

No, not Louise—because Louise would simply change his shunt mixture if she'd wanted to wake him, not shake him by the shoulder. He opened his eyes. It was dark, save for the light of a nearby LED that lit the silhouette of Audrey's fuchsia hair bright pink against the murky, blue-gray night. Ernest almost reassured her that he was still alive, but at the last moment, changed his response to, "I'm awake."

"Do you feel any better now that you've slept? I've never seen anyone hurling like that. That's not really an idiom, more of a slang, but don't you think it's a good one? Hurling?"

Ernest's abdominal muscles ached with the memory. "Yes. It's pretty accurate." He wedged an elbow under himself, levered up and found the flask of water Will had left beside him. The thought of putting anything else in his stomach brought back, if not the illness itself, the memory of feeling queasy. But his mouth was so dry, he was so acutely thirsty, that he was totally willing to risk another round of hurling. Once he tipped the water back and attempted a small sip, his thirst overtook him, and he ended up gulping down the entire flask.

He still felt nauseated from drinking—but not to the degree he would have a few hours before. "Sorry. I don't think there will be any more hurling to see."

"Oh, that's not why I woke you." Audrey took him by his dominant arm and helped him to sit up. "The degaussing coil is finished. Will said Martha would have wanted you to be there when we demagnetize her body."

Ernest decided he must have been asleep a very long time. The buried railroad tracks were nearly uncovered now, and the way would shortly be clear to travel on. Will worked at chopping earth with a sharp-edged POD fragment while Benjamin hauled the chunks of sod aside. A few yards away, on a flat stretch of grass, Martha's body lay upon its silver blanket, unwrapped. It looked bloated and mottled, though not quite as bad as Ernest's clearcoated arm. Abraham knelt on one side of her, Elizabeth on the other.

Audrey led Ernest closer, and he saw there was one more in attendance on Martha: Charlie. His processor, bundled with the electronic device Ernest had discovered at the ancient, radiation-contaminated shop, sat on the ground beside Abraham. The front of the device was a liquid crystal display that was currently cycling through a series of patterns like a black and gray kaleidoscope. Charlie had a viscreen again, archaic but functional. His voice, small but still audible, piped through a speaker opening on the front of the device's casing.

"Here's another option. Build a cairn. That's a pile of rocks to cover the body and prevent predation."

Abraham shook his head wearily. "That sounds even worse than burying her." His gaze was fixed on a small data screen in his lap. Ernest had assumed he was simply reading, but then noticed the scanner beside him, loosely hooked to the data screen in a trailing chaos of wires, which seemed to be Audrey's signature style. Abraham's fingers keyed nearly as quickly as Ernest's might have, though what he was programming, it was impossible to determine without seeing the screen.

"It would be dry," Charlie said, in defense of his cairn idea. "And you could take some aesthetic license in the arrangement of the stones."

Abraham rolled his eyes. Ernest barely caught himself before he asked his long-gone AI to help him research the subtler meanings in the expression. "No holes in the ground, no fires, and no cairns." He keyed even faster for a short burst, and then sat back on his heels, satisfied. "I've reprogrammed a batch of nanites to decompose her body instead."

Nanites? Ernest was intrigued. "I could check those over," he said, and the rusty sound of his own voice startled him. "If you want me to."

Abraham's expression shifted—unreadable, something with twisted up eyebrows and tightly clamped lips—and he stared at Ernest for a long, agonizing moment. Finally, once Ernest had prepared himself for a horrible tirade, Abraham said, "Yes. You know the most about nanotechnology programming. Have a look."

Ernest took the viscreen and scanner from Abraham, doing his best not to glance down at Martha's face. He couldn't help but look, though, and while it was only a glimpse, it was enough to see that her features were puffy, and her expression, if there were any thought behind it, would have been dismayed.

He took the scanner far enough away that he could no longer see Martha's face, and tried not to think about it. A mind, however, was not exactly like a piece of circuitry. It couldn't be erased so simply.

He checked through the nanites' routines. Their program wasn't written exactly as he might have done it himself, but it would certainly do the job—even to the point of making them shut themselves down once the fuel of Martha's cells was digested, and decomposing their structures until they dispersed as harmless molecules of hydrogen and carbon. "Yes," Ernest said. "It's good."

Abraham nodded curtly, and picked up the degaussing coil. It was a simple tool, really, only a coiled copper wire with a small solar battery hooked to the end. "You'll tell me when the magnetic charge is gone," he prompted Charlie. His voice was thick.

"Of course."

He began at Martha's feet, holding the coil just above her body, running it carefully up one leg, then the other.

The grass rustled beside Ernest as Will crouched beside him and put an arm around his shoulders. Benjamin stood to one side, feet planted, arms crossed over his chest.

"That's fine," Charlie said. "Keep going."

Abraham ran the coil over her hips and abdomen, her chest and each of her arms. And finally, very carefully, he swept it in a circular motion around her face.

Elizabeth tilted her head as if to determine whether Martha's body looked different without her soul in it. Ernest found himself doing the same.

How was it, he wondered, that something so significant could be so difficult to process with his own senses? Facial expressions and idioms. Radiation. A soul.

Charlie's voice broke the heavy silence. "Very good." His tone was gentle, even nurturing. "It's done; she's free."

Abraham continued to stare down at Martha's body, which lay there as still as one of the mannequins. The radiation poisoning made Ernest dizzy, and he held himself very still as he wondered if it would be all right for him to lie down again, or if it would somehow be interpreted as a lack of respect, when finally Abraham said, "I'd like to move it off the blanket before I start the nanites. Put it directly on the ground. I think she would have liked that. She was always fascinated by the edges of the city."

"I will assist," Benjamin said. His loud, clipped voice startled everybody. He'd trained all his life to speak like that, and had no other inflection to use. "You," he pointed at Abraham, then stopped to consider what he wished to say. Then he swept his arm in an arc to include everyone. "You think I'm still an op. But this thing that happened..." he pointed at Martha's corpse. "I didn't do it. Not me."

"We know," Abraham said dryly. But Ernest wondered, did they, really? Or was Benjamin sensing what they all, on some level, still thought of him?

Abraham took Martha's body by the shoulders while Benjamin hefted her legs, and they lifted it up while Elizabeth pulled the blanket out from beneath it. The smell was strong, and disturbing.

They set the body directly on the grass, and Abraham placed her arms neatly at her sides. He smoothed her hair, and gave her cheek a final caress. If she'd been vertical, Ernest thought, and not so discolored, she might have looked like she was just sleeping.

Abraham swiped a syringe over the transfer port of his handheld to program the nanites, then turned Martha's shunt arm so the shunt faced him. He considered her face for another long moment, then introduced the nanites to her shunt.

If Abraham's nanites functioned as they were meant to, Ernest realized, it would be a much more compassionate ending than the infernos of Reclaim.

They didn't have long to wait. The change, initially subtle, cascaded rapidly once they perceived it. Martha's mottled, ruddy, decaying flesh went silvery and lustrous, like the shell of a brand new POD. For a single moment, her corpse was beautiful.

And then her features softened. The silver of her newly converted skin dulled. The tips of her hair stirred and broke off, carried away like ash on the wind. Slowly, at first, she began to erode, but the process soon sped as the nanites replicated themselves exponentially, one billion becoming two, four, sixteen and so on.

Less than a second after her features began to sag, the surface tension broke, and everything that was once flesh, hair, muscle and bone collapsed, like piles of sand. And soon those sandy granules decomposed farther still, until they became powder— and the powder broke down even more, until it was smoke.

And then Martha was truly gone.

⸝⸝⸝CHAPTER THIRTY-ONE⸝⸝⸝

THE TRAIN CAR GLIDED forward, occasionally swaying. The movement felt surprisingly POD-like, and Ernest's eyelids grew heavy where he sat, propped against Will at his side, with the wall of the car pressing into his shoulder blades. Even Will, who claimed that he hadn't slept in a POD in over four years, had trouble staying awake—though every time his head dropped forward, he jerked back to attention and blinked.

"You should sleep," Ernest said. "Last time we stopped, you cleared more of the blockage than anyone else. You must be tired."

Will ground his thumb into the corner of one eye. "I'm fine. How about you? Are you feeling okay?"

Ernest was nauseated and his head throbbed. "Yes. Good."

Will's arm tightened around his shoulders. "You're such a liar." He pressed his face into Ernest's hair. "Just so we're clear, I'm still livid about what you did back there in the radiation."

"Will...."

Will breathed into his hair, hot against his scalp. Ernest thought maybe he was trying to convey whatever it was he wanted to say through touch, but after a long moment he spoke again, quiet and desperate. "I can't lose you. Do you get it? Because everything we've done, recruiting the specialists and salvaging the PODs—everything I've ever worked for...." He squeezed Ernest against him so hard it was painful.

"Will...."

"None of it means a damn thing if I can't share it with you."

Ernest pulled out of Will's grasp so he could turn and face him. Will's eyes glittered in the LED beam. "We are sharing it," Ernest said softly. "Look how far we've come." He thumbed a half-formed tear from the corner of Will's eye, considered it for a moment, then touched it to his tongue.

Salt.

Will cupped a hand around the back of Ernest's head and drew him into a kiss. A gentle kiss—because he was being tender, or because he'd realized they were most definitely not immortal, and even though he'd lured Ernest away from his POD and away from the city, it might not have been enough—and Ernest could very well be the next to die?

Eventually, though, exhaustion overtook grief, and Will's mouth slid from Ernest's as he sagged against the fiberglass wall in fitful slumber, brows hitched as if he couldn't let go of his worry, even in his sleep.

Ernest propped a pack of spare clothing under Will's arm and carefully extricated himself from their entanglement. He cast around to see if there was anywhere he might reasonably expect to rest himself, and noticed everyone else was asleep— everyone but Abraham.

Abraham glanced over the top of Charlie's old, cracked viscreen. To his side, his fingers twitched as he keyed, slowing as he made eye contact with Ernest, though not stopping. He looked back down at the screen.

How much had he heard? Everything, Ernest supposed. He'd need a VR helmet to block out a conversation in such an intimate space. And how much had he seen? His eyes flicked up to meet Ernest's gaze, then back down again. No doubt he'd seen everything, too.

"What are you writing?" Ernest asked—because it seemed that anything would be preferable to the awkward silence.

"Maybe a gig of nothing. We'll see when I'm done."

Ernest moved to the front of the train car and pressed his eye to the hole. Even with an LED mounted on top of the bin, it was impossible to make out much more in the dark than fleeting shapes. Besides, Ernest could swear he felt Abraham's gaze on him like a physical weight. He turned. Abraham was looking, but his eyes dropped down to the viscreen just as Ernest faced him.

"Why are you using the screen without the audio?" Ernest asked.

He'd expected the reason to have something to do with conserving solar charge, or maybe even the desire to keep quiet so everyone could sleep. But instead Abraham said, "It's more efficient."

That made no sense. Abraham was supposed to be as intelligent as he was. "Can't you parse written and verbal data at the same—"

"Of course I can." Abraham keyed even faster while he spoke, though he scowled down at the screen, not meeting Ernest's eyes. "If I had my own processor, I'd do it. But Audrey's got her POD-mind so heavily modded it would probably want to inflict some sort of grief counseling on me or sing me a lullaby instead of helping me write a routine."

Judging by Abraham's scowl and stiff shoulders, not to mention his tone of voice, he disapproved of Charlie's mods. Ernest, however, felt no impatience, only an empty, poignant longing. What if he could have afforded to mod Louise to that extent?

She'd still be with him. Not the whole POD, not unless it was in pieces. But Louise...the strings of code that made her who she was...if only he'd known the truth about Reclaim, if only he'd known about the tattle-strip so he could disable it, he could have taken steps to keep her from being erased.

"As it is," Abraham said, "the damn thing keeps making winky faces at me."

"I'm sure Audrey built in a bypass. Even as creative as she is, I don't think she'd sacrifice functionality for—"

"It's fine. Forget I said anything."

Forgetting on command...that would be quite a trick.

Ernest settled back against the wall of the train car and shut his eyes, and tried to pretend he was back in his POD. The rocking motion of the car nearly lulled him to sleep. His consciousness flirted with the fringes of dreams, and if he ignored the hard fiberglass floor against his rump, he could almost pretend he was cruising down a magnetic strip, shunted, sedated, climate-controlled, and blissfully vertical.

The train car's clumsy, shuddering stop plucked him out of that fantasy. Audrey was the first to her feet. "What now?" She pressed her eye to the hole in the front of the car and sighed. "I can't tell what it is. Too dark."

She stepped over Will's legs and pushed the side flap open, but Benjamin, moving more quickly than he looked like he should be able to, grabbed her by the upper arm. "Stop. Be careful."

Audrey chafed at the spot he'd grasped. "But we're out in the middle of nowhere. Isn't that the best idiom ever?"

The expression was lost on Benjamin. "You don't go first, you're small and weak." He pointed to Will. "Him. Me. With Tasers."

"He's right," Abraham said before she could object. "You'll just have to 'hold your horses.'"

Will shook off his drowsiness when a Taser was pressed into his hand. He and Benjamin slipped out of the train car to assess what had stopped the railroad this time. Even the few moments they were gone made Ernest's pulse begin to race, and unease fluttered in his chest.

The melodramatic things people said and did in those old-time feeds made more and more sense every day. He wrung his hands to see if the action would help quell his anxiety. While he couldn't be sure if the motion really did any good, it at least distracted him for a moment—until Will pushed open the flap, confident as you please, and said, "It's all clear. And, get this: it looks like a *building* fell on the tracks."

It wasn't a modern building, not exactly, but it wasn't an old-time wood and brick building, either. Ernest wasn't totally clear on the timeline, but he suspected the building couldn't have been more than a couple of centuries old. The health monitors had been housed in a structure such as this, with polymer-infused cinderblock walls and compressed Styrofoam roof shingles. Though the construction methods had since been banned to keep the city from being buried in non-bio-degradable materials, it didn't make sense to simply abandon the buildings that already existed. Ernest had read they were actually quite sturdy, if ungainly and utilitarian.

Not sturdy enough to resist the creep of the wilderness, it seemed. This building had been tumbled by trees that hadn't even existed when it was originally erected. Many of the bricks were still whole, and though some had fragmented into a few pieces, they didn't show the erosion and wear that the old structures at the edges of the city did. Or the other city, the radiation-poisoned city.

Ernest felt queasy.

"Why was there a building in the middle of the forest?" Elizabeth demanded, as if the discovery of something unexpected annoyed her.

"Maybe it used to be in the city, but someone moved it," Audrey suggested. "Or maybe it was here for maintenance on the tracks. Or maybe there were more buildings, but they've all fallen down and this is the last one left. Or maybe—"

Abraham checked Charlie's viscreen. "Radiation levels are normal. It's almost morning; we might as well spread our solar panels. Those bricks are twice as heavy as they look. Clearing the tracks is going to take a while."

He plugged in Charlie's audio, and the AI said, "There's fresh water nearby. You might as well get comfortable. And, by the way...I wouldn't dream of singing you a lullaby."

Will slung his arms around Ernest from behind, remembering the clearcoated surgical wound only at the last moment. He hugged Ernest close, back to chest, and leaned his cheek into the top of Ernest's head. "I'll handle the solar panels. You need to rest."

Ernest strongly suspected the "hurling" might begin again if he got too comfortable. He took a deep breath to quell the nauseated sensation. "I think I smell that water Charlie's talking about. I'm going to go look."

The sky was pre-dawn pink, and the shapes of trees and landscape that had been hidden by moonlight and the harsh focus of their LEDs rose, mist-like, from the darkness. Ernest found a gap in the undergrowth with mammal tracks pressed into the earth. If Louise were there, he could have scanned them for her and asked her about them. But of course, she wasn't. He ducked a branch and followed the gentle curve of the dirt path. The sound of Benjamin and Will sizing up the bricks—discussion about how old they were, how many, and how to move them— was swallowed up by the forest more quickly than Ernest would have thought possible. The vegetation was not terribly dense, and red motes of sunrise began to shine through gaps in the leaves, twinkling, illuminating the trees.

The light shimmered through a gap, and Ernest squinted and averted his eyes. Green afterimages in the shapes of the spaces between the leaves danced beneath his closed eyelids.

Now that his eyes were shut, the scent of the forest flooded his senses. He'd never thought about water having a smell. He'd never thought about so many things. His nose guided him deeper into the undergrowth, and though he did need to open his eyes to avoid tripping over tree roots and rocks, he didn't lose the scent.

He walked, and walked some more, and finally, there was water. He tested the earth that bordered the creek. It was spongy, but it would hold him. The water's surface was nearly half a meter down from the bank, but if he knelt, he found he could reach it. He skimmed the surface with his fingertips. Cold. Water bugs danced away from the ripples his touch created.

He only had one flask with him, he realized. But that was fine. He'd fill it, and now that he'd found the water, he could go back for more. Several trips, if need be, because he couldn't carry much. Audrey wasn't the only one in the group who was "small and weak." And, unlike him, she had full use of both her arms, and wasn't lightheaded with radiation poisoning.

The ripples slowed and stilled, and he paused to stare at his reflection as he bent to fill his flask. He hadn't realized he looked quite so worn and intense—though once he bent closer still to get a better look at himself and the reflection didn't move, he realized that it was not his reflection at all, and he flinched back, startled.

He turned and found Abraham standing behind him. Not

some other C754, some stranger, he told his pounding heart. Just Abraham. Unfortunately, his heart wasn't at all reassured by that knowledge.

"Why were you so interested in what I was working on last night?" Abraham asked. "I'll bet you could read my keying hand, even upside down."

"No."

"No?" He narrowed his eyes and raked them over Ernest, who wondered if perhaps he would feel less vulnerable if he stood, or if he'd look like he was trying to be threatening—when the last thing he wanted to do was make Abraham feel angry or threatened. "Are you sure? Because if I'd been stuck cleaning data fifteen hours a day for the past twenty years, I'll bet I could."

"You're you. I'm me."

Abraham gave a laugh that had a bit of humor in it, but only a bit. "How true."

Perhaps so, but when he squatted down beside Ernest, the way they balanced their weight on the balls of their feet and planted their elbows into their thighs, they seemed more like mirror images than two separate beings.

Abraham pulled his handheld from his pocket and passed it to Ernest. "It's ready now. Have a look at the code."

Ernest read, scrolled, and read some more. "Are these the nanites you programmed for Martha?"

"No. They're based on them, though."

Ernest read on. The routines where the nanites would undergo fission and render themselves into carbon looked consistent with what he'd seen at the funeral, but the rest of the program...he wondered if he was reading it correctly. "This is for decontamination."

"And once the nanites do their job, they'll break down so you can breathe them out like spent flavor nanos. No dialysis."

Ernest scanned the routine again, tweaked a command, and saved. "You ran sims?"

"Of course. So what do you say—are you willing to give it a try?"

"Yes," Ernest said, dazed. "Good."

They straightened their legs to stand, both shifting their

weight to their heels at precisely the same moment. Ernest, though nauseated and woozy, needed to press his lips together to keep from whooping with joy. Abraham watched Ernest's reaction, and allowed himself the shadow of a smile.

Back at the railroad, Elizabeth seemed pleased enough to stop hauling bricks so she could double-check the program. "Add in a sleep routine. Decontamination will go faster if it's the main process your body is focused on."

While Ernest suspected his physical body was a lot like Charlie running on a too-small processor—no better at healing itself while at the same time trying to speak and think and digest and whatever else he did while he was awake—the notion of allowing himself to be mechanically sedated made him anxious. "We don't really need to, do we? I'll stand very quietly. I won't talk. I won't even think. About anything."

Abraham asked him, "How many nights did you shunt in and trust yourself to your POD?"

Ernest considered. "Seven thousand, three hundred, twe—"

"Then what's one more nap?"

Slumber without a POD was scary enough—horizontal and exposed—but out in the open without the capacity to awaken if need be, it was positively terrifying. Will's voice rose from the brick pile on the tracks, mingling with Benjamin's as they bickered over their task. Ernest turned and looked toward Will, what could be seen of him around the train car.

Yes, Ernest decided. He would allow himself to be vulnerable. He would accept being exposed. He would surrender control to this group of individuals rather than an AI. And if it were only his own life at stake, maybe he'd decline the nanites and let nature take its course...but seeing Will hauling bricks, perspiration glistening off his brow, his cheekbones, and his chiseled bare arms...knowing how much Will had invested in Ernest's recovery, how could he refuse?

Elizabeth set him up inside the train car, so it wasn't quite as frightening as lying there, splayed and exposed, in the open air. Even as hard as Ernest tried to rationalize that the train car was really a giant POD, he still needed to swallow back his panic with his nausea. Elizabeth scanned him and went over his readouts while Abraham swiped a foil square over the nanite port of his handheld. It was a small thing, innocuous...the same sort of medium fastened to the exterior of the simulated coffee drips Will once sold in his shop. Ernest tried to assure himself that the procedure was all quite safe, though deep down he knew, even with the sims they'd run, it had its risks.

Outside, there was a crash of stone on stone, and then the bellow of Benjamin's voice calling, "Health Monitor!"

Audrey pushed open the door flap, stuck her head into the train car, and said with obvious delight, "Come see all the blood!"

Elizabeth set down the readout and sighed in exasperation—and Ernest noted she responded to the title Health Monitor these days as if she'd trained for the position herself, and not merely that of an aide. "Go ahead and get started without me," she said. "I'll be back soon. It can't be all that bad out there. The screaming's already stopped."

She eased her stiff joints and brittle bones out the door flap, and suddenly Ernest found himself alone, yet again, with Abraham. "Why?" he blurted out, and then he realized it was probably such a broad question it made him look foolish.

"You're part of my team. I'd do the same for any of us. Even Benjamin." Ernest studied Abraham's eyes, and wondered if maybe the set of his mouth was not quite so harsh as it had always seemed to him, and if maybe there was a kindness to his eyes. "Besides, if anything happened to you, Will would be useless." He handed Ernest the foil square. "Go on. No sense in wasting any more time."

The last foil square Ernest pressed to his thumbnail port had given him a flood of false flavor information. This patch was different. It didn't feel quite like shunting in; it was connected by much smaller vessels, and though the nanites were many times larger than flavor-nanos, they were still far too diminutive to actually feel them entering the bloodstream. But the effects of the sedation routine were obvious enough. He meant to speak, to ask Abraham to bring Will in one last time, so he could say goodbye in case the experiment didn't work, and the next batch of nanites he received were the same as those that turned Martha to silvery ash. But he got as far as drawing breath to say Will's name, and then everything went black.

⸗CHAPTER THIRTY-TWO⸗

ERNEST STRUGGLED TO OPEN his eyes, to make sense of what he was hearing and feeling. Breaking through his nanite-induced stupor was not unlike prying himself out of the Diaconate holding cell with the twisted wreck of his own shunt. Painful, difficult...and necessary.

He was horizontal. He noticed that first—not because it was uncomfortable, which it was—but because his sedated mind had been somehow convinced upon waking that he was back in his POD. The sensation of being vulnerably supine shattered that illusion as his internal sense of spatial orientation engaged.

So, why would he have thought he was in his POD? Maybe it was the radiation sickness confusing him...although, honestly, the nausea did seem much improved. Maybe, then, the obliterated feeling of forced slumber reminded him of his POD's embrace. Though how the mere fact that he was sedated could overcome the awkwardness of the horizontal position, Ernest wasn't sure. Or maybe it had something to do with....

"Ernest, can you hear me? Ernest? Baby?"

Whoever that was. It must have been Audrey, or maybe Elizabeth. But to his confused senses, it sounded exactly like... "Louise." His voice was a dry whisper.

"He's awake! He's awake! Elizabeth! Will!"

The ceiling swam when he forced his eyes open. He'd

expected the ceiling of the train car, so again he needed to readjust his reading to compensate for what he saw. Bricks. Windows. He was in an old-time building—or was he? The place was much smaller than all the old-time buildings he had ever seen. And it had the air about it of something that had been recently constructed; the bricks were stacked as if they hadn't quite had the chance to settle.

He raised his head to get a better look at his surroundings, and the voice that sounded so much like Louise's said, "Lie still, Ernest. You're safe. Just rest."

Weakness (rather than obedience) caused him to comply, but as he lay his head down again, a silver curtain was dashed aside with a loud crinkle, and muted daylight filled the room. There in the doorway, broad shoulders and spiky hair backlit, was Will. "You're awake?" He sank down to one knee and gathered up the hand of Ernest's shunt arm in both of his hands—only now, Ernest saw, his shunt arm was no longer brownish red and shiny with clearcoat, though a few flaky remains of the bandage clung to the downy hair on his forearm. His arm bore a long scar, and seemed thinner and more fragile than it had before he'd torn his shunt loose, but it was no longer a mangled tube of clotted blood.

"Does this mean I'm cured?" Ernest said. He'd been aiming for a light tone, but his throat was so rusty with disuse he had to force it out a word at a time.

Will, for once at a loss for words, could only press his cheek to Ernest's chest and stroke him everywhere he could reach—hair, face, neck, shoulder and arm. Ernest wondered if he actually was real after all, or if perhaps the last firings of his neurons had been devoted to spinning out some kind of strange fantasy with Will and Louise, and once he was demagnetized, the fantasy would fade, like mist in the sunrise.

And then Audrey pushed into the enclosure and said, "You look like death warmed over." She hugged herself with glee. "I've been waiting to say that all day."

"Oh, Ernest." That voice again...just when Ernest had convinced himself he was lucid.

"I keep hearing things."

Audrey said, "I guess that means your ears are functional."

Ernest sighed. "Not necessarily...I think I'm hallucinating. It sounds like Louise is talking to me."

"Surprise!" Audrey stepped over Will so she could tweak a few dangling wires in a jumble of plastic, copper, fiberglass and other materials, bundled together with strips of silver blanket and a few patches of clearcoat, hanging from a peg on the wall. She licked her thumb and buffed one of the connections with her saliva. "Doesn't the audio sound amazing? Almost as good as your old internal POD speakers—not that they were top-of-the-line. All from spare parts."

"You're such a smart girl," Louise said. "You're lucky you have such good friends, Ernest."

"Are you sure you didn't reprogram her so she'd brag about you all day?" Will asked. If Ernest needed to reassure himself that Louise's return was more than neurons firing in his dying brain, all he needed to do was analyze Will's expression. Annoyed. But resigned.

"Nope! I erased all the Diaconate blind spots, updated her vocabulary, and created some preference files. I left those empty, since I figured Ernest would want her preferences to develop organically. That's what I did with Charlie, and that's what I like best about him. He's his own person."

Ernest strained to get a better look at the mass of components that held Louise. Not the L0U15E-model POD anymore. Only the POD-mind. If he didn't see it working, he would have assumed it was a tangle of discarded components. Something swelled inside his chest at the sight of the untidy bundle, something warm and wonderful, and painful too, but mostly joyous. "I don't understand. How did you salvage her hard drive while her tattle strip was screaming out to every op in the sector?"

"Oh, Ernest." Was it just his imagination, or did Louise sound ashamed?

Audrey said, "This isn't her original drive. It's part of the clock radio microwave MP3 player you found in the old store. It's amazing how much computing power they wasted on those old-time languages. She fits in the circuit board with room to spare." Audrey caressed the bundle, and tweaked another connection. "I always back up an AI's data first thing when I open 'em up. Accidentally deleting someone's POD-mind," she shrugged in embarrassment, "that's something you only do once."

Ernest gawked at the intricate mass of parts and wondered when Audrey had found time to assemble it. Then he reviewed the rest of his surroundings—the walls, the polymer-shielded windows, the doorway with its crinkly silver curtain. "How long have I been in forced slumber?"

"Five days, ten hours, twenty-eight minutes," Louise said, and the memory of awakening from his last forced slumber caused the skin to creep on the back of his neck. She added, "Welcome back. It's wonderful to see you again. I was so worried."

"You built this in five days?" Ernest wasn't sure if he was asking Audrey about Louise's new processor or Will about the shelter. Maybe both.

Will turned, with his head pillowed on Ernest's chest, and gazed up at the ceiling. "We're running out of food and it'll take time to synthesize more soy, so we figured we might as well stay here a while and rest. The security ops would never make it this far, plus we've got water nearby, and all this polybrick from an old train station just lying around waiting to be stacked."

Louise said, "I still think it's safer to stay in the train car with Elizabeth and Audrey."

"Don't be so sure of that." Audrey lifted Louise from the wall. She cradled the AI in the crook of her arm as she plucked the fine web of sensors from the wall and hooked them onto her shirt for safekeeping. "As soon as I get that protein tank online, I'm plotting out my own house." She stepped over Will and paused in the doorway, beaming. "Isn't that exciting? A house. Just like an old-time pioneer."

Ernest followed Will's gaze up to the patched-together Styrofoam ceiling, considered Audrey's question, and said, "I suppose it is. Where are you going with Louise?"

"Mission one, complete. She was monitoring you during your recovery—we could hardly put Charlie on that detail with Louise around. But you're awake, and you seem relatively intact. Now her main duties begin."

"She has...duties?"

"Well, sure. You're not a big larva anymore that needs an AI to take care of every little thing for you. Abraham says Louise will run the protein tank."

"I'll miss you, Ernest." Louise sounded truly pained. Her speakers might be small, but she'd never had that much inflection in her voice. It brought a lump to his throat.

Audrey said, "I think we can spare enough power to have her transmit to your earpiece. That way you can hear her from anywhere in...is this a city? Our own city?"

"Cities traditionally contain at least ten thousand people," Louise said in her dictionary voice. But then she added, "Cities, plural? How could there be more than one?"

"So what do you think," Audrey asked Ernest. "Audio link?"

Ernest looked down at Will, who was watching him quietly. Before Ernest had met Will, the only person in his life was Louise—and he did very much consider her to be a person. But if he wanted there to be room for both of them, and everyone else in their group, he could no longer be hardwired to Louise. "I don't think so. Louise will have more of a chance to build her preferences if everybody can hear her, and she's able to interact with all of us."

"No better way to build up her files," Audrey said. Ernest thought she sounded pleased.

Will gave a wavery smile. He looked relieved.

"She's staying here when she's not at work," Ernest informed him.

Will's smile broadened. "I suppose I've cached enough badass reputation that I can risk sharing a home with my mother-in-law."

"What law?" Ernest said, though he supposed from the way Audrey's face brightened, it must have been an idiom.

"GOOD MORNING, ERNEST. TIME to wake up. The temperature outside is 21.4 degrees. Sunrise occurred at 5:32 am. Sunset is predicted at 8:29 pm. Current time is 7:00 am. Would you like to hear some music?"

"No, thank you." Ernest pushed aside the crinkly blanket and knuckled the dry-grit remains of sleep from his eyes. While at first the necessity of doing such things for himself had seemed inconvenient as well as unsanitary, he now saw the value in being able to care for himself, rather than entrusting all his functions to a POD.

As for other details, he didn't exactly relish the sensation of sleeping horizontally—but he was accustomed to it.

"Where's Will?" He smoothed the blanket over Will's side of the bed, something he seldom got a chance to do, since Will always clung to sleep much more tenaciously than he did.

"Did Will go somewhere?" Louise replied easily. "I hadn't noticed."

If there was one thing Ernest couldn't have imagined in his wildest dreams, it was that Louise could have the capacity to be playful. He did his best not to seem choked up when she showed off her lighter side.

"He's not out digging again, is he?" Their house had become so full of old-time artifacts, Ernest had needed to institute a one-piece-in, one-piece-out rule.

"Why don't you go see for yourself?"

Ernest opened the door—which didn't have a W3 lock on it like a modern door, nor did it even have hinges and a doorknob like a historic door. Even so, the slab of Styrofoam blocked the sounds of their neighbors pretty well, and kept the building cool on the warmest days. And since it weighed far less than a polymer door, Ernest could lift it aside with no problem. He'd eventually bulked up a bit, since his days of having testosterone filtered from his system were long gone, but he'd never be as big as Will. Pronounced musculature just wasn't in a C754's genetic makeup.

Scratching sounds drifted over from the train car, where Elizabeth swept soil and dried leaves from the perimeter of the door flap with a bundle of fine twigs. Everyone else had learned to live with the constant creep of dirt, grit and dried organic matter that resulted from homesteading in the wilderness, but Elizabeth had proclaimed that cleaning was her hobby, and the subject was tacitly dropped.

Nothing else moved in the communal area between the buildings, until Will, crouching on the ground, took two bare wires from a bundle of components and brought them together. There was a loud pop, and a wisp of smoke curled up. It smelled of burnt polymer.

"What are you doing?" Ernest knelt opposite the strange pile of stuff. "And why is Audrey letting you launch one of her projects without her?"

"She'll be along soon. I'm just making sure everything's ready."

Ernest recognized a solar panel and a heating coil, but the glass and plastic tubular thing with the water in it was nothing he'd ever seen before. "Did you find that behind the train station?"

"Yep."

"Any idea what it is?"

"French press."

"What are Frenches?"

"If I told you," Will said, "it'd ruin the surprise."

Audrey returned from the well-worn path to the stream

with a tray of small polymer containers that sparkled with waterdrops. "Are you doing some kind of experiment?" Ernest suggested.

"You'll see." Will held his gaze for a long moment and treated him to a secret smile.

Audrey set down the tray, took the two wires from Will and tapped them together until sparks fell from the connection and shimmers of intense heat rose in the air around the coil. The French press went opaque with steam, then cleared again as the water began to boil.

"Now we're cooking with gas," she said. Ernest didn't ask her to clarify. He couldn't keep up with her idioms, so he'd learned to parse tone rather than her vocabulary. "All ready," she declared, and Will squared his body over the antique press and pushed down on a plunger. The water turned a deep, rich brown.

Will chafed his hands together. "Okay."

"Okay?" Audrey repeated. "That's it?"

"That's it. Go get Abraham. He won't want to miss it."

Audrey scampered off to the tiny house at the edge of the woods. Ernest looked from Will to the French press and back again, but it wasn't until Will poured some of the brown water into one of the makeshift cups that Ernest smelled, and he understood.

"Coffee? Real coffee?"

Will held the cup under his nose and inhaled the steam. "I'd stashed some away, hoping to celebrate someday, but then I got so caught up in all the work around here that I forgot about it—until I found this." He patted the French press with affection, though he pulled his hand away quickly when it scalded his fingertips.

He handed the cup to Ernest. "I want you to be the first."

"Me? Oh, no. I can't. This is yours. You're the coffee expert."

"And seeing you smile is the light that powers the solar panel of my heart. Besides, I still owe you a brew. So drink up."

Ernest could hear Audrey's bright voice rising and falling, mingling with Abraham's and Benjamin's lower, more subdued tones. Even the rasp of Elizabeth's broom had stopped. In a moment everyone would be huddled around the coffee device, but right now it was just Ernest, and just Will.

Ernest raised the cup to his lips, and drank.

And nearly spat it back out. Hot. Bitter. Hot and bitter. Very bitter. Horribly bitter. He swallowed convulsively to try to choke the coffee down. Tears sprang to his eyes as his throat seized around the bitterness, and his tongue felt like it would shrivel in on itself and disappear.

"Good and strong?" Will said.

Ernest handed the cup back to him and turned away, gasping.

Will tipped the cup back, drank, and said, "Ah." And not like he'd just been poisoned, either. "Don't worry. Remember what I told you the first time you had a rush? It's an acquired taste."

Ernest pressed his knuckles to his lips and nodded vigorously. Choking sounds fought to escape him, and while he was sure Will had seen it all before, it didn't seem polite to retch.

"I remember my first cup of coffee," Audrey announced, crouching beside Ernest. She chose a cup and held it out for Will to pour. "That's when I learned the saying, *Bouncing off the walls.*"

Benjamin and Elizabeth elected to try smaller samples of the brew, while Will poured Abraham a brimming cup. Abraham smiled his sad smile—the one that meant he was remembering something he and Martha had once done together—took a careful sip, and nodded. He didn't choke at all.

Elizabeth finished her coffee in small sips. She declared it was "interesting." Benjamin seemed more leery of the beverage, but he certainly wouldn't allow himself to be outdone by a fragile slip of a woman like her. He pronounced it, "good," though his eyes were watering.

Conversation turned to whether coffee could be synthesized (maybe) and whether it was worth the effort (most definitely, at least according to Audrey.) Once all the coffee had been extracted from the precious grounds and the components of the heating apparatus disassembled, the neighbors all went their various ways, and Ernest and Will were alone.

"It looked so good in old-time feeds," Ernest said. "I really wanted to like it."

Will laughed. "You were almost fodder for the Reclaim machine, and now here you are: no Diaconate filling your head with lies, unplugged from the W3, living in an actual house, programming our nanites yourself instead of just cleaning up the code of other programmers..." he eased himself closer to Ernest so they were side by side, and slipped an arm around him. "Who gives a damn about the coffee?"

Will was still smiling—he smiled a lot now, not a smirk, or a grin, but an unmistakable, genuine smile—when he leaned in and pressed his mouth to Ernest's. His lips were warm, and his breath had an earthen coffee bitterness that was much more appealing than the coffee itself, because it tasted more like the coffee shop had once smelled, and beneath that, like Will's kisses.

Ernest cupped Will's jaw with his fingers so he didn't break the kiss. Their tongues touched and slid. Saliva mingled. Will breathed the air that Ernest exhaled, and Ernest took it back and breathed it again. The aftertaste of coffee lingered, mellowed by their kiss.

Bitter, but good. Yes. Definitely good.

|||ABOUT THE AUTHOR|||

AUTHOR AND ARTIST JORDAN Castillo Price writes paranormal sci-fi thrillers colored by her time in the Midwest, from inner city Chicago, to various locales across southern Wisconsin. She's settled in a 1910 Cape Cod near Lake Michigan with tons of character and a plethora of bizarre spiders. Any disembodied noises, she's decided, will be blamed on the ice maker. She is not very good at camping.

Jordan is best known as the author of the PsyCop series, an unfolding tale of paranormal mystery and suspense starring Victor Bayne, a gay medium who's plagued by ghostly visitations. Also check out her fascinating psychological M/M thriller, Mnevermind, where memories are made...one client at a time.

ıııABOUT THIS STORYııı

FROM 2008 TO 2010, I published a writers' podcast called Packing Heat. During one of the early episodes on developing creativity, I was explaining to the listeners how almost any story prompt could be used to spark a writing session. From the outrageously quirky and creative website Seventh Sanctum, I generated the following prompt:

This is a gross-out story. This story is about an organized spy, a comic, and an artificial life form. It starts in a coffee shop. The religion of the world will turn out not to be what it seems.

As I went on with the podcast, the idea kept nagging at me. That awkward prompt could totally work. I could see exactly how to do it.

I needed content for my new newsletter, so I began writing a serialized story. And I decided to go with that randomly-generated prompt.

Eventually I stopped trying to shoehorn in the "comic," though you could argue that Audrey inadvertently provides pretty good comic relief. I get a big kick out of how innocently gleeful she is whenever someone gets hurt. And I didn't go out of my way to make it a gross-out story, though the shunts are fairly nasty, and I didn't hold back when Ernest encountered the Reclaim machine. The "organized spy" became Will, the artificial life form was LOU15E, the religion of the world was the magnetic soul theory, and the coffee shop was...the coffee shop.

Zero Hour developed into a bizarre mashup of Logan's Run, The Wizard of Oz, Alice in Wonderland and Soylent Green. As innocently unlike my typical protagonists as Ernest turned out, I felt he had a certain appeal. I know that I, for one, can identify with the individual who realizes they're surrounded by people hell-bent on marching into the gruesome reclaim machine even after they learn it's the opposite of the big reward they've been promised.